EyeCu Presents

STORIES OF THE DEAD

A TRIBUTE TO GEORGE A. ROMERO

**EDITED BY
DAVID OWAIN HUGHES
& DUNCAN P. BRADSHAW**

Stories of the Dead First Published in 2018

Published by EyeCue Productions

Stories of the Dead Copyright © 2018 David Owain Hughes and Duncan P. Bradshaw

The EyeCue Logo Copyright © 2016 Duncan P. Bradshaw

Copyright of each story belongs to its listed author.

All rights reserved. No part of this publication may be reproduced, stored in a retrieval system, or transmitted, in any form or by any means without the prior written permission of the author, nor be otherwise circulated in any form of binding or cover other than that in which it is published and without a similar condition being imposed on the subsequent purchaser.

All characters in this publication are fictitious and any resemblance to real persons, living or dead is purely coincidental.

Cover illustration by Kevin Enhart
https://kevinenhart.deviantart.com/

Overall Design by EyeCue Productions

ISBN 978-1-999751210

All proceeds are going to the American Cancer Society.

CONTENTS

Grounded – *Dan Howarth*	**- 1**
Beekman's Diner – *Jeff C. Stevenson*	- **19**
Mama – *Nikki Tanner*	- 34
The Last Scare of Jonny Blair – *Nathan Robinson*	**- 49**
Collateral Damage – *Anthony Watson*	**- 60**
WGON TV: Off Air – *Duncan P. Bradshaw*	**- 69**
Fuel – *Jason Whittle*	**- 90**
Not Anymore – *Rachel Nussbaum*	**- 102**
Safe Zone of the Dead – *David Owain Hughes*	**- 106**
Last of the Day – *Chad A. Clark*	**- 127**
After Us – *Emma Dehaney*	**- 141**
A&E – *Tony Earnshaw*	**- 160**
Once Bitten, Twice Die – *James Jobling*	**- 170**
Who They Were – *Rich Hawkins*	**- 181**
Hopelessly Devoted – *Kelly Gould*	**- 200**
Dead Harbor – *Patrick Loveland*	**- 221**
Eternity – *Thomas Vaughn*	**- 244**
Roll Credits – *Kenneth E. Olson*	**- 252**
Afterword – *Jonathan Maberry*	**- 268**

Through all the reminiscences prompted by George Romero's death there runs a constant theme: gratitude. The people who love his movies are grateful for his art. The people who worked with him are indebted to him for the supportive, adventurous, and welcoming atmosphere that he created on the set.

George did for zombies what Edgar Allan Poe did for Gothic horror: he took an old tradition and made it speak to modern times. His zombies are the perfect metaphor for the fear of apocalypse that humans are dealing with today. The zombies arouse our fears, let us have fun with them, and help us face them more confidently in the real world.

He had a big heart and a keen social conscience. His casting of African-American men as heroes and his lampooning of rampant consumerism urged us to see some of the lapses of modern society.

May you rest in peace, dear George. We'll treasure the legacy you've left us.

David Crawford
'Dr Foster' in Dawn of the Dead.

A few years ago I was a guest at a convention in Maryland. It was almost like a George Romero retrospective. Most of the cast of Night of the Living Dead, Dawn of the dead, Day of the Dead, Land of the Dead, Survival of the Dead were there. Everybody in those rooms was from the Romero family of movies.

I looked at each of these actors from the various films and thought, 'man he did a great job', and 'she did a great job', and 'he did a great job', and 'she did a great job', with their roles in the progression of Romero films.

I was in such awe of everyone, and I realized that one person in that room was responsible for *everyone else* being in the several rooms of the Romero retrospective.

Then when the crowds trickled away later in the day, I was able to meet up again with George Romero. It was the first I'd seen him in more than 30 years, since the making of Dawn of the Dead. His smile, his big bear hug and genuine connection almost brought me to tears. He had that kind of effect.

Fans know me, and the other actors, because George Romero made movies. Not only did he have a huge impact, in creating the films he made, but also the people that he brought together, as actors and fans, as friends and new relationships.

And even though he's not here with us, a bit of him lives on in each of us who enjoyed his films and the way he helped us find our common bond.

We lost George in 2017, but we have each other.

Thank you, George. And thanks to each of you, who form part of the fabric of the George Romero legacy.

Jim Krut
'Helicopter zombie' from Dawn of the Dead.

To the one and only George A. Romero.
You showed us that anything was possible..

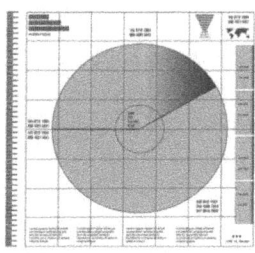

GROUNDED
BY
DAN HOWARTH

Mission Control, Houston, Texas
1st October 1968

Anderson removed his glasses and rubbed his nose, the skin was sore and red. He took the opportunity to close his eyes and felt the hand of sleep immediately pull at his consciousness, clawing at his senses. He snapped his eyes open. It was professional suicide to fall asleep at your terminal. Long hours and no rest were an unspoken part of any NASA contract. The expectation was that you dropped anything you were told to do, when you were told to do it, even if it compromised your physical or mental health.

Re-entry was always the most gruelling part of the process and Anderson slurped on some coffee from the mug on his desk, wincing at its tepid temperature. He checked nobody in his row was looking and slapped himself around the face a couple of times to wake himself up. He figured he was probably at least twenty-four hours away from being able to get any rest, if not closer to forty-eight. Mind over matter was the only thing that would get him through.

Tension hung thickly in the air of the Operation Control Room. Around him, people barked instructions, senses dulled from lack of sleep, tempers flaring needlessly and regularly. Cigarette smoke shrouded everything, the grey-blue tint lingering in front of screens and gathering near the ceiling. Ashtrays overflowed and assistants were sent on runs for more packets and cups of coffee. Around him, monitors flickered and flashed with streams of numbers and data, buttons lit up and went out when pressed by the flurry of his colleagues. At the front of the room, high above the rows of desks where he sat, the trenches as they were called, three large screens showed radar pictures and sine graphs of the probe's progress towards Earth.

The atmosphere in the room wasn't helped by a strong military presence, something Anderson had never seen in his time working on the Gemini or Apollo missions. There was always an element of martial representation and interest in any space mission, as long as those Commie fucks in Moscow were trying to get ahead, but the interest in the return of the Boreas probe was beyond anything Anderson had ever seen. The back of the room, normally reserved solely for the top brass at NASA was packed with uniformed men. Members of the Military Police flanked both sides, mingling with officers of various ranks including General Thorpe, the head of Texan operations and liaison to the White House itself.

Anderson swivelled in his chair to look at the military men. They had a distinct look. Even out of uniform, they were easy to identify with their thick necks and shaven heads. They all had a similar attitude from Anderson's experience, something totally contrary to how he saw himself. He and his team were creators, working to build or do something new for America, heck, the human race.

A TRIBUTE TO GEORGE A. ROMERO

Whereas the Army guys were here to protect, to kill if need be. They didn't have the same aims and certainly didn't see things as he did. He leaned back in his chair and lit another cigarette, breathing in deeply and enjoying the burn of too much smoke in his throat. At the front of the room, Director Kranz still had three large jars of peanuts on the table under the screens. Anderson sighed, knowing he was a long way away from his bed if the lids were still on the jars. Peanuts were a superstition at NASA and were only broken out when a mission was in its final throes. A last minute good luck charm.

An assistant he didn't recognise tapped him on the shoulder, interrupting his thoughts of home and duvets and pillows.

"Erm. Sir?" The lad could only be in his early twenties and judging by the shake in his voice, extremely new to his role. Anderson turned to look at him. The boy shrank back visibly. "I'm sorry to disturb you but would you like some more coffee or cigarettes or anything else?" Anderson noticed the lad eyeing his screen, his gaze flickering around the various controls and buttons, drinking in the detail with an almost-childlike thirst.

"No, no. Thank you. I need to stretch my legs. I'll get my own."

"No problem," said the assistant, beginning to swivel away, notebook in hand.

"What's your name, son?"

The assistant turned back. "Michael. Sir. Michael Hicks."

Anderson nodded, removing his glasses and rubbing at his nose again, feeling the skin flake under his touch. "You picked a hell of a mission to start on." He smiled. "It will get easier you know."

"I know," said Hicks. Smiling in a way that made him look not only confused but younger than his years.

"Just don't screw up anyone's coffee order and you'll be fine."

3

"Thanks," said Hicks, turning and heading busily away, his pen already poised to take the next order.

Anderson went to leave his trench, negotiating his gut past a number of colleagues, he was almost out of the room, his bladder throbbing, when the alarm sounded. Instinct made him turn and look for the poor soul whose job it would be to fix the problem. It was only when he saw, Keith Parry, his nearest colleague in the trench turn and wave him back to his desk that he realised, with a flood of tension, that it was his station sounding the alert.

"Fucking hell." He muttered as he broke into a trot across the room, avoiding wires and kinetic interns, as he went. Suddenly, he didn't need to piss.

A small red button flashed on his console, a throbbing crimson light that kept the rhythm of his headache. He tapped a couple of buttons, watching numbers pour down the monitor in front of him. A cascade of data threatened to drown him. Sweat formed on his brow, his shirt was clammy around the arms and back. His eyes searched the numbers desperately, trying to find the problem. As he struggled, the alarm beeped louder, more urgently. Its harsh voice grating in the inside of his skull.

At first, nobody paid him any attention. Minor alarms and alerts were part of any mission. They were deemed routine, unless they escalated. Now, heads were starting to turn in his direction. He felt the gaze of not only his NASA superiors but the unwanted, questioning stares of the military men at the back of the room. His skin itched at the thought.

Relief washed through his mind as he isolated the problem. He put his fingers against the screen as he read, checking and double checking. His chest tightened, the euphoria of discovering the dilemma had been replaced by the worry of whether he would be able to fix it or not. He breathed in deeply, feeling his ribcage relax as he exhaled. He checked for a final time as he saw Director Kranz marching down from his position at the front of the room, manoeuvring his way through the trenches to Anderson's desk.

"Fuck," he muttered as he rested his chin on his hand, his palm slick with sweat.

"What's the issue here, Anderson?" He put his hands in the pockets of his white waistcoat, his arms sticking out at cockeyed angles.

"There's been a breach, sir. Quite a serious one."

"Where?"

"Systems are saying there's a biological presence. Nothing sizeable but it's there. I'm running a report now."

"Biological?" Kranz rubbed the back of his head, his flattop haircut remained immaculate. His voice was strained, higher than usual.

Anderson studied the data, running a hand through his own greasy hair and wincing at its texture. "But this doesn't make sense? It says that the hull was permeated in space, near Jupiter, but the biological presence has increased sevenfold in the last twenty minutes. But that's not possible."

"Unless the biological presence was too small to be measured at first."

"But how did it permeate the hull?"

Kranz rubbed his head again. His face was devoid of colour. "It could've come from a piece of debris, rock or something else floating through space. Probes come back all the time full of dings and dents. Maybe the hull wasn't breached, only weakened enough to emit something."

"It could be a microscopic hole. Something the sensors can't pick up?"

"But what could survive out there? An organism?"

"A virus of some kind? It would explain the multiplication"

"Jesus," muttered Kranz. He lit a cigarette, exhaling a cloud of white smoke through his nostrils. Anderson lit up as well, unsure of what to do. "This is serious," said Kranz, cigarette butt wedged between his teeth. He put his hands on his hips and looked up at the nicotine stained ceiling, obscured by the fog of smoke.

"Do we need to abort, sir?"

"Abort? *Pah*. The probe is in orbit, Anderson. It's being pulled in by earth's gravity. Even if it runs out of fuel it will still re-enter the atmosphere. We need to quarantine it on arrival somehow."

"How quickly can we get a message to the recovery crew?"

"Pretty damn fast. The only issue is that we might need further input. The World Health Organization need informing, they'll want to coordinate the response. I'm trying to remember if we even have a protocol for something like this. Professor Wilson in Biology is only ever concerned with the health of astronauts, we've never even *considered* anything extra-terrestrial." He spat into the overloaded ashtray on Anderson's desk.

"But if there's a perforation in the hull, what can the quarantine team do? Surely whatever it is will escape regardless?"

Kranz looked down at Anderson. Any humour that had previously lit his eyes had disappeared. "Unfortunately, there's not really anything we can do about it. It's a problem for the WHO now." He pulled on his cigarette and looked away.

Anderson let the words sink in; knowing the fallacy of what Kranz was saying and assuming that knowledge was mutual. It was certainly not just a problem for the WHO. His stomach churned, he sat back, trying to breathe in deeper.

"I think I need to call Professor Wilson." Kranz stubbed his cigarette emphatically, adding it to the pile in the ashtray and stalked back to the front of the room, already signalling to one of his assistants to get the telephone ready.

Anderson sat in his chair, watching the LED screen displaying the probe's progression towards its inevitable touchdown. In a few minutes, it would be within earth's atmosphere. The stage of a mission that generated the most optimism, the most relief, was now bringing dread and fear to the staff.

A hand fell on his shoulder, derailing his train of thought. He jumped, knocking his cup of coffee across the desk, causing a dark pool to spread over the surface. He looked up into the cold, meaty face of one of the military men, which seemed many feet above him. The man's uniform was heavily decorated. His skin was purple and looked swollen, flushed with too much blood. His eyes held a look of disgust as Anderson swivelled round in his chair, drinking in his gut and flabby arms.

"What have you found, son?" Anderson would have put the man at barely ten years older than he was, yet the man spoke to him as if he was a newly graduated temp.

"Erm. I'm sorry?"

The man sat down heavily in the chair next to Anderson, it groaned beneath the man's weight. His arms and shoulders were muscular but his stomach bore the trademark rotundness of a prize fighter who'd gone to seed. His enormous hands gripped the chair's arms; a solid gold wedding ring adorned his left hand, glinting in the sterile light of the control room.

"I'm Major Whatcroft, here with the military detail." Anderson thought about offering his hand but saw the man hadn't moved in any way, an air of violence hung around him like the cigarette fug in the room. "We couldn't help but hear," his mouth turned upwards in the faintest semblance of a smile, "about the quarantine. What's happening?"

Anderson looked round hopelessly, like an antelope penned in by lions. Kranz stood at the front of the room, his back to the trenches, his shoulders hunched as he chuntered into the phone's receiver. "I don't know what to tell you, sir. I don't know what I can tell you."

Whatcroft banged his hand down on the arm of his

chair so quickly and forcefully that Anderson flinched backwards. Before he could speak again, Whatcroft had reached forward and hooked one large hand around the back of Anderson's leg, digging his fingers into the sensitive tissue and ligaments at the back of his knee. Anderson let out a stifled grunt, his eyes filling immediately with tears. Whatcroft pulled his face close to Anderson's, his breath warm and heavy with the muddy reek of coffee. "We're discussing a matter of national security, you fucking egghead. You can and *will* tell me anything I want to hear. Do you understand?"

Anderson nodded, his bottom lip moving involuntarily. "Y-y-yes".

Whatcroft grimaced and gave Anderson's knee a final spiteful squeeze. "Sir."

"Sir." Anderson agreed.

Whatcroft pushed himself backwards, away from Anderson and smiled. "You may begin."

"There's something on the ship. A virus or bacteria. Something perforated the hull, allowing it entry. The sensors have picked it up but the probe is in orbit, it's out of fuel now. It's coming down. Sir."

Whatcroft's facial expression didn't change, his placid expression reminding Anderson of an ex-cop that he used to play cards with, his features inscrutable as if carved from stone. "So this probe, it won't burn up in the atmosphere? Not with its perforated hull and all?" There was a sarcastic, mocking tone in the Major's voice that made Anderson want to rebel, to lie or ignore his question, yet the throb in his knee made him remember how out of his depth he was.

"No sir, I'm pretty confident. Very confident in fact that this probe will land safely and soundly on Earth."

Whatcroft rubbed his flabby chin with the side of his hand. His eyes were unfocused, looking past Anderson rather than through him. Anderson shifted in his chair, adjusting his weight. Whatcroft snapped back into focus.

A TRIBUTE TO GEORGE A. ROMERO

"Thank you for the intel, son." He rose out of his chair, his body stiff and angular, his shoulders hunched and tense.

Anderson watched him walk over to the General and call a scrum of senior officers around them. At one point, the General looked over at Anderson and he immediately turned away to look at his terminal, tapping away meaninglessly at buttons and taking down superfluous readings to look busy. On the large screen at the front of the room, the LED display estimated twenty-five minutes until the probe touched down. Kranz stood at the front of the room, still talking into the phone with his hand cupped around his mouth. The rest of the room was quiet, people busied themselves on their individual stations, ticking boxes and pressing buttons. Anderson lit another cigarette with shaking fingers and felt the throb of his knee as time ticked down.

He'd smoked another three cigarettes by the time he saw General Thorpe walking down through the trenches. Anderson felt himself shrink in his seat but nobody in the General's entourage paid him any attention bar Whatcroft who looked at him stony-faced as he walked past. The General marched up to Kranz, stepping between desks and over wires. He took the phone from Kranz, surprising the Director who hadn't seen him coming, and pulled it from the wall by its cord. The General slammed the phone to the floor and the military party surrounded Kranz and his assistant. Without realising that he had stood up, Anderson crossed the room in a trance, never taking his eyes from the scrum on the small stage at the front of the room.

"This is a national security issue," barked the General,

his face puce and barely two inches from Kranz's who flinched away from the volley of spittle that followed the words.

"Sir, I am in charge of this mission and cannot and will not abort it until the Director of NASA authorises the decision. The fact that you are here now shouting at me, does not change the chain of command. We've had our best people on this and the decision is still being made."

"It's extremely simple. You must destroy the probe. There is an extra-terrestrial lifeform onboard that cannot be allowed to interact with humans."

Kranz took a pull on his cigarette, the exhaled smoke causing the General to step back slightly. "Sir, I repeat, it is beyond my authority to sanction anything to happen without the sign-off of the Director of the Agency. I appreciate your concern but this mission is beyond your control. And mine."

The General stepped forward, jabbing a finger into Kranz's chest, prodding the NASA badge neatly sewn onto his cream-coloured waistcoat. "You'd better remember who you are speaking to here, Kranz. I report to the White House. Funding can be pulled like that." He snapped his fingers sharply. "Jobs can be lost. Amongst other things."

"There is no room for your threats here, sir. In front of my staff. Where NASA's authority is key."

"I report to the goddamn White House! You have no higher authority."

"If there is no scientific autonomy and integrity then we will lose the space race."

"And if you don't listen to what I'm saying, an extra-terrestrial lifeform could destroy our planet. It must be incinerated."

"And the Agency must decide this based on scientific merits. This decision is not yours or mine."

"The General of the Army, my boss, has authority from the Military Secretary and Chief of Staff to destroy this probe. Now, for the love of God man, step aside and let me communicate with your Director."

Kranz stepped in front of the General as he made to walk past and pick up the phone from where it lay sprawled on the floor, their chests bumped and Kranz moved his arm to block the General's progress. The two men wrestled briefly, the General's superior strength put to the test by Kranz's determination. Anderson stepped forward, unsure of whether or not to intervene and help Kranz. A military man stepped in his way. As he did so, the General stepped back from the scuffle and produced his revolver, shooting Kranz twice in the stomach.

"*No!*" screamed Anderson as Kranz doubled over, his face draining of colour. When he lifted his head up again, Anderson could see the claret stains on his waistcoat. He reached out once for the General and collapsed onto the floor, facedown. Anderson freed himself from the grip of the solider, racing to Kranz's side. By the time he got there, Kranz was unconscious. His eyes closed, his breathing shallow and hoarse.

The General put his gun away, looking round to take in the shocked faces of the NASA staff. "Lock the doors," he said to the Major who quickly dispersed soldiers to man exits. "And get that phone plugged in. We need to get the order out to destroy the probe."

"But you can't," said Anderson, his voice more shrill than he could remember it being since he was a teenager. "It might not kill whatever's on the probe."

"Shut up." said the General, "we've listened to arguments on both sides. We can incinerate this probe and burn up anything on it in the blast."

Anderson went to talk again, his voice weak and flat. The General cut him off. "I'm sorry about your Director, I am. But this is a security issue now so let us do what we do."

Anderson turned away, looking back at Krantz, pushing his hands through the blood, to stem the wound.

"Please, just call an ambulance. Get medical support."

"After the order is given," replied the General, turning to use the phone as Anderson's arms covered up to the elbows in blood. Sobbing, he pushed his hands down on the bullet holes, praying for the flow to stop.

Less than ten minutes later, the probe was destroyed. The news filtered through from the military men accompanied by firm handshakes and smug tones. Anderson continued his vigil with Kranz as the man's life slipped away, determined to provide him with some comfort before he died. Finally, only a couple of minutes after the probe was confirmed as destroyed, Kranz stopped breathing. Anderson let go of his boss, folding Kranz's hands on his body, closing his eyes in the way he had seen in a movie. Rather than being angry, Anderson felt hollow, he walked back to his desk and slumped into his chair, putting his head in his hands and letting the tears flow. The military men continued to crow and strut, celebrating successfully destroying a severe threat to humanity, not noticing or caring about the human cost, the price NASA would have to bare in its continual fight against the Russians to conquer the final uncharted frontier.

On the stage, the General stood talking on the phone, his voice loud and knowing as he barked his report. "Yes, Mr President. Completely destroyed. We are confident America is safe again, sir."

A few yards away, Kranz's prone corpse lay discarded and ignored. Anderson sat staring at it, willing his boss to be alive again, wishing this day was just a bad dream, a nightmare brought on by too much work and too little rest. It was him that saw the movement first. Kranz's hand moved slightly, twitching. Anderson blinked, took his glasses off and rubbed his eyes. As he did so, he saw Kranz's fingers shudder and then tighten into a fist. The movement made Anderson's own skin tighten, his senses sharpened despite the lack of sleep. As he watched, Kranz sat up, his waistcoat caked in blood, his face a monstrosity, devoid of anything that had made him human. Kranz moved onto all fours and crawled slowly behind the General who was in the process of hanging up the phone.

To Anderson's rear a few soldiers began to yell but the General never heard them. Kranz was on him before he realised, his momentum combined with Kranz being slightly off balance allowed him to tip the General over. Before the General could make a sound, Kranz was on top of him, his face buried in the skin of the General's neck. Now the General was screaming, his voice thick in the air, dominating the room's atmosphere. Anderson saw Kranz's face was red with the General's blood, he was devouring the man, ripping at his throat and shoulder with his teeth.

Around him people started yelling, running for the exits. Anderson's own fear bubbled up in him, like a champagne bottle waiting to burst. He felt suddenly delirious, unsure whether to laugh or cry or run or fight. Chaos reigned as staff abandoned their posts and fled for the doors. The soldiers manning them, confused and frightened, produced their weapons, pumping rounds into the onrushing workers, dropping them to the floor clutching chests and legs and arms as they went. Anderson watched, cowering behind his chair as friends and colleagues alike were mown down. He saw the intern take two bullets in the shoulder and one in the neck as he rushed to get out. By the time the violence was over, the smell of cordite and smoke had mingled with the stench of cigarette fumes and body odour. The soldiers manning the doors stood shocked, their faces ashen, their rifles hanging limply by their sides as they comprehended what they had done. Bodies lay on the floor, some moaning in pain, others prone and silent.

STORIES OF THE DEAD

On the stage, Kranz slowly worked his way through a large piece of flesh pried from the General. His innards were scattered in a splattered pile in the corner of the room, encircling the phone he had used to speak to the President. Anderson whirled round at a noise behind him, those who hadn't charged towards the exits were now hiding under desks or in the corners of the room, holding themselves and shaking or crying and praying. A heavy hand fell on his shoulder and Anderson spun round, his arms instinctively going up in front of his face. When nothing happened, he opened his eyes. Major Whatcroft stood in front of him, gun in his meaty hands, sweat pouring down his jowled face.

"What is going on here, science boy?" he muttered. The authority and confidence stripped from his voice, leaving nothing but the slight twang of a Boston accent.

"I'll be damned if I know," said Anderson, pulling himself to his feet. "Something to do with the virus from the probe."

"Your man Kranz is one tough son of a bitch, to live as long as he did."

"He died. He died in my arms."

"No, he must've faked it. The strength to attack the General like that…"

"What living person would kill and eat another, Major? Have you ever seen that before?"

"No," the Major admitted, keeping his gaze on the ground.

"It was the virus. It must've brought him back from the dead or taken him over before he died."

"It brought him back from the dead? I don't fucking believe you. Something else must've happened."

"No," said Anderson, almost shouting. "He'd died. I felt his pulse. He was gone."

"We need to regroup and get the fuck out of here."

"Wait," said Anderson. "Those people. My colleagues. They were gunned down. The dead ones, they might –

come back like Kranz did."

The Major looked over the top of the trench towards the door, the pile of bodies in front of the three soldiers guarding the exit had begun to twitch and writhe like maggots in a bait box. The injured tried to crawl away as the dead began to reanimate, their eyes hungry, their movements intent on harm. Anderson and the Major watched as the reanimated began to feast on the living, hands gouging and scraping, teeth sinking into soft flesh. The sheer weight of the dead outnumbered the living, pinned them down and exposed limbs and necks and faces to biting teeth.

The soldiers guarding the doors froze, acting too late as the dead rose to their feet and advanced, clawing the air whilst reaching for the fresh meat. The troops unleashed a volley of bullets, tearing into the dead, skin and blood flying out of the walking cadavers but never doing anything more than slowing their progress. The soldiers were swamped, pulled down onto the floor, guns still firing as their faces were ripped from their skulls and arms wrenched free of their sockets.

Anderson stared like a rubbernecker staring at a car crash, unable to look away from the carnage but appalled by everything he could see.

"We have to go now," hissed the Major, cocking his gun. "Whilst they're distracted."

"What about everyone else?"

"Nobody else has even moved. They're gone." He tapped the side of his head. "Up here. I've seen it before. We have to save ourselves."

"But—"

"Do you want to live?"

"Yes."

"Then we leave right now."

The Major led the way as they scuttled to the door, bent low, Anderson following behind, feeling his heart pumping in his chest. He couldn't remember the last time he had attempted to run anywhere. The dead had ripped the soldiers to pieces and Anderson stepped over the bodies and remains of most of his colleagues to get close to the door. As they neared the exit, the Major began to fire bullets into the crowd of bodies. Those that reached for him shrank back before trying to grab him again.

"Keep up with me." He roared as he kicked and stamped at hands and faces trying to attack him. He got a hand on the double doors and plunged it downwards, the door cracked open, revealing the harsh light from outside. Anderson squinted and the Major, temporarily blinded, lost his grip on the handle and fell onto his hands and knees. As fingers reached out of the crowd of bodies, an arm hooking around the Major's knees, another joined it, pallid digits reaching for his throat. Another figure rose, stumbling on jerking, twitching legs, shuddering as it lurched and fell, cascading its weight onto the Major's back. The Major fell face first onto the floor, shrieking as the creature on top of him sunk its teeth into his neck. More arms and faces appeared, drawn by the noise. Nails and teeth ripping, pulling, snagging the soft exposed flesh of the Major's face and arms and neck. His skin came away from his neck and cheeks in small sheets, dripping with blood and exposing nerves and tendons beneath. The Major screamed again as Anderson stood, defenceless, watching the world fall apart around him.

From his prone position on the floor, the Major threw his pistol at Anderson, where it bounced off his shin. The dull thud broke Anderson out of his quiet stasis.

"Run, you fucking idiot!" the Major yelled from the floor, the bodies piling on him now, clawing at each other to try and get closer to the ragged form of the Major.

Anderson bent and picked up the pistol, its angles unfamiliar and strange to his hand. He pointed the gun ahead of him and charged forward towards the door, his legs pounding, his heart racing. He couldn't remember the last time he had exercised but as he ran now, powered by adrenaline, he felt young and free as if he was back in high school trying out for the track team again. He hurdled the scrum on the floor and forced his shoulder against the door, staggering as it swung open, allowing him out into the lobby of the building. He panted, breathing heavily, forcing himself out through the glass double doors and into the fresh air.

The wind nipped at him as he raced through the complex, sweat patches on his back and underarms made him feel exposed to the elements. He forced himself forward towards the car park, aware that his run had slowed to no more than an agonised jog. He was barely moving beyond walking pace. His chest was on fire, his lungs thrashing against his ribcage, a stitch working its way up his side.

He found his car, dropping into the driver's seat so heavily he heard the suspension creak under his weight. The keys were behind the sun visor, as always. He sighed and started the engine, pulling his seatbelt on as he drove away. All he wanted was to be from here, to be safe, to lie down somewhere quiet. Music blared from the radio and he snapped it off, listening to the consistent thrum of the engine as he pulled through the small roads of the NASA complex towards the entrance.

He drove past the front doors of Mission Control, the windowless building looked the same as it had every day he had ever worked there, nothing betraying the carnage that was happening inside its walls. As he looked, a small crowd of corpses surged against the glass doors, mashing their faces and hands and legs against the glass as the car glided past. The Major stood amongst them, his tattered face hanging slack as he pounded mindlessly on the window. Anderson turned back to the road and pulled out of the complex onto the highway, heading for home.

He looked at the gun on the seat next to him and wondered how many bullets would be enough to survive whatever was going to happen next.

DAN HOWARTH

Dan Howarth is a writer from the North of England. Like all Northerners he enjoys pies, rain and the tears of his enemies. He has co-edited two anthologies, *The Hyde Hotel* and *Imposter Syndrome* with James Everington. His fiction has appeared in *The Hyde Hotel* and *No Monsters Allowed (edited by Alex Davis)* as well as numerous places online. He has recently completed his first novel.

MEMORIES OF ROMERO

For me, George Romero's films started as a social thing. Staying out at a friend's house as a teenager, a group of us watching a zombie film and discussing how best to kill the undead whilst drinking a few illegally purchased beers. George's films are the foundation of my horror education.

They drew me in as a kid for their gore and violence but I came back to them again and again as an adult for the social commentary and the way they make you stare unblinkingly at some of the worst aspects of humanity. Romero's films are not an easy watch, they contain little comfort, but for me - they will always be essential viewing.

His DIY spirit and refusal to conform should stir the spirit of every aspiring creative. Budget and resource should be no object, believe in what you have to say and force it out into the world.

Few films end as darkly as Night of the Living Dead and as a writer, what better education can you ask for? Rest in peace, George.

Beekman's Diner

BY
JEFF C. STEVENSON

The Cooper family was lucky to be in a booth toward the back of the Beekman's Diner.

Harry Cooper dropped the quarter into the tabletop jukebox, began to search through the options.

"What are you going to play, Dad?"

"I paid for three songs, Karen, so why don't we each pick one?"

His wife, Helen, said, "Anything by Dionne Warwick for me."

"What's that coo-coo-ca-choo song?" Karen asked.

"'Mrs. Robinson,' and they have it, so that's one," he said, entering punching in the numbers. A few seconds later, the intricate acoustic guitar introduction began. Karen grinned, nodded her head to the beat. Helen smiled at her.

Pushing the buttons on the machine, Harry said, "And next we'll learn the way to San Jose, courtesy of Miss Warwick."

Helen nodded. "Thank you." The therapist had said

she needed to communicate more with her husband, acknowledge him more often. Even the little things matter, she'd been told. "Please" and "Thank you" and "That's a good idea".

Harry peered closer at the selections, grinned suddenly, and made his choice.

"What did you pick?" Helen asked. *I don't care,* she thought, *but I'm trying. God knows, I'm trying.*

"You'll see. Now, are we ready to order? I want to eat, get to the motel before dark."

After the waitress—an attractive redhead that Harry was especially friendly to—had come and gone, he leaned back in the booth, stretched his left arm behind his wife. She stiffened. He pulled his arm back, exhaled, stared out at the huge front window of the restaurant.

It was close to eight. Daylight saving time had just kicked in so the sun would still be around for a bit. That was always nice, he liked the light in the evenings, felt like he had more time to each day. While Helen and Karen chatted, he glanced around. Beekman's Diner wasn't very busy, fewer than a dozen people. Their booth was the only one playing music. It was a necessity. He tried to fill his world with sounds or distractions to offset the silence that usually nestled in close to him and Helen. Things weren't going well, hadn't been for several months, ever since she'd found out about Heidi. Not that he was trying to hide it, didn't really care. Besides, it was over by the time she discovered what was going on. Now it was therapy, together and apart. He told the guy Helen was cold, ignored him, never wanted any affection, or never showed any. He had no idea what Helen said about him.

The food came, they started in on it. They were taking Karen out of school for a few days for a short vacation. She had picked up on the tension in the marriage, was acting out at school, bickering with her friends, her grades had changed from mostly B's to mainly C's, even a few D's. It had been going on for months. The therapist suggested some time away as a family might help them bond or re-bond.

"Or rebound?" Helen had said. "Bounce back to where we used to be?" She had been grim whenever she and Harry were together in counseling, didn't like looking at him. He had admitted several times that he had made a mistake, what else could he say or do? They had reached an impasse. That's when the focus had shifted to Karen, her needs, what was going on with her.

"Can't this trip wait until the spring break?" Helen had asked.

"It's better if this is thought of as a special time for your family, not time off that every other child will have," the therapist had explained. "It'll show you value her, yourselves, your family."

They had talked about where to go, what to do, allowed Karen to choose. She had always been interested in history, suggested they visit Washington D.C. or Boston or Philadelphia. Since Harry was doing all the driving, he recommended suggested Philadelphia. It was closest.

"Liberty Bell, Independence Hall, American Revolution," he had said.

"And Pittsburgh," Karen had insisted. "I want to see where the Underground Railroad was!"

The therapist seemed to have been correct. Karen's enthusiasm for the vacation broke her out of her distracted, angry slump. Helen asked her to work out the schedule for the trip, so every day after school, she and her friends would pour over the Rand McNally map, figure out the miles between home and their first stop. Then they looked through library books to determine which attractions she wanted to see.

And here we are, Harry thought, still irritated that Helen wouldn't even let him put his arm across her shoulders. She held the affair up to him like a shield, blocking him from getting close to her. He acknowledged to himself that she had him dead to rights, would ride that horse for as long as she could. Which was fine. There'd be another Heidi or Suzanne or Melissa. There always was.

"Excuse me?" Helen called out to the redhead. "Someone left that newspaper behind. Would you mind?" Harry and the waitress looked over at the next booth. The empty plate, discarded paper napkin were partially covered by the front page of the local paper. The headline read: *First Photos of Viet Mass Slaying.* Below it was a large, grisly image of several corpses. The waitress grimaced, swept up the paper and plates, disappeared to the kitchen.

"I'm so tired of those horrible photos being publish in the papers and shown on TV," Helen said. "They can tell us without showing us." She wanted the war to be thousands of miles away, not in her living room each evening. Of course, Harry insisted on watching Walter Cronkite report his gruesome stories every night. Helen protected Karen from the horror and violence. While the news was on, they did the dishes. She and Karen weren't going to expose themselves to such gory events.

The song at their booth changed to tapping drums, a trumpet, twangy guitar. Harry's selection was on. He bopped his head to the opening beat as the O'Kaysions started in on "I'm a Girl Watcher." He twitched in his seat, snapped his fingers, sang to Karen, "'I'm a girl watcher, I'm a girl watcher, watching girls go by, hey, my my.'" Karen rolled her eyes at his antics, giggled, then matched his seated movements. He was glad he'd made the choice after the way Helen had rebuffed him. Without looking, he knew she was furious with him, knew he'd landed a punch.

While Harry and Karen kept their eyes on one another, jiving to the music, Helen looked away. She was the first to see the commotion through the large front window of Beekman's Diner.

A small crowd had suddenly materialized in the parking lot, their silhouettes shimmering like dark flames against a twilight sky. Instead of moving to the left toward the entrance, they continued walking until they smacked into the glass. More piled up behind them. The few customers with their backs to the window turned, startled by the noise.

Oh, God, not another protest, Helen thought, annoyed. That was all that was on the news. Students against the war or fighting the police. There were marches everywhere, groups like the Black Panthers, the Yippies and SDS, always gathering to voice their opinion for or against something. She watched the large window for their placards to be revealed, indicating what their cause was. Patrons remained in their booths, unclear what was happening. Helen noticed a woman in a yellow dress who kept a spoonful of food held halfway to her mouth, just frozen in place, uncertain what to do. Everyone seemed to be motionless, waiting for something to happen.

Outside, those who'd gathered continued to line up, two or three deep. Their hands were pressed on the large panes of glass as if they didn't know what it was.

What's wrong with them? Helen thought, the first tingling of unease beginning.

Then those outside began pounding on the window, dull, drumbeat-like thuds.

"What the hell are they doing?" Harry asked.

Karen turned around. "What's happening?"

The huge window reflected the lights of the diner; it danced madly in response to the steady, persistent pummeling of hands and fists. Seconds later, it abruptly cracked, then shattered in place, transformed into what resembled a gigantic spider web stretched across the front of the restaurant. Shaken from their stupor, customers cried out, stood from their tables and booths, but still didn't know what to do. It was all so unexpected. No one knew what was going on or why.

Those from outside continued to push against the glass until the entire section exploded inward, raining shards everywhere. Then, like sleepwalkers, they stumbled over one another as they made their way inside. Arms outstretched as if blind, they only moved forward, forward, forward, as if on a conveyer belt that deposited them into the establishment. They had no reaction as they cut and sliced their flesh on the dagger-like edges of the broken glass. They didn't bleed, didn't say a word. They shuffled awkwardly, weaving a bit, off balance as they invaded the space.

People were now screaming, backing away from the strange group who showed no emotion or reaction to the commotion they'd caused. The patrons formed a small, terrified cluster. The others surrounded them. Harry counted at least twenty of them, all shapes and sizes. Men, women, teenagers, children. Without hesitation, the people from outside began to relentlessly attack the customers. But instead of hitting them or fighting, they began to claw at them, pull at them, take bites out of them. Harry couldn't believe what he was seeing. The diners raised their arms to protect themselves, but it was useless. With three or four of the creatures attacking each person, they had no chance against the slow-moving throng.

Harry saw one woman in a yellow dress push away a young girl who had bitten her hand. A man grabbed her by the shoulders, took a chunk out of her neck. She sank to her knees, was immediately set upon by three teenagers. The place was now filled with shrieking cries for help. Everyone was being clawed at, the blood splashed about along with bits of flesh and internal organs. It was unbearable enough to see the bodies torn apart, but the monsters then fell to their knees in some kind of blasphemous devotion and began to devour what they'd had just killed.

Harry watched it unfold but it was impossible to process what was occurring right in front of him. Bewildered, he wondered, *Was this slaughter really happening?* His mind and body tried to shut down. Vaguely, he was aware his right hand was violently twitching, his fingers snapping together like a fresh-hauled fish. It took him a moment to realized it was a reflex to what he was seeing. At home, his right hand controlled the TV remote. He stood there with a desire to change the channel, find a different image to watch. *I'm not home,* he comprehended. *This is really happening...*

Abruptly, he pushed Helen out of the booth. She grabbed Karen's hand. "In the back!" he yelled, "the kitchen." He was thinking knives, iron skillets, weapons. The two waitresses and three kitchen crew were just coming out to see what was going on. It had all happened in less than a minute, but everyone seemed to be reacting so slowly. Karen was crying, Helen was holding her close, pushing her face into her bosom, trying to protect her from the sights and sounds. The staff only stood there, watching the chaos, mouths agape in dull shock, blocking Harry's way. He pushed past them, dragged Helen and Karen along. The double-swing saloon doors to the kitchen flapped closed behind them.

On the other side, the staff had seen enough. They were now screaming. They charged back into the kitchen. Harry knew they needed to block the swinging doors. He shouted that to them but they only stared at him, wide-eyed, trembling. They didn't seem to understand what had gone on out there, what was about to occur again if they didn't secure themselves.

"We have to block this entrance!" he yelled at them again. He looked around but all the stainless-steel sinks and counters were mounted, the chopping table was too heavy to move. He felt his heart pounding hard against his chest, he was panting, wished he'd had a cigarette, anything to help him calm down, to think, think, think.

The doors suddenly burst open and arms—so many of them—reached in, seized what was nearest. The redhead. Hands clamped all over her body, her shoulders, chest, waist, legs, her face, her eyes, her mouth. For only an instant, Harry saw her eyes go wide with shock when she was first grabbed, then they opened further in terror, and just as she started to scream, both of her eyes were torn from their sockets as she was dragged away from the kitchen. Urine poured from between her legs. Crying and yelling hysterically, the blonde and the kitchen staff backed away.

Harry stepped past the traumatized diner workers, peeked through the swinging door window. On the floor, the monsters had quickly dissembled the redhead, torn off her head, had begun to consume her. He glanced up to the front of the restaurant, saw that dozens more of the fiends were pushing their way in through the broken window. He noticed the woman in the yellow dress was up, wandering around like the others. *Hadn't she been attacked? She was still alive? Why was she shuffling around with the rest of the hoard? Didn't—*

"Harry?"

He turned from the carnage. An odd thought had started to form, one that was quickly forgotten, a piece of a puzzle that he couldn't use at the moment.

Helen grabbed his arm. "Harry! We have to get *out* of here!"

The double-swing doors crashed opened again. Eager, outstretched arms appeared. With barely a thought, Harry moved behind the blonde and kitchen staff, shoved all of them into the embrace of the slow-moving things. They were immediately enfolded, dragged away to the other side of the door. It reminded him of how quickly a sea anemone or Venus fly trap held, then devoured, their prey. Seconds later, even before the screams had stopped, blood gushed from under the door, spread across the floor. A sickening stench filled the room.

The doors eased open. A woman with glassy eyes, bloody scratches on her neck and arms reached for him. Harry grabbed an empty pot from the stove, slammed it across her face, then down on her head. The arms kept seeking him. He continued to batter the skull until she was still.

A TRIBUTE TO GEORGE A. ROMERO

"This way!" Harry prayed the rear area outside wasn't infested. Karen was whimpering, Helen was trying to calm her. "Quiet!" he hissed. He didn't know what kind of infection the sick people had, didn't know what was wrong with them, but he thought they could still hear sounds.

When they reached the service door, they waited a moment. Behind them, they heard the sound of unsteady feet shushing on the kitchen floor, dull-witted bodies bumping off of the tables and walls like pinballs. Harry cautiously opened the back door. The cool evening air—fresh, free of the vile odors they had been inhaling—was a relief. He breathed deeply, glanced around, no movement. He pulled Helen and Karen behind him, closed the door. A large, empty dumpster was nearby. The three of them strained hard against it, managed to position it against the door just as it was pushed outward. They heard the repetitive thud of many bodies bumping against it, trying to gain access outside.

"That ought to hold them for a little bit," he said.

"What's wrong with them?" Karen asked, shivering against her mother. "Are they sick?"

Helen asked, "What are we going to do, Harry?"

"The car's in the front. If all those things have moved inside, maybe we can get to it, make a run for it."

The dumpster rattled.

Harry said, "I'll check to see how the front looks." He ran around the side of the diner, stayed in the shadows, moved as quickly and quietly as possible. Tall shrubs provided a hiding place.

When he saw the front of the restaurant, he gasped. There must have been close to a hundred of the dazed creatures fumbling about the parking lot as they sought entrance to the building. A handful were still cutting themselves to ribbons trying to climb in the broken window. The place was filled with them. He could see they were moving as one toward the rear where'd they'd join those in the kitchen who were seeking to break through the service door barrier. They didn't speak. Some of them had terrible injuries. Arms or legs had chunks missing, some had extreme facial disfigurations, others had spines that appeared to have been twisted. A few were clad in their underwear, others were dressed for a night on the town or an evening in, watching television. They all seemed to be mesmerized or in a daze, as if programed to keep moving no matter what the obstacle was.

Harry spotted his car; it was surrounded but didn't appear to be damaged. Across the road from the restaurant was an open field. By the moonlight, he could see more were approaching from that dark pastureland. Slowly, methodically, silently, they were arriving.

He headed back to Helen and Karen, told them what he'd seen. The screech of the dumpster alerted them that the back entranced was almost breached. They saw arms reaching through the partially opened service door, flailing about, reaching, grasping the air.

"Come on!" The three of them hurried to the shrubs in the front where they watched the ever-growing mass of shambling figures.

"What's happened to them?" Helen whispered.

"Infected with something, I guess. It's like they're slow-moving, rabid animals or something. And whatever it is, it turns them into cannibals." He recalled his puzzlement over the woman in the yellow dress who he thought had been dead. But then she'd been up, seeking human flesh like the others. How was that possible?

Helen said, "It seems they are attracted to movement and sound. Watch. See how they get caught in like a...a whirlpool when they get close to those trying to enter the diner? They just get sucked in, become part of the flow of activity the others are doing."

Harry nodded. "We need to make sounds to distract them. What if we break the windows in the car near ours? When they go to explore, we should have time to get into our car, drive off." Anxiously, they watched as more and more of the shuffling figures wandered out of the darkness into the front parking lot. "We better hurry," Harry said.

They stealthily began to collect large rocks and bricks. When they had a good pile, they huddled and whispered their plan again, confirmed they all knew their part. They would throw the rocks and bricks as far as they could, aiming for the blue Ford Mustang. Once the shufflers started toward that car, Harry would climb into their Oldsmobile. Fortunately, it was parked on the end. Helen and Karen would get into the front seat next to him.

"All of this as quickly and quietly as possible," Harry cautioned. "Once we're in the car, I'll start the engine. Ready? One, two, three…"

The first rock landed loudly on the hood of the Mustang. The second hit the automobile next to it, cracking a window. The response was immediate, a slow mass turning as one. Arms outstretched, they weaved and bobbed their way toward the Mustang. More stones were thrown, more of the monsters were distracted. Harry slipped away first, soundlessly climbed into the driver's seat. All the things had their backs to him, focused on the sound of rocks clunking against steel. Seconds later, Helen and Karen scooted in next to him.

Harry started the car, backed it out, but it immediately came into contact with half a dozen slow-moving men. He gunned the engine, knocked a few of them over, but all of the others in the parking lot turned around at the noise, began to lumber over.

In her haste, Karen hadn't completely closed the door. It was pulled open. She screamed, pressed back against her mother who fell on Harry, who was trying to steer the car out of the lot. The lady wearing the yellow dress reached in for Karen, who cried out, pushed her away. She lunged at Karen, latched onto her arm, tore away a piece of her flesh. Karen shrieked in pain. The woman, still chewing, leaned in for another bite. Helen reached over her daughter, shoved hard at the woman. More of her kind had crammed in behind her, so she tripped over them, fell to the ground. She immediately tried to get back into the car, her head and neck taking the full impact when Helen tried to pull the door shut. But the bulk of Yellow Dress's head wouldn't allow it. Her mouth remained intent on poaching another piece of Karen while behind her, others lined up outside the car, surrounding it, drawn to the screams and activity.

"Help me!" Helen cried to her daughter, who was weeping, her arm covered in blood.

Together, they kept pulling and releasing the door, gradually crushing the woman's head and neck even as her dull, white eyes stared dispassionately at them, her teeth chattering with anticipation.

With one final yank, they were able to shut the door. The severed head landed at Karen's feet, still chewing what it had taken from her earlier. Karen squirmed in disgust, kicked at it, but Yellow Dress's mouth continued its ghastly movements.

Helen was babbling, sobbing at the blood that dripped off of Karen's wound. "Do we have a first aid kit?" The bite mark was deep, harsh-looking. Karen was withering in pain.

Through the front windshield, Harry could see an onslaught of shapes approaching, the moonlight giving them an unsettling sheen like characters from an old, flickering silent movie. The slow-moving shambling figures had surrounded and immobilized the car. The tires were simply spinning in place. Arms extended, they began to claw at the windows, the trunk, the windshield. The Oldsmobile began to rock, the back window shattered. The things started to pile up on the side where Karen was, as if the still-chewing head at her feet was calling to them. The car began to lurch, to tilt.

"It's going to flip over!" Harry screamed. "Get out, get out!"

He dragged Helen out after him, felt the fingers of the

monsters eagerly tugging at him, the hands seeking him, the mouths chomping the air near his face, his neck. He prayed Helen was pulling Karen after him as he forced his way through the thick, sludge-like forest of beings that were so slow, yet so unrelenting in their desire for him and his family. The hungry, populated darkness swarmed around them.

When they reached the back of the diner, the things had broken through the service door, pushed aside the dumpster, were loitering about.

"We have to get Karen to a doctor," Helen whispered as they crouched behind a broken fence. "Baby?" she murmured. "Say something." Karen was slumped over, unconscious. Harry felt his daughter's forehead. It was hot to his touch. She groaned restlessly.

"They're coming from that direction," Harry said, indicating the field in front of the building. "Our only option is to head out into the fields behind the restaurant." He picked Karen up, cringed. She was like a lifeless doll in his arms, only a warm bundle of legs and arms. He and Helen plunged into the woods. The moonlight illuminated the trees, tall grass, weeds, and the vast expanse of wide open fields that surrounded them. Twice they stopped, looked back. All they heard was their own frantic breathing. Karen remained unresponsive.

After a moment, Helen said, "If she dies…"

"What?"

"I said, if Karen dies…it's all on you…"

"How can you say that? I have nothing to do with this!"

Helen was weeping now as she caressed her daughter, but she was furious. "You have *everything* to do with this! You're the reason we're here, why we took this trip in the first place. If you hadn't…" She took a breath, finished by saying, "Just remember that, Harry. This is all on you. Whatever happens."

"Come on," he snapped. He picked his daughter up.

Dead to rights, he thought bitterly. *Helen will ride this horse for as long as she can, all the way to the end.*

They trudged on through the darkness, stopping every few minutes to catch their breaths, listen for sounds of pursuit.

Fifteen minutes after their last short rest, they came upon the silhouette of a two-story farmhouse. It was imposing against the starry sky. No lights were on.

"Think anyone's home?" Helen asked, not caring, only wanting there to be a phone, access to a doctor, someone to care for her daughter.

They walked briskly toward the house. It was surrounded by trees. The foliage could be hiding the creatures. They stopped again, listened. All was quiet except for the usual night sounds of insects, the wind in the trees.

They stepped gingerly onto the front porch.

Harry settled Karen with Helen. He reached for the doorknob, turned it.

The Cooper family cautiously entered the farmhouse.

A TRIBUTE TO GEORGE A. ROMERO

JEFF C. STEVENSON

Jeff C. Stevenson is a professional member of Pen America, an active member of the Horror Writers Association, and a finalist for the Best Published Midsouth Science Fiction and Fantasy Darrell Award. Jeff has published more than two dozen dark fiction stories and has been included in anthologies alongside Clive Barker, Ramsey Campbell, Richard Chizmar, Jack Ketchum, Brian Lumley, Adam Nevill, Graham Masterton, Edgar Allan Poe and Algernon Blackwood. Jeff is the author of the Amazon #1 bestselling *FORTNEY ROAD*: The True Story of Life, Death and Deception in a Christian Cult. His first novel, the supernatural mystery, *THE CHILDREN OF HYDESVILLE*, will be published summer 2018 by Hellbound Books, who will also publish his suspense thriller, *I'LL COME BACK TO GET YOU* in late 2018. Jeff also writes mainstream fiction under the pen name of Mary Saliger.

MEMORIES OF ROMERO

I remember that George once said that, "the family unit in NIGHT OF THE LIVING DEAD completely collapses. That's what we were focused on." I was always fascinated by the Coopers, the family in the basement. Why were they so angry with one another under such horrific circumstances? What had happened to them before they sought shelter in the farmhouse? Since George was fixated on the family unit, I followed his lead and focused on Harry, Helen and Karen Cooper and their lives before the zombies tore them apart.

BY
NIKKI TANNER

They held hands in the dark, listening to the footsteps coming down the hall, closer and closer until the light under the door darkened. Sarah squeezed Karen's hand tighter and started to shake. It was her turn tonight.

Karen gripped back and whispered, "Think of Mama. That always helps."

Sarah nodded and wiped the tears from her eyes. Daddy didn't like it when they cried, and if they fought back he threatened to give them to Mama.

The knob turned and the room filled with light. They closed their eyes and pretended to be asleep. Daddy stood over their bed and grabbed Sarah's arm. "Let's go," he said.

Since Mama left, he didn't have to hide his intentions. There was no one to stop him from taking what he wanted. Sarah whimpered as he dragged her from the bed and into the hallway. The door slammed closed, and Karen wept softly.

A TRIBUTE TO GEORGE A. ROMERO

It started about two years ago, when the twins were eight. Karen had noticed Daddy watching her and Sarah with a peculiar look in his eye while they played in the yard. That afternoon he asked Karen to sit on his lap, which she'd thought was strange because they were getting too big for that. Mama told her later that he was wistful about them growing up and was trying to hold onto his little girls a bit longer, before they grew into young women. Karen had felt proud then. It became a frequent request; whether he was sitting at the table or watching television, he always had one of his girls on his lap. That is, until Sarah complained about something poking into her back. He blamed his belt buckle, but Mama had a suspicious look on her face and called Sarah over to help with dinner. The twins heard Mama and Daddy arguing that night, which was not uncommon in their home. They couldn't hear much through the walls, and their bedroom was upstairs, but before the tell-tale slapping and crying that always ended their fights—with Mama cowering in the corner—Karen heard Mama say he wasn't wearing a belt.

The sun woke Karen bright and early. Birds were singing in the trees and she smiled, forgetting for a second that it was the end of the world. Then she heard the faint moans from outside and it came crashing back. She turned over and saw Sarah sleeping peacefully beside her. Well, as peacefully as she could in the nightmare they were living. Sarah's face was red and streaked with tears from the night

35

before, but there was a trace of a smile on her lips. Karen let her sleep, so she could forget for a few hours. She got up and went to the window. She did this every morning. It gave her some peace. Her eyes darted from face to decaying face until she found her. Mama was shambling in the backyard, dragging one foot behind her as she bumped into neighbours, townsfolk, and strangers, all trampling what used to be a vegetable garden. Occasionally one of them would look up and see Karen in the window, sparking a frenzy, and they'd start banging on the side of the house, the door, and the broken windows, which Daddy had boarded up to keep out the marauding ghouls who wanted nothing more than to tear them all to pieces.

"Buncha overblown nonsense," Daddy had said when the newsman interrupted *The Lone Ranger* to report on the attacks. "Drugged out lunatics, that's all. City folk got too much time on their hands, if ya ask me."

Mama smiled and nodded, but her face betrayed her fear. It wasn't until Old Man Andrews wandered onto the farm that afternoon and tried to bite Daddy that he changed his tune. Within a few hours, half a dozen had made it to the backyard.

Daddy set up shop on the doorstep with his shotgun, picking off anything that moved, while Mama paced in front of the television set and mindlessly chain-smoked, jumping every few minutes when Daddy fired. Somehow Sarah had managed to sleep through all the excitement and was passed out on the couch clutching a pillow. She often shut down when she was upset, and Karen envied that a little. She wished she could escape, just for a while. Instead, she sat in the rocker and watched the newscast with her mother, waiting for the news to turn good.

A TRIBUTE TO GEORGE A. ROMERO

Someone off-camera handed the newsman a piece of paper—a special bulletin. *It's over*, Karen hoped. Instead, the man said that people should head to their nearest rescue station, and a list of locations flashed on screen. Mama stopped pacing and knelt in front of the set, murmuring the place names as they popped up.

"Hampton!" she gasped. She jumped to her feet and rushed to door, opening and closing it quickly behind her. Karen heard Mama's muffled voice sounding excited, so she slid off the rocker and went to the window. She couldn't see her parents but could make out their words.

"It'll all be over soon, Martha," Daddy said to Mama as he reloaded. "'Til then, we got chickens in the coop, cans in the pantry, and water in the pipes. We'll be fine."

"But the man on television said to go to a rescue station. Hampton's only a few miles! We'll make it in no time."

"What'd I just say?"

"Henry, please! We have to get the girls out of here. Those... those *things* just keep coming!"

"Listen to me, woman." He cocked the gun. "I make the decisions round here. I'm not leaving this place open for folk to ransack."

"But Henry—"

A slap interrupted her protest.

"Don't sass me, woman," he said, the anger in his voice rising. "Get back in that house and get started on supper. I'll take care of this."

"Yes, Henry." Mama sounded defeated. The door opened, Mama came in, and it closed behind her. She went into the kitchen without looking up and soon cupboards were banging. Karen followed her.

"Ah, just the girl I was looking for," Mama said with a smile on her red, welted face. "Help me with supper, will you? We need to keep our strength up. Can't sit around watching that blasted television all night. What should be make, hmm? Mashed potatoes? Roast?"

"Sounds great, Mama," Karen said. After ten years in the Wayfair house, she had learned to play along, for her mother's sake.

Supper was ready as the sun started to set, and Daddy came in for the night, shotgun never leaving his side. Mama put on a cheerful demeanour but never took her eyes off the weapon. When their plates were clean, Mama left the dishes in the sink, a rare event, and resumed her pacing. Daddy stood guard at the window by the door while Mama split her time between the television and Daddy's post. The lights were off and the curtains were drawn, except for where Daddy sat. "No sense attracting moths to the flame," he said. In the distance, the wind carried intermittent screams and gunshots, but the nearest farmhouse was miles away and no one had wandered onto the property for hours.

"This'll all be over soon," Daddy said again. "Already less of 'em than before. It'll be normal by morn. You'll see."

Mama put her hand on Daddy's shoulder and stood still. "Do you hear that?"

"Hear what?"

"Listen." She pressed an ear to the glass. "Sarah, honey, turn off the TV."

Sarah scooted off the sofa and snapped off the set. They sat in silence, listening intently, while Mama and Daddy stared into the moonlit darkness.

"Look!" Mama cried suddenly. "Someone's coming!"

Daddy squinted and cocked his head. "Runnin' this way."

"Is that... William Doherty?" Mama asked.

"Looks like it."

"Henry!" William was screaming Daddy's name.

"Dang fool's gonna bring them things here in droves if he keeps carrying on like that."

"Henry, let me in!" William's voice was getting louder. He was almost to the house.

Mama went to the door and tugged at the lock. "I can't get it. Henry, help me open this!"

"What the hell do you think you're doin', woman?" Daddy hopped to his feet.

Mama looked puzzled. "I'm letting him in, Henry."

"No, you are *not*. Sit back down."

"Henry, come on, you can't be—"

Daddy pointed the shotgun at her chest. "As a heart attack. *Go sit down.*"

Mama gaped at Daddy, her mouth trying but failing to respond. Her eyes darted to the living room, where the girls were watching the scene unfold. Her hands dropped to her sides and she backed away.

William had made it to the porch and was banging on the door. "Henry! Are you there? Henry, let me in! They're gonna get me! Please!"

"Get on home, now, Billy," Daddy said, raising his voice enough to be heard through the window. "There ain't no room in here."

William's face appeared in the glass. "Henry, please! They've overrun my house! My family's dead! They're all dead! Please, let me in!"

Daddy aimed the gun at William's face. "I don't care where you go, Billy, but you're getting the hell off my property. You've got to the count of three. One."

William looked behind him and sobbed. "They're coming, Henry! Please!"

"Henry, for the love of God, he's our neighbour! Let him in!" Mama begged.

"Two."

William hesitated as moans filled the air. Then he was gone, his footfalls thudding on the porch as he ran away from the house. Mama rushed to the side window and parted the curtains, Karen not far behind her. William Doherty's silhouette dashed into the field. He was almost out of sight when several shadows surrounded him and swarmed. William fell to the ground, his screams echoing through the night. Mama wept and covered Karen's eyes as William was torn apart.

"And that," Daddy said, suddenly behind them, "is why we're staying right here."

After seeing what the ghouls were capable of, Mama returned to the topic of the rescue station.

"Please, Henry," she said, tears streaming down her face, "I don't want to die here, not like this. Not like poor William!"

"Billy Doherty is—was—a damn fool who should've been more prepared. And who died, in case you didn't notice, because he left his house."

"He said it was overrun! How do we know that won't happen to us?"

"Dammit, Martha, what did I tell you? If anyone's gonna take care of Henry Wayfair's family, it's gonna be Henry *fuckin* Wayfair, not the God dang government or mayor or King of England." He jabbed his thumb into his chest. "*Me.*"

Mama closed her eyes and shook her head. "No," she said, "it's not." In a cat-like movement, she grabbed the gun out of Daddy's hands and pointed it at him. "It's going to be *Martha* fucking Wayfair. Girls," she called into the living room, "get your coats."

Karen and Sarah exchanged looks, knowing what the other was thinking. They had never seen Mama stand up to Daddy like that. He was mean to her, and she usually cowered, except where the girls were concerned. After the belt buckle incident, Daddy never asked either of them to sit on his lap again, and Mama was responsible for that. Martha Wayfair didn't care what anyone did to her, but when it came to her daughters, all bets were off. And when

A TRIBUTE TO GEORGE A. ROMERO

Mama was mad, the twins knew she meant business. They did as she said.

Mama grabbed the truck keys off the hook, gun still firmly pointed at Daddy, and herded the girls behind her.

"We're leaving. You can stay and be a hero, or you can come with us. But *we* are *leaving.*" Mama glanced out the window and moved to the door, still shielding the girls. With one hand on the gun, she tugged at the lock with the other, but it wouldn't budge. Her struggle was all Daddy needed. He shoved the twins away, grabbed the gun, and slammed Mama's head against the door. Blood poured from her forehead, and she struggled to stay on her feet. Daddy held her steady by her hair.

"You want out so bad," he said through gritted teeth, inches from her ear, "here ya go." He turned the lock easily, opened the door, and shoved Mama onto the porch, slamming and locking the door behind her.

Sarah sat on the floor where she landed, sobbing and crying for her mother, while Karen pounded on her father's leg. He grabbed Karen's arms with one hand and held her still. She wrestled from his grip and took a step toward the door but stopped when her father pointed the gun in her direction.

"You want to join her, little miss? Because that's what'll happen if you touch that door."

"Henry?" Mama's muffled voice called from outside. "Henry, I'm sorry. Let me in. You're right, we should stay here!" She pounded on the door, her voice becoming more panicked. "They're coming! Please, Henry! I'm sorry!"

"You better get runnin' to that rescue station, Martha! Hope you run faster than ol' Billy!"

"Please, Daddy," Karen said, "Let her in!"

Sarah continued to weep, her hands over her ears.

"Henry! *Please!*" Mama's cries became more desperate. "No, no, please, get away from me! *Henry!* For the love of God!" The sound of shuffling footsteps filled the air, and Mama's begs turned to screams.

"Daddy!" Karen cried. "Open the door!"

Mama stopped yelling and fell silent, and the only sounds from the porch were the tearing of flesh and the moans of the dead.

Daddy's visits started that night. Sarah was first. She was catatonic and unable to process what was happening to her, but Karen knew what was going on down the hall. She stood at their bedroom window and stared at their mother's lifeless body, still lying on the porch below. She watched the ghouls wandering through the yard and wondered if they were the lucky ones. They weren't afraid of anything, inside or outside of the farmhouse. She watched as night birds picked at her mother, pulling on veins until they snapped. And she watched as Mama's body twitched, stood up, and shambled away.

Yesterday, Karen caught Mama's eye and was sure Mama recognized her. But she, too, started clawing the side of the house, hungry for those inside. Karen understood that Mama, as she knew her, was gone, but it comforted her to know that she was still out there, in body if not in spirit. Sometimes she imagined opening the door and letting her in, or going out to join her. It couldn't be any worse than staying with Daddy.

Something stirred, and Karen turned. Sarah was sitting up in bed, watching her.

I have to be strong, she thought. *I can't leave her alone with*

A TRIBUTE TO GEORGE A. ROMERO

him. She was five minutes older than Sarah and was very protective of her little sister.

"Mama out there?" Sarah asked, rubbing her eyes.

"Uh-huh."

"Good." Sarah lifted the covers and swung her legs over the side of the bed. Karen's face fell. There was blood in the crotch of Sarah's nightgown. Sarah followed Karen's gaze and her face crumpled. Karen went to her and held her as she cried. *It's not going to get better*, she thought. *We have to get out of here.* She kissed the top of Sarah's head then looked toward the window. *Any way we can.*

They sat on the floor, facing each other as the sun went down. They were holding each other's left hands, their knuckles white. In their right, carving knives, both freshly sharpened that afternoon. They stared into each other's eyes, Sarah's face frightened, Karen's determined.

"You're sure you want to do this?" Karen asked.

Sarah tried to respond, but her voice cracked and a sob came out. She nodded instead.

"There's no going back," Karen pressed. "You have to be sure."

Sarah took a deep breath and this time found the words. "I'm sure. I wanna hurt him like he hurt Mama."

Karen forced a smile. She wasn't sure she wanted to go through with it, but knew she had to. She might have been able to bear her father's abuse alone, but she couldn't let it continue to happen to Sarah.

"OK. Just like I told you. Count of three?"

Sarah nodded.

"One." They lifted their knives in front of them. "Two." They held the blades to each other's throats.

"I love you," Sarah said.

"I love you, too." Karen squeezed her eyes shut and took a deep breath. "Three!"

Karen felt the blade open her throat as she sliced Sarah's in return. Her eyes popped open and she gasped for breath, but none came. Blood poured down Sarah's shirt and she was gulping like a fish out of water. *Like looking in a mirror*, Karen thought. Her grip on Sarah's hand loosened and the world faded from grey to black.

Daddy crept down the hall toward the twins' bedroom, right on schedule. He opened the door and was hit with the smell of copper. He knew that scent. He slaughtered the chickens himself and there's no mistaking it. He snapped the light on and screamed. Their once pink and frilly bedroom looked like a slaughterhouse. Blood spattered the walls and soaked the floorboards and hook rug. The girls were standing side by side, eyes glazed and jaws slack, like a demented Diane Arbus photo.

"Oh, my God," he said, hand to his mouth. "What did you *do?*"

Karen took the first step, but Sarah wasn't far behind. They shuffled, hand in hand, toward him, their expressions blank and emotionless.

Daddy backed into the hallway and hit the wall with a thud. "Oh my God, oh my God," he repeated.

Inch by inch, the girls grew closer. Karen raised a hand and light glinted off the blood-stained blade of the carving knife.

"Oh, sweet Jesus," Daddy cried. He backed down the hallway and paused at the top of the stairs.

"I didn't mean it!" he said, attempting to reason with his undead daughters. "You have to believe me! I did it because I love you! I'm sorry! Please God, I'm sorry!" His eyes darted around, looking for a weapon, anything to fight them off with. His eyes settled at the bottom of the staircase, by the front door: the shotgun. He started down sideways, not taking his eyes off Karen and Sarah, who were slowly gaining on him. His foot slipped on the second step and he reached for the bannister to steady himself, but his fingertips only grazed the wood and he tumbled, ass over teakettle, down the stairs, cracking his skull and shattering his right knee as he made his way to the bottom.

When he hit the floor, he struggled to get to his feet, but the pain in his knee was excruciating and his legs wouldn't work. He tried to drag himself toward the gun, but the floor was wet with blood from his head wound and his hands slipped. All the while, the twins descended the steps, footfalls careful and well placed, until they stood before his struggling form. He turned to see them towering over him, flanking his crumpled body.

"No," he repeated. "No, no, no! I'm sorry!" His cries fell on deaf ears. They raised their knives with both hands and brought them down on him as he begged for mercy. When his screams died, they feasted.

The next day, it was all over. The National Guard and groups of local men with guns took care of the ghouls in town, eventually making it to the farms on the outskirts. Hundreds of thousands of lives were lost all over the country. TV crews interviewed the local sheriff as men threw bodies onto bonfires. One newspaper photographer was lucky enough to get a Pulitzer-winning shot out on the Wayfair farm. It showed the bodies of three ghouls, a woman and two little girls, lying together behind the house, their arms wrapped around each other with matching bullet holes in their foreheads. Although there was much debate at the time, and continues to be fifty years later, all three appeared to be smiling.

A TRIBUTE TO GEORGE A. ROMERO

NIKKI TANNER

A former Haligonian, Nikki Tanner lives in Fredericton, New Brunswick, with her partner, Glenn, and their two cats. By day she is a law librarian and instructor, and by night she reads and writes scary stories, listens to new wave and old-school Goth music, and watches horror movies. She is obsessed with David Lynch and likes her coffee black as midnight on a moonless night.

MEMORIES OF ROMERO

I'm still surprised that I'm a horror fiend because I was always so afraid of everything. When I was little, I loved Halloween and "safe" scares, but even then I was terrified by cartoons every October (*Garfield's Halloween Adventure*, I'm looking in your direction). The nightmares were non-stop. In my teens and early twenties, zombies invaded my dreams, and I'd wake up terrified at least 2-3 times a week. I loved scary movies, looked like Morticia Addams, and was in love with Vincent Price, but I couldn't handle zombies or gore. But everything changed when I was introduced to George Romero.

One afternoon, my Greek History professor announced that we were going to watch *Night of the Living Dead* in class. Apparently the premise of a group of people surrounded by the enemy with one on the inside is like a Greek battle we were studying. My stomach dropped, but I played it cool and watched with my friends in the back of the room. It was creepy and unsettling, but it wasn't what I'd expected. It was more than just a horror movie (not that there's anything wrong with simply being a gorefest— Lucio Fulci is a god in my home). It was political, not nearly as gross as I thought it would be, and the end was crushing. I loved it. A few weeks later, I skipped a different class to stay home and watch *Dawn of the Dead*. Again, it wasn't as scary as I'd expected, and, although I kept looking over my shoulder for zombies ready to pounce, I wanted more. All of the movies I had always wanted to see, but was too afraid to, were now up for grabs, and I watched everything I could get my hands on. And then my zombie nightmares stopped.

If it weren't for George Romero, I would never have faced my fears and come out the other side. In a way, he taught me that I can overcome obstacles. Every time I stand in front of 45 law students to teach them the horrors of legal research, it's because George Romero pushed me forward. He's the reason I write what I do, and I'll be forever grateful.

THE LAST SCARE OF JONNY BLAIR

BY
NATHAN ROBINSON

His grey eyes opened to darkness, but he wasn't awake in the normal sense.

The evening air was chilling, but he didn't feel it, for he was already colder than the night.

The man formerly known as Johnny Blair twitched. A memory remained, but faded the more his dying synapses tried to cling onto it.

A girl's face, plain, but pretty. She meant something to him, but the image of her was moving away, like passing a roadside advert. Bright, up close, then fleeting.

"Ba..Ba...Bar..Be."

He groaned, mouthing a recollection that was fast fading. But the words wouldn't come. Couldn't. Can't. He no longer had the capacity for fine speech, just the sound of dead air leaving his lungs, carved by whatever shape his mouth was making at the time. A fragment of muscle memory helped shape it.

"Bar...Ba...Ba...Bar...Be...Ba..."

The attempt at the word descended further into nonsensical grunts. His mouth was dry, his tongue flapping like a piece of old jerky.

He tried to move, but was restricted somehow.

He couldn't feel it, but something anchored him. Not his legs, they kicked out, his heels stabbing into the dirt for purchase. He rolled his hips, outstretched his hands, fingers clawing into the earth and grass as he attempted to free himself.

The obstruction felt behind him, not holding, but pinning him. He lifted his head up and away. A wet sucking noise fell deaf on his ears as shards of skull and chunks of loose unused brain fell away onto the gravestone beneath him.

He'd lost his glasses during the fall. His eyesight wasn't awful before his first death, but he wouldn't have driven at night without them.

Johnny Blair sat up, alone in the desolation of Evans City Cemetery, the landscape illuminated by the moon glaring down from the twinkling tapestry of a starry night.

He groaned and got to his feet, his knees buckling as if he were a new born deer. He started to topple and swayed, legs pushing him one way as he acclimatised to the unbalance of himself and getting a grip on motor functions he had forgot.

His hand lurched out and latched onto a tombstone. He carried on moving, his fingers struggling to listen to his commands. He tore dead flesh from his palm, the skin folded and creased, the flap hanging back. He didn't bleed, but seeped a dark, dire jelly that clung in clumps around the wound.

Johnny paid no mind to the injury. He found his graveyard legs and carried on his wayward stumble, until he found a rhythm he could use without falling, holding his arms out in front for balance. Not something he'd thought of, but what the body needed to do in order to move more freely.

The Evans City Cemetery sat on a hill, facing the

expanse of Pennsylvania. Encumbered by gravity, Johnny Blair felt the pull and went where his legs took him.

Downhill.

He fell a few times as his speed got carried away and his legs became twisted around one another, but within half an hour he found the perimeter wall and followed it in whichever direction he was facing until he came to an open gate. Seeking to flow outwards into the world, he bent around the wall and onto Sycamore Lane.

There was a new light. Not the moon. It startled his eyes and caused him to shift direction. He veered off Sycamore Lane, through a copse and onto a road he would have intersected anyway. However, the glow was far too interesting to follow the curve of the highway. He needed to investigate, his primitive interest piqued.

Now he was closer, a smell invaded his olfactory senses, filling him with the potential of what could be called satisfying another need; a basic happiness.

The bus was upturned, aflame at the front where it had collided and moulded around a tree which had joined the fire. Bodies and broken luggage lay in a scattered semi-circle upon the surface. Dead-alive bodies were crouched over the recent dead, working fingers into wounds and tearing stubborn flesh. Some had crouched to feast, as if in prayer, taking a mouth-on approach to eating.

Johnny stopped at the first body he came across on the outskirts of the accident. Many of the victims had three or four diners enjoying them on this midnight feast, but Johnny's only had two. He slumped to his knees to join them, taking the head end for himself. To him, it was sexless. It was food. He felt nothing. It was a thing for fuel. The others at the mock tarmac table felt the same.

STORIES OF THE DEAD

One chewed on a socked but shoeless foot, giving an extreme pedicure. The other feasted on a hole above the crotch, unspooling links of intestine, and chewing on them with a look of abject boredom and necessity.

The face of whomever it was had been cut open by glass. Deep and fatal gouges had marred and pared their features into a jagged jigsaw. This was where he was, where he started.

He dug his fingers into the ruined face, pulling flesh from the cheek. He ate into the night, defacing the stranger until only scraps of muscle clung to a wide-eyed pink skull. Johnny plucked the left eye form the socket, tugging at the fibre that held it until snapped with a sick ping. He was busy chewing when the body shifted. The cyclops glared at him, not in annoyance, but to determine if the man eating them was considered food or not. The half-eaten human, devoid of sex, rolled and tried to stand, collapsing into a pile as their legs, stripped and denuded of muscle, crumpled and splayed outwards. Unperturbed, the ruined being began to crawl away from the fire and into the woods.

In a previous life, Johnny Blair would have thought this humorously rude.

He moved on, crawling on his hands and knees to join another, less mobile meal. This time his hands quested inside a broken chest cavity, gorging himself on the meatier, more substantial nourishment found in the floppy sacks of the lungs, which sighed blood when squeezed.

Before dawn, a vehicle came hurtling down the hill from where Johnny had come. Seeing the gathered crowd, it swerved and slipped on the tableau of gore, the bald tyres losing traction as it power slid through half of the diners with a series of grim thumps, knocking them like skittles and ploughed sideward into the burnt-out bus.

The fuel tank ignited instantaneously, the resulting blast sent the still chewing witnesses that remained on the roads into the woods. The explosion knocked Johnny backwards, the alveoli he'd been gnawing was thrown from his mouth and lost in the darkness.

He landed hard on his right shoulder, his legs flung over the top of him and he flipped once more before folding into the dirt on his front, tearing his shirt open and scouring the fabric from his trousers.

He lay stunned for a moment while he collected what was left of him. Jaw rolling, he unchewed a mouthful of dirt soaked in blood. He tried to sit up, pushing himself on his right-hand side, but collapsed back into the mud and leaves. He used his left-hand side with more success, rising steadily to his feet.

The explosion had sent a puddle of fire in every direction. Any of the bodies caught within the circumference of this lethal bay were now burning. Some of the dead groaned and rolled away, others lay still and succumbed to the flames because they were already too dead or had yet to awaken in their renewed mortality.

Johnny Blair viewed the inferno with suspicion. Light meant civilization and food. But some deep seeded fear warned him to keep away from such a brightness. It made him wary. A knowing that still held fast in his decaying mind. Whatever decision-making functions were left within, his path had been chosen.

He shuffled up the incline but away from the burning wreckage and past the far end of the bus. The primitive side of him understood that this was the safest way.

He left the blaze behind and walked towards the dawn, the distant fire that seemed safer.

The scream caused him to turn his head. Johnny Blair shifted direction and moved towards the noise.

Movement.

Something fast and spry. Others like him milled about, shuffling and shambling, searching for direction.

They found it.

The girl screamed as she ran across the road and Johnny fixated on her movement, quickening his pace to a light jog. He raised his arms to steady his balance with the increase in speed, but found only his left limb would raise up. The right hung limp, impotent from the shoulder. Johnny remained unconcerned. The fleeing food was the matter in hand.

Emerging from the forest that bordered the road, the girl's foot caught in a pothole, a symptom of an unkempt road. She skidded onto the tarmac, arms outstretched, she utilised her palms and knees as brakes to slow her impact. The rucksack on her back fell and burst open, scattering tinned food and other assorted survival items she grabbed in a hurried escape. She screamed again as blood bloomed on the four points of contact, then shrieked once more as the dozen or so shuffling ghouls descended on her.

Johnny cheered an excitable groan as she posed on all fours, the enthusiasm becoming a form of rage as she struggled to her feet, moving towards an abandoned car that sat with two flat tyres at the roadside. With her grazed knees, she moved about as fast as her pursuers.

The crowd advanced, becoming animated as the notion of nourishment surged within.

The odds changed though when the young girl removed a pistol from a holster on her hip. It had been her father's, a man she had loved and shot in the head only hours ago. She still had speckles of his blood on her sundress.

But her tale wasn't theirs to worry about. She was food.

Seeking vengeance on a multi-faced enemy, the girl levelled the gun and shot the closet attacker, an obese farmer's wife in a ripped floral dress. Her face exploded outward and the farmer's wife dropped with a sudden violence upon the tarmac.

A TRIBUTE TO GEORGE A. ROMERO

The young girl aimed again, taking out more of her assailants with precision headshots. She drew the gun on Johnny Blair, the next in line for lead between the eyes.

Johnny felt zero fear. He didn't recognise the gun a threat. It wasn't fire. It was too sudden for him to consider it an immediate danger. He wasn't aware that the others had been dropped. He continued his advance. Even as she pulled the trigger, he didn't falter his shambling, eager gait.

The gun clicked.

Empty.

The girl screamed and turned. She tore at the car's door handle. Luckily for her the previous owners had neglected to lock their vehicle before abandoning it. She scrambled inside. Slamming a bleeding palm down on the raised lock.

Johnny and the rest of the great unshot arrived at the windows a second later, slapping grey, dirty palms on the glass.

Inside the girl hurried about checking locks and making sure all windows were up. She searched for keys but found none. She released the handbrake, but to no avail as the backroad was on a zero gradient. Unless the crazies wanted to offer her a push, she was going nowhere.

The group, including Johnny, smacked at the windows and bodywork of the vehicle, frustrated at the prize awaiting inside that they could see but not get at.

With the girl's screams and the hungry tattoo drummed on the bodywork, the noise attracted more wanderers to the crowd, surrounding the car three people deep.

As long she kept yelling and moving inside, they would be interested. Darkness might shroud her and dampen their interest, but that was hours away.

The crowd jostled one another in the frenzy, leaning too far one way. One tripped on uneasy legs and took Johnny down with ten others. They fell to the dirt, tangling legs and arms, bouncing heads off one another.

Johnny came to rest, his skull inches from a fist sized rock. His eyes viewed the stone, taking in its jaggedness and harsh edges. He didn't clock the potential danger for him if he'd fallen a few inches further forward, but an understanding formed in his rough excuse for a mind.

Fire meant people. Fire meant danger.

It was a cause for potential. Objects and elements had more than one use.

The food had trapped itself within the car. They didn't have the cognition nor the strength to smash the glass or bend the metal.

Johnny picked up the rock in his good hand.

He had a key.

Sat up on his knees, Johnny drew the rock back and slammed the sharpest edge into the closest window. Glass exploded inwards with ease, giving immediate volume to the girl's fresh screams.

Johnny clawed up the door, his fingerprints shredding as he pawed over the jagged remains of window. The teeth of glass shredded his shirt and cut his bloated belly as he wormed his way inside.

There was the girl, eyes and mouth wide and screeching fear. Johnny lurched forward, fingers and mouth open in hunger. She tried to fight him off, but he had her backed against the door, his good hand pinning her down, the other flopping useless at his side. He went in with his teeth gnashing. She turned, panicking hands scrambling for the lock and handle. She found purchase, and as soon as the door had opened a crack, the clawing hands waiting on the other side fell upon her with gruesome enthusiasm.

Her cries became lost in the blood in her throat.

Johnny feasted.

They all had a taste.

Of the girl, they left nothing but bones, buttons and

A TRIBUTE TO GEORGE A. ROMERO

buckles. Awash with the blood of another, Johnny left the carnage and walked on, separating from his fellow diners who'd joined him at the last supper.

He moved through the trees without direction, occasionally tripping over dead wood and protruding rocks which altered the desire line he was taking. The alarmed chirp of nesting birds altered the flow of his journey as well; the tweets caught his attention, so he followed his ears to the noise before another distraction grabbed hold.

A few other wanderers crossed paths with him during his ramble, all of them as dead as him. As they approached, they sized one another up, determining whether they were food, friend or foe.

All friends here in woods.

Gunshots rang out far and high in the distance, now losing their meaning since Johnny had lost his mind.

It was noise.

And as light meant sustenance, so did sound.

A farmhouse appeared behind the trees. To Johnny however, it was only a shape, but some deep recognition told the animal part of him, the ever hungry, growling stomach, that it contained food, that the square shape was more than a form. It was a container for nourishment.

This was where the noise was coming from.

The shape, the noise. Johnny got excited and hurried his gait.

Figures became apparent, filling the gaps between the trees.

Not his own lumbering kin, but live flesh. Tens of them.

No. His own kind was here. In the trees, hanging from the branches like the strangest fruit.

Some of the others, the food, moved closer towards him.

The primal part of him became animated, getting tunnel vision on the closest one.

It laughed. But to Johnny, the chuckle was noise,

nothing more sinister than a crow's caw.

Amongst the crowd behind, a figure stuck out.

Johnny slowed to trundle, staggering to stop.

The figure turned his way, but no acknowledgment dawned upon that plain and worried face, which had become hardened and deeper set since he'd last seen it.

The unknowing wasn't mutual.

It was deep within him.

A notion of recognition. A sound. A word. Something that he remembered last and had somehow stuck like glue to his new primitive self.

"Ba."

"What you saying boy? What you saying you freak?"

"Ba…Bu..Ba…"

The man who had come to face him, turned and called his brethren.

"Hey, I didn't know that these freaks can talk!"

"Bu…Ba… Baa..."

"What the fuck you singing boy? Ba Ba Black Sheep. Get fucked."

The man moved, raised something up to his shoulder. It clicked. The noise meant nothing.

Johnny was transfixed, this food was different. It meant something other than sustenance. It wasn't just food, although she could be. He knew her, like he knew light and noise meant food. Like he knew that eating flesh was important to him.

"Barbara…"

There was a new noise. But Johnny Blair's head didn't stay in one place long enough to hear it.

A TRIBUTE TO GEORGE A. ROMERO

NATHAN ROBINSON

Nathan Robinson is a father to amazing 8-year old twin boys, and they are his world. So far he's had over thirty short stories published in various anthologies, zines and web publications. His novellas Starers, Ketchup on Everything, Midway and his short story collection received much acclaim upon release. His novel, Caldera, however, did not.

He lives in Scunthorpe, England.

MEMORIES OF ROMERO

I don't know what year it was. I can't remember how old I was. 14? Probably younger. I've seen a lot zombie films since then. It was Dawn on the Dead and I remember it was late at night. I'd seen screen shots in the various horror film books I'd ravenously collected. Of course, the film was much better than I could imagine. It gave me my first taste of the apocalypse. It was primal, it was fun, and it gave me characters I cared about, then turned the screw on them until their island of safety became a place to fear.

COLLATERAL DAMAGE

BY
ANTHONY WATSON

Bill O'Dea says he seen it but he is—and always has been, pardon my French—full of shit. Such is, I don't believe a word that comes out of his mouth near on ninety nine percent of the time anyways so when he tells me he saw a light in the sky and an explosion on the night that probe or whatever it was was supposed to have been blowed up I took it with—what's the expression—a pinch of salt?

Thing is, despite bein' a full time liar by nature, Bill was at the time of his relatin' this story, well into his cups – as the pile of crushed *Coors* cans behind him would testify to. Myself, I'd consumed my fair share too, so was willin' to let him ramble on just so's he could finish his story and we could get back to drinkin'. He surely was convinced by what he was sayin', I'll grant him that but even in my own state of mild tipsification I knew the truth was so far from what he was tellin' that it might as well have been up in the sky alongside that probe, wherever it was when they blew the thing up.

See, what they're sayin' is somehow that explosion

caused all this stuff that's happenin'. That maybe it picked up something from Venus – which is where it had been. Or so they say. My pa says that whole space thing is just a made-up story too; a cover for the government to explain away all them tax dollars they actually spend on themselves. What happened was, when they blew it up, this stuff got into the sky, and drifted down to Earth and then seeped into the ground bringin' about the dead risin' up and killin' folks.

Seems to me them scientists are even more full of shit than Bill O'Dea – 'cept they get to call themselves doctor or professor and have fancy letters after their names.

Anyways, irrespective of who's full of shit the most, the dead surely are risin' from their graves and, let me tell you, many of them ain't that pretty to behold. The scientists tell us it's only the fresh 'uns who can do it but havin' seen some of what I have of late I'm keen to hear their precise definition of "fresh". Course, all this information is comin' from the radio and TV, which means it's probably a pile of horseshit too. It's another of pa's beliefs that all them media folk are government shills, spreadin' propaganda – and not the good kind like in the war. Pa, of course, has a lot of funny values. Seemed to have more of 'em after his accident at the sawmill for some reason. Maybe I'll ask that reporter fella tomorrow, Billy Whatsisname. He's bound to be taggin' along behind the militia again, always askin' questions, always tellin' that fella with the camera where to point it.

When Sheriff McClelland put out the call for men, I was first in line. Well, okay – not exactly first, but what I'm tryin' to say is how eager I was to get signed up for the militia and kill me some of them dead folks. I could see he was surprised to see me there. Didn't seem too happy about it truth to tell – probably on account of all them run-ins we've had in the past. Still, these are desperate times – he said so himself when he made that little speech to all of us –distressed enough for him to give me a badge anyways. Some of 'em there needed guns havin' arrived weaponless, so they handed them out, made them sign a little chitty. Of course I already had mine. Didn't have a fancy bandolier though, not like the sheriff. I figured he thought it made him look important but to me he looked like a Mexican Bandeedo – 'cept without the sombrero.

We was split up into groups, posses I guess you'd call them, and off we went, huntin' down dead folks. Weren't long before we came across the first 'un and Karl Streiner shot him right there and then. That dead fella kinda folded up as he went down; there weren't no histrionics to it. Karl gave out a rebel yell at that and one or two of the others joined in. Not me. It weren't the first thing I'd seen killed, not by a long shot and as such I wasn't that given to celebratin' it none. Don't know why he had to do no rebel yell anyways; this is Pennsylvania, not Georgia or somesuch place.

It was an old fella that he shot, bald 'cept for a wisp of grey hair right in the middle of his pate. Anyways, we all ran up to take a gander but nobody recognised who it was. Or had been, if you get my drift. Soon enough, someone's on the walkie-talkie thing, callin' it in. Wasn't sure what all that was about at the time but now I know of course.

Man, them pyres are a sight to behold. It was a first for me, and that's no lie. Ain't never seen a body burn before, not up close an' all. Hell, I been to funerals enough but let me tell you there's quite a difference seein' a coffin goin' behind them big purple curtains and knowin' what's goin' to happen to it and seein' the deed done right there in front of you.

And the smell. Oh lordy.

Seems it's the best way to make sure that them dead folks don't come back again. What with them havin' done it the once already. Better safe than sorry, as my pa is fond of sayin'. They look kinda pretty at night, all them fires. Shame about the smell.

That old codger was the first but there was plenty more

where he came from. It's surprisin' just how many dead folks there are. Plenty room for some more now I guess, what with all them graves bein' newly empty.

It wasn't long till I got me my first dead one. This was a fella too, though not as old as that first one. Just wanderin' through the woods he was, goin' real slow so it weren't that much to get a sight on him and squeeze the trigger. Damn near took the top of his head off! His hair kinda flew up when my bullet hit and it looked funny. Least ways it did to me, made me laugh. And that got me some black looks I can tell you. "This is serious business," Walter Reade said — but then he always has had a stick up his ass so I didn't pay him much heed.

I guess some of that laughter came from somewhere else though. This bein' the first actual person I'd ever killed it was somewhat of an event for me that's for sure. I mean, I'd thought about it plenty enough and have killed many other things but I can tell you straight, shootin' a cat or a dog ain't the same.

Anyhoo, we radioed in the kill and went on our way. We all wandered around for some time after that but we didn't find any more dead folk and people started gettin' a bit bored. Karl was the first to leave — which came as no surprise because he ain't never had any kind of stayin' power and then, not long after, Keith Hirzman upped sticks and went.

After that, well I didn't really know anyone else that was left so it was me who was the third to go. It was on my way home that I saw another of 'em. Some old lady it was, wobblin' her shaky path along the road. Well, it didn't take me but two ticks to shoulder my rifle and line her up in my sights.

Pow! And down she went.

Man, the thrill I got at that one was better than the first. Soon as I saw her drop I was runnin' over to get me a better look. As I got closer I could tell somethin' wasn't quite right. Them others that got shot well, they didn't bleed none – well, not as much as might be expected from a gunshot wound. I'm guessin' that was somethin' to do with them bein' already dead and their blood would be, what's the word? Conjoined. But this one was different, even before I got within twenty feet of her I could see the blood gushin' out of her, like someone had put a faucet on her head and turned it fully open.

Well now. Seems I'd made somewhat of a mistake. Turns out the old lady I'd shot wasn't one of the risen dead. She was more than plenty dead now of course but this was on a first time basis if all the blood was anythin' to go by. It wasn't all bad though, at least I'd been on my own when it happened. Still, it was somewhat of a dilemma I was in. How best to sort it out?

I didn't have long to ponder that question cause no sooner was I stood there lookin' down at her than I heard an engine approachin'. Not wantin' to be found at the scene of the crime so to speak I skedaddled out of there into the trees. Not a moment too soon because seconds later that big ol' truck come round the corner, the one they were usin' to transport all them dead-again folks to the fires.

The truck pulled up next to the body and my heart was hammerin' away just like them dogs' legs did when I was holdin' their heads under the water. And wasn't I the relieved one when they got out of the truck and hefted her up onto the back with all them other bodies piled up there. They didn't even bat an eyelid, just threw her in with the rest and drove off.

Well now, there was a thing…

I went over to where the old biddy had been layin', looked down at the bloodstain left behind in the dirt. There was other stuff mixed in there too, bits of bone and mushy stuff which must have been brains. Shee-it, I was quite the marksman. Of course, I had to touch it, to feel what it was like. Jello, as it turned out. I'd had my hands on plenty animal guts of course but this was different. Not in the feel of it—which was pretty much the same—just different, because this was from a person, a human bein'.

I kinda liked it.

I realise now that moment was like the one Paul had on his way to Damascus, the one they told us about in bible study. That was the moment he realised who he was and what he was meant to do and that's exactly how I felt, rubbin' that old lady's brains between my fingers. Sometimes it's adversity that brings out the best in a person—that was somethin' else they told us in bible studies—but it was only at that moment I realised the truth of what it was they were sayin'.

I wiped the blood and brain off on my pants and set off along the road filled with an excitement more than I'd ever felt. (Even more than when I'd killed that bull and I thought I'd never top that).

Either they hadn't seen all the blood or they had – but weren't bothered none by it. Given that it was all over the road they couldn't *not* have seen it—they would have been treadin' in it too—so my opinion was it's the second of those two options which was the truth of things. Hell, if that was my job I'd want it doin' as quick as. I had no reason to suspect otherwise of them two who were actually doin' the clean-up work.

Man, was I buzzin'! Some might have seen this as the end of the world but for me it was the beginnin' of a whole new one. Pa always tells me that I'll never amount to nothin', never find my true callin'. Says that's why mama drinks so much too, on account she feels the same way and I'm such a disappointment to them both. Well now, I don't give two shits what those two think—about me or anything else for that matter—but as I walked along that road I knew that I *had* found a callin', and maybe it wouldn't make them feel any prouder of me but it would damn sure make me feel good which, at the end of the day, is all that really matters.

When I saw Wayne Russo walkin' towards me I knew

what I had to do and my rifle was up on my shoulder before he even got his hand up to wave to me. I didn't shoot straight away, took a moment or two to enjoy the look of shock on his face. He called out to me and I could hear the tremblin' in his voice. Havin' been on the wrong end of many of his beatin's in the past, what with him bein' all cool and always surrounded by his friends and me bein' – well, me I guess, I have to say I enjoyed hearin' that fear, it gave me a nice, tingly feelin'.

He turned to run but never made it given as how I took that moment to squeeze the trigger and blew his head off. Man, that was even better than the old lady. This time I knew what I was doin' and so could appreciate it more. The shot made him fly forwards into the ground and he threw up a cloud of dust when he hit. Not so cool now, Mr Russo.

And that was it. Cool was the word. I felt cool. Somethin' that was new to me, truth to tell but somethin' I liked very much. So cool I didn't even look down at Russo sprawled there in the dirt, now minus his head, just walked on by. He'd be on the truck soon enough, on his way to the fire. Me? I was on my way to a nice, cold sixpack.

Maybe Bill O'Dea is right. Maybe this is all down to that space probe explodin' and spreadin' some weird kind of shit all over. If that's the case then I figure this is a much bigger problem than even Sheriff McClelland might realise. Hell, this could be happenin' way beyond Butler County – maybe the whole state of Pennsylvania is affected. Shit, maybe the whole country! That's the case, this emergency could go on for plenty time to come; we could be huntin' down the dead for days or even weeks.

Bill O'Dea is full of shit. Most of the time. Sometimes though, he's right.

Maybe he's right this time.

I surely hope so.

A TRIBUTE TO GEORGE A. ROMERO

ANTHONY WATSON

Anthony Watson has placed short stories in various indie press publications. He has also seen publication of his war/horror novella *Winter Storm* in a six author collection *Darker Battlefields* from The Exaggerated Press and has completed another, *The Lost*, for inclusion in the follow-up volume.

His weird western novella *The Company of the Dead* made up a double-header with Benedict J Jones' *Mulligan's Idol* in Volume 1 of *Dark Frontiers*. Work has begun on Volume 2.

January 2018 saw publication of his novel, *Witnesses*, by Crowded Quarantine Publications and he is currently working on a second which will feature demons, angels, scientists, sailors, mercenaries, ships and planes. And lots of snow.

As well as writing, he runs a horror review blog "Dark Musings"

(found at: http://anthony-watson.blogspot.co.uk/).

MEMORIES OF ROMERO

I knew the storyline, and pretty much every scene in *Dawn of the Dead* before I'd even seen it thanks to my mate Kevin. Kevin had seen it, more than once, and he'd spend every break at school regaling me with the wonders he'd witnessed on screen. "A helicopter blade! A screwdriver!"

I'm pretty sure Kevin had an eidetic memory given the amount of detail he provided when describing the plots of the films he'd been to see and as a result I often felt it unnecessary to actually go and see them myself. This one was different though. A helicopter blade? A screwdriver?

Thus it was that we (yes, he wanted to see it again) made the journey to Newcastle to watch *Dawn of the Dead* and, despite having intimate knowledge of what was going to happen, I was utterly enthralled by what I was watching. I'd never seen anything quite like it —certainly in terms of the amount of gore being sprayed around the screen. Of course, I was only fourteen at the time but this was nothing like *The Omen* which we'd sneaked into the year before.

It was a profound moment but not quite the same as when I saw *Night...* a few years later on TV. What I watched that night in student digs was – and remains – one of the darkest films I've ever seen. Being a little older I was able to appreciate the real horror of the film – yeah, the risen dead were horrible but there was so much more to it than that. The scenes which affected me most profoundly were the closing ones, that final montage of still photographs and then the closing shot of the pyre…

Having revisited the films so many times since, I can appreciate just how clever they are. It takes real skill to convey subtext and important messages in film without detracting from their entertainment value and that's what George A Romero did in amazing fashion. His films provided me with so much in terms of how I approach, and appreciate horror and I am forever grateful to him for that.

OFF AIR
BY
DUNCAN P. BRADSHAW

Richard fussed and preened at the Doctor's stained suit, dabbing a towel against a large coffee stain, "Heck, I'm real sorry about that. This whole jawn has everyone on edge, you know?"

The Doctor placed a hand on top of the studio director's shoulder, "So much for trying to help you people. Look…I get it, I just want out of here."

Stepping back to admire his handiwork, utterly oblivious, Richard sized up the soiled suit, "It ain't perfect, but it'll do."

Foster folded his arms, "The exit, where is it?"

"Oh right, of course, Owen here will walk you to your car, make sure you get out of here safe." Richard raised his hand and clicked his fingers, trying desperately to get the attention of the security guard, who was doing a quick headcount of the remaining studio crew. He clocked Richard's furious gesticulation and ambled over.

"Say, Doctor, where you off to next? Got another interview lined up?"

Buttoning his jacket up, Doctor Foster shook his head, "Are you crazy? You saw what this bunch of crazies were like. You think I'm going to put myself through that again? Not a chance. I'm heading back to DC. At least I'm appreciated there."

"Hey, I didn't think it would go this way, everyone's all riled up, that's all," Richard protested.

Pinching his nose, Foster sighed, "Fine, whatever. Please, heed what I said, you and your staff have to get out of here, this is madness! It's only going to get worse out there."

As the guard led the flustered man away, Richard called after him, "We're only here till midnight, the emergency networks take over then." Foster waved a hand dismissively, before he disappeared through the doorway out of sight.

Richard turned on his heels and stormed across to the few crew members that were still milling around the studio. He grabbed hold of the cameraman, and shouted, "Nice one, idiots! That guy came here to try and help and all youse did was berate him. You should be ashamed."

Spinning his camera around, Todd shirked free from the grip, "Don't get fresh with me, man, I'm just trying to do my job. You know that you should've sent us all home by now, don't you? We got families, man. People are freaking out over here. The last thing we need is Doctor Beardy coming in here telling us we gotta kill these geeks. That's not cool, man, not cool at all."

"Fine, Todd, look, we got a few hours left until the network pulls the plug, let's just keep going until then, okay?"

Todd looked up at the control booth, "Fine, but then I'm going home. So should you."

"You bet your ass I am," Richard slapped Todd on the back and ran his hands across his bald pate; dribbles of sweat ran into the thatch of hair that still clung to the sides of his head. After wiping his hand on his trouser legs, he looked from a monitor showing the current programme, up to the elevated booth, "Hey! Why is the rescue stations crawl not back on?"

George cupped a hand over his microphone, and shouted over his console, "Fran told us to turn them off, said that most of them aren't responding any—"

"Jesus H Christ. Who gives a shit what she said? Who's in charge here? Huh?"

Turning to his colleagues and muttering something which made them snigger, George shouted back, "I guess that would be you, *Dick*."

"Damn straight. Where the heck is Franny anyways?"

Looking over his shoulder, George shrugged, "No idea, think she stepped out a little while back, when Stephen came by."

"Fine, I'll remind her of her duties later. Now please, get those goddamn rescue stations scrolling again. People need information, and if they're not getting it from us, they'll change channel and go elsewhere, okay? Jeez..." Richard tugged at his tie, feeling as if it was trying to constrict him, and walked across to the semi-circular table, which was the focal point of the studio.

Talk show host, Danny Berman, was tapping at a cigarette as if his finger was a woodpecker, the stubborn kernel of ash clung onto the smouldering cherry, "What if he's right? What if we missed our chance and it's all too late now?"

"I've seen all kinds of shit go down in Philly, we're gonna be just fine. This thing'll blow over in a few weeks, you'll see," Richard patted himself down, eventually finding his pack of cigarettes in an inside pocket. With shaking fingers, he took one out and lit it, the flame danced in time with his trembling.

Snapping the Zippo shut, he saw Berman staring back at him, "Sure thing, *Dick*, sure thing."

Straightening his tie out as best he could, Richard took a drag before pointing at Danny, the cigarette spewing curling smoke into the air, "Cut the crap, and just make sure you're ready for the next segment, okay?"

Danny pushed back on his chair, "Who we got this time?"

"Another petri-dish botherer, Millard Rausch, or something. From what I've heard, if you thought the good Doctor Foster was a tightass, this guy'll blow you away."

"Great, another egghead, just what we need right now," Danny smoothed down his waistcoat, and began to pick through his notes, puffing out smoke rings from the corner of his mouth as he read.

Richard leant over the front of the desk and knocked the steeple of cigarette ash into an empty coffee mug, "Look here, it's all people are talking about, not as if we're gonna get the Flyers centre in here right now, is it? Just do your fucking job, and we'll get through this, okay?"

Danny held his hands up, "No worries, man, I'll do what you want me to," he nodded at the vacuous studio, "though if anyone else splits, you're gonna have to put Owen on camera detail."

Daring to turn around, Richard took in the set. Normally, it was a hive of activity, people practically falling over each other as they worked to get the current affairs show on air. Today, it was a ghost town. Those who had stuck around to hear what the scientist had to say had left, leaving crumpled scripts, stage directions, and Styrofoam cups on the floor. Todd and Danny aside, there were three upstairs in the booth, Connie from make-up and a couple of other guys who Richard was convinced didn't actually work for WGON, and were seeking a brief respite from whatever the hell was going on out in the streets.

As Richard took another pull on his cigarette, his wandering thoughts were shattered as a solitary gunshot rang out. As one, the room hushed, and everyone looked to the doorway. The second shot made everyone jump, the expectancy of it doing little to mitigate the reality. There was a muffled shout, before a third bang sounded. Richard marched towards the doorway, clutching a microphone stand in his clenched fist, "Everyone stay calm, I'm sure it's—"

Owen rounded the corner at pace. Using it to steady his aim, he pushed his shoulder into the jamb, peered back down the corridor, and loosed off another round, his hand recoiling with the force. "What the heck is going on out there, Owen?" Richard demanded, waving the microphone stand at the guard.

Ducking into the studio, Owen ran his free hand round his belt, searching for more bullets, his ashen face looked across to Richard who was still advancing on him, "It's—"

An abyssal moan echoed up from the corridor, funnelled down its concrete lined oesophagus and into the studio, erupting into the room like a foghorn. Owen gulped, his Adam's apple rippled in his throat. Richard stopped dead in his tracks upon hearing the sound, making him fiddle with his tie again. The security guard pointed behind him at the open doorway with his revolver-laden hand, "It's them, Mr Degale. They're in the building."

The room gasped as one, the inhabitants looked from one to another, seeking assurances which no one could provide. Another bassy rumbling shook them from their reverie, Owen spun round in time to see a woman standing in the doorway. Her cheeks had been torn open, her mouth now ratcheted open to an impossible angle, rows of shiny wet teeth glistened from the harsh overhead lights. Dried blood caked her chin, as if she had been gorging on a jar of strawberry jam. A floral blouse splattered with blood and stringy pieces of flesh sagged from her shoulders.

Her dead eyes regarded the occupants of the room with little more than a flicker of recognition, before her hands, twisted into feral claws, raised towards them at the prospect of fresh meat. Her right leg, the knee buckled inwards, lurched forwards, her motion like a ship listing on choppy seas. Owen took a step back, closed an eye and aimed at her head.

The revolver's retort was near deafening, amplified within the bowels of the room. The woman's head rocked backwards, the pale blue wall behind her was pebble dashed with chunks of her skull and brain. She took another step forward before her legs gave way, her body smacked into the floor, slumped against Owen's feet. A pool of black coagulated blood slopped from the wound in her forehead, now pressed against the concrete ground, the lumpy viscous liquid oozed out.

The security guard looked down instinctively, before hopping backwards, every step away from the woman's body left a bloodied footprint on the grey floor. Richard placed a hand gently on the small of Owen's back, trying to not frighten him, but the man jolted at the touch. He spun around. Richard looked into the frenzied eyes of the security guard, his mouth carved into an O.

"Easy, son, easy now," Richard laid a hand on top of the revolver, and angled it away from his body, gently applying pressure on the weapon, until it pointed at the floor. "Good work, son, you did good. Now, let's get this show on the road. We're back on air in five, with or without that damned Rausch."

Richard went to walk past Owen, who grabbed the director's bicep in a vice-like grip, "I don't think we're going to be able to, sir."

Feeling his heckles rise, Richard ground his teeth, and glared at the guard, "And why not? Hmmm? Give me one goddamn reason why not."

A chorus of moans echoed from the corridor in response, grey pallid hands slapped against the doorframe, broken nails and shorn off fingers seeking purchase into the room. "There's a whole ton of them in the building, sir."

Richard's mouth fell open, and the cigarette which had been clamped into a corner of his mouth drooped, before tumbling onto the floor, the cherry exploding in a shower

A TRIBUTE TO GEORGE A. ROMERO

of fiery sparks. A businessman dressed in a smart suit, save for a blood stain which made his shirt look like a bib, appeared in the doorway. A switchblade, shoved in so deep that the top of the hilt was buried within his body, jutted from the shoulder. Though that palsied arm hung slack, the other was out in front, groping the air, pointed towards the people in the room who were rooted to the spot.

Owen shoved Richard behind him, took aim and fired, the bullet ripped through the man's throat, shattering the spine and making him fall to the ground as if he were a puppet who'd had his strings cut. Even with the loss of his legs, the businessman craned his head upwards. A rasping wet moan resonated from the bullet hole and his wide-open maw. With his one good hand, he began to drag himself across the floor, pushing past the body of the previous intruder. "For God sakes man, finish it off," Richard shouted. Owen squeezed the trigger, the businessman's back shuddered from the impact, but still it continued its inexorable path forward. "Hurry up, man! Kill it."

The security guard cracked his head to the left and right, planted his feet, and closed an eye, aiming for the businessman's head. Sure of his aim, Owen squeezed the trigger once more.

CLICK.

Owen held the gun to his face, and examined it as if it were a carton of milk on the occasion of its expiry date. Seeing the businessman pull himself closer, Owen took a step forward, and pressed the barrel against the top of the prostrate man's head.

CLICK.

"Oh my god," Richard looked at the doorway, now blocked with more of the shambling dead. The only respite came from the walking corpse's eagerness to get to the warm flesh, which meant they were sandwiched shoulder to shoulder between the doorframe. A surge from behind pushed the first two into the room, like a freshly unblocked hose, the undead ambled inside.

CLICK

CLICK

Owen felt cold fingers press against his calf, which began to gouge into the muscle. Turning the revolver round, so he held the barrel like the handle of an axe, he roared and pistol-whipped the man's skull. There was a crack like ice being dumped into warm Cola, and another as Owen brought the weapon down again. This time though, there was a slurp as it broke through the bone and into the ribbed organ within. A few more lusty blows and Owen felt the pinch on his leg cease. He shook the hand free from his trousers and staggered backwards into Richard.

The undead, like an evening tide, swept into the room. Pete, who had only been with the network a few months, was set upon first. He hadn't moved a muscle since the first of the dead had been felled, and was swarmed, pinned to the ground and devoured, still clutching a clipboard to his chest. Ropes of intestine were pulled from their cavity and dragged across timetables and Neilson charts, as keen fingers rent him open.

"Come on, people, we have to push them back, we gotta get them outside or we're all goners," Todd shouted.

This stirred a few people into action, seizing hold of anything they could get their hands on. Poles from lighting rigs, a mop, the end snapped off so it was a crude spear, all wielded with a degree of uncertainty. Owen flicked open the revolver and shook out the expended shells, before fumbling fresh rounds into the chamber. Richard retreated into the room, eventually butting against the half crescent desk, where he sunk to the floor and pulled his legs to his chest, sobbing gently.

George from the booth slid down the ladder which ran to his little nest, a paperweight in hand. He bellowed a series of expletives, before charging the nearest zombie, and set about caving in their skull with the glass orb. This spurred on the others. Todd, who was armed with a small hand camera, rallied a few people, "Pete's a goner, but we can use him as a distraction. Focus on the doorway, okay? Will, get jabbing at them with the mop handle, Sam, the same with you and that pole. Try and get those geeks out into the corridor. If we can close the door, then we can deal with any stragglers left in here, okay?"

Buoyed by instruction, even if they were still filled with fear, people began to fan out. Todd joined George and began to tackle those who were in the room already, and were eager for their own piece of meat. Will and Sam, after avoiding the attentions of a former policeman, another in the nameless ranks of the undead, skulked towards the doorway, trying to push the horde back into the corridor.

Another scream curdled everyone's insides as Connie tangoed with a portly man, dressed only in a pair of tight shorts. His chubby hands turned her head to one side, letting him sink his teeth easily into her neck. With blood trickling from the wound, he pulled his head backwards, ripping out Connie's jugular. Arterial spray painted his blue face, red, as he sunk to the floor with his prize. Podgy fingers rooted inside the freshly created wound, delving within for chunks of warm flesh. Connie's eyes flared once with a last spark of vitality, before they dimmed, and she sunk into her killer's embrace, who continued to pick and pull at her now lifeless body.

Owen, with a freshly reloaded revolver, ducked beneath the lazy swipe of an undead mailman, smacking him on the back of the neck as he went. The momentum sent the postal worker to the ground, where Owen placed a foot on the base of the man's skull, before blowing it open with a well-aimed shot. He didn't even give the man a second glance, as he strode over to the doorway, where Will and Sam were still trying to keep the murderous advance at bay. "Get ready," Owen warned, then worked his way from left to right with three more shots, each sent their targets spinning into the corridor. "Now, goddammit, now," Owen shouted. Shouldering his weapon, Will grabbed hold of the door and swung it shut.

There was a dull thud as it bounced off an arm which had been reaching out for Sam. Pushing all of his weight against the door, Will edged towards the obstruction, "A little help here?" Owen slammed into the door, stopping the reapplied pressure from outside putting paid to their good work. Sam started to smack the invasive limb with the bloodied metal pole. The arm remained, fingers curled and flexed, certain that sustenance was within reach.

Will got to the edge of the door and turned to Owen, "On three, let the door open a little and I'll grab him, okay?" The guard nodded, Sam continued to flail at the hand which was beginning to bow from the attack, the bone within fractured, like broken pottery in a sack of skin.

"One…two…three…"

The two men let the pressure off for a second, long enough for Will to grab hold of the intruder's forearm and yank him into the studio, "Take care of him will ya, Sammy?" His friend nodded, standing over the stricken zombie and lashed out with the metal pole. Will grabbed hold of the edge of the door, let out a scream, before slamming it shut. With his back to the barrier, he slid down it, coming to a rest.

Owen appeared in his eyeline, "You did good."

Will began to sob, holding his hand up, Owen winced, the top of the man's index finger was missing; a rough bite mark and tattered skin heralded its demise. "Just go, help the others," Will demanded, he pulled his tie off and wrapped it round the finger, desperately trying to stem the bleeding.

Turning away, Owen took in the sights. George and Todd were with a few other men, splattered in blood, dealing with the stragglers. He chuckled to himself, as the gateway to insanity buckled within. The dead, who were being obliterated, paid their attackers no heed. One, a prim and proper looking woman, had pulled off Connie's arm at the shoulder, and was languidly chewing on the meat as if she were having dinner whilst watching a TV show. Her mouth continued to work, even as George caved her skull in with the paperweight. The woman sagged under the assault, finally expiring, again, in a crumpled heap of blood, shattered bones and limbs, some of which were not her own. As the last sounds of violence subsided, there was a collective intake of breath, a stock take of events.

There was a wide swathe of human devastation in a fifteen-foot arc from the doorway. Blood, both fresh and bitter, mingled together on the floor, separating out from each other like the foam and coffee in a cappuccino. Those who bore them, checked their weapons, and then themselves for signs of injury, patting each other on the back when their inquiries were complete, only to tut and moan when they saw Will, cradling his hand, the blood seeping through his tartan tie. They offered regret and remorse, though in their heads, were relieved it was not them.

Like surfacing from underwater, there was a pop, and the silence was broken. Hands began to pound and scrape on the door. Teeth grazed against the paintwork, fingernails gouged away, eager to get back into the room, and finish what their kin had started. The survivors looked from one to another, panting, unsure as to how much they had left to give. From behind them, came clapping, "Well done, everybody, well done," Richard said.

George looked around slowly, a grimace fixed to his face, his fingers squeaked against the gore spattered paperweight, "Why, thank you, *Dick*, what an outstanding effort you made. I really must commend you on a job well fucking done."

Even Will forgot the burning pain which had started to worm its way down his arm, through the network of blood vessels, and stood up, regarding the man who still continued to applaud. Richard finally got the message and ceased, he wiped his sweaty palms against his jacket, "I mean...I would've helped, just...you know, you guys looked like you were in control."

"I ought to smash your face in and leave you with them," George pointed to the pile of bodies, the undead and dead crocheted together in a grisly tableau, "least you know their intentions, you? Who knows?"

Richard gulped, "Say now fellas, let's not be so harsh, I mean, not everyone's cut out for this, you know?"

Owen stepped in between the two men, his weapon holstered, "Come on now, that door ain't gonna hold forever, and I think our luck is in limited supply. We need to get out of here. And the only way we're gonna do that, is by everyone pulling together, you hear me?"

Still glaring at Richard, George reluctantly nodded, "Sure thing, just keep him away from me." With that, George shuffled across to the desk, taking a welcome cigarette from Berman, who had a broken bloodied chair backrest lying on his knees.

Richard looked side to side, eager to make sure there was no one in earshot, before sidling up to Owen, "Say, son, weren't you in 'Nam?"

The soldier in him snapped to attention, "Yes sir, two tours, sir. Air cavalry. Never seen anything like this though. Spent most of the time watching forests and villages burn to cinder, never had to...up close I mean. Never had to..."

With an arm around his shoulder, Richard pulled Owen in, "Mighty proud of your service, son. We all are. Me especially, heck, that's why I insisted they employed you, you know? Got to look after our vets, that's what I say."

"Why thank you, sir, I don't really see how this is going to help all of us."

"I think you'll find that there's something a man of your talents can help with. In fact, you might be the only one who can save me...I mean us. All of us, what do you think about that, soldier?"

A TRIBUTE TO GEORGE A. ROMERO

Owen looked from the sweaty director across to the other survivors, Will was slumped against the desk, whilst Sam stood in front of the door, trying to will the scratching and scraping to cease by mind power alone, he nodded, "I'd like that very much, sir. You just tell me what I need to do."

Richard squeezed Owen's shoulder, "Not just yet, son, all in good time. We gotta see how this plays out for now, okay? These folk are too skittish for my liking, we gotta deal with it just right, you hear me?"

"Yes sir."

"Good, now, let's go see how everyone's doing," Richard patted Owen on the back and walked off to the table, where the remaining survivors were gathered.

"So how many ways out of here are there?" Danny asked.

George pointed to the door which vibrated and shimmered with every battering, "That is one of two, though the other, above the booth? That only leads to the roof, there's no way we can get past those things from up there. Unless any of us has sprouted wings, then I think our choices are somewhat limited."

"The longer we wait, the more we're going to have to face," Sam added.

"The way I figure it, we have two choices: we either barricade ourselves in here and wait them out, or we try to fight our way outside. The car park is right by the entrance, providing there aren't too many of those things, we should be able to get away pretty easy," George said, peeling strips of skin and gore from the paperweight in a slow deliberate way.

"I for one say we go out fighting, we ain't got many supplies in here, no food at least, plus it's only a matter of time before that door goes and then the decision is made for us. The longer we leave it, the worse it's gonna be. We can use these, here," Owen tapped the top of the table, lifting up some of the panels. "We have a couple of folk up front, block them off with these, use them as shields. It should hold long enough while those behind try and spear 'em. With a bit of luck, and some elbow grease, I reckon we can clear a path outside."

George nodded, "Think that's about as good as we're gonna get. Okay folks, look around for something you can use as a weapon. The longer the better, if you can, grab something smaller you can use up close if you need to. No idea what we're gonna face when we get outside, it'll be every man for himself," he glowered at Richard, "should suit you down to the ground, huh?"

The group began to peel away, scouring the studio for anything they could use as a weapon. Sam crouched by Will, who was coated in a fine sheen of sweat, his head lolled to one side. Trembling fingers clutched his injured hand to his chest, which was rising and falling quickly, "Hang on in there, we're gonna get out of here, you'll see, then we'll get you fixed up."

Shivering, Will looked up at the silhouette of his friend, "Too…late…for me, Sammy." Blood slick fingers reached up to the face which loomed over him, "Please…take care of me…before…before I come back. I don't want to…not…like that…"

"Shhh, you're gonna be fine, it's only a nick, there's no way that a little scratch like that is gonna turn you into one of those things, I promise."

Will's glazed eyes shimmered as they tried to focus on Sam's face, "Please…Sammy…please."

"How's he doing?" Richard's voice boomed behind Sam, who jumped at the noise.

"He's got a fever, he should be fine," Sam smoothed down Will's hair, tucking it behind his ear.

Richard gasped, "Jesus H Christ, he's bit! We gotta isolate, knock him out, or…"

Sam stood up, nose to nose with Richard, "Or what?"

"You know," Richard raised an eyebrow and nodded down at Will, who sunk lower to the floor.

"No, go on, tell me."

Grabbing hold of the pole, Richard mock swung it, "Take care of him," he hissed, "before it's too late."

"Be my guest," Sam stood to one side, allowing Richard to stand over the now unconscious man. Richard first licked his lips, before rubbing his moustache, stepping to one side, then the other, trying to work out the best angle of attack. Settling on a position, he raised the bar above his head, and held it there. He stared down at Will, who had slumped forward, the crown of his head presented itself perfectly. Richard's hands tremored before he took a sharp intake of breath and staggered back, lowering the pole, "I can't…"

Sam snatched the weapon back, "Exactly, not so easy is it? Besides, he's just resting. We'll get him to a rescue station when we get outta here. They'll patch him up. You'll see."

"But the rescue stations—"

"What?" Sam snapped.

Richard gulped, trying to find some saliva to moisten his dry mouth, "Oh nothing, don't worry about it."

"Are you two ready?" George shouted across. The few who had survived were standing by the doorway, which creaked on strained hinges. The thumping of balled fists, the scrape of tooth and nail reverberated through the room.

"I guess so, I'll just get Will," Sam knelt down and heaved the deadweight up, bearing the load on a shoulder, so Will's feet scraped across the floor.

Danny and George were at the front, each held a crude rectangular shield fashioned from the table leaves, handles made from duct tape and telephone receivers. "Owen, you go get the door, but be ready for the surge, we'll try and pin them in. Everyone behind us get ready to spear those deadheads, you hear me?" There was a low murmur of agreement, George fixed Richard with an icy stare, "By everyone, I mean *everyone*, clear?" Richard nodded, snatching the broken mop handle spear from Danny, who finished his cigarette and flicked the butt away.

"Good, now, let's go," George and Danny readied themselves a few feet back from the door. "Now, Owen."

The security guard ducked in quick, fiddled with the door latch, and twisted the handle. The door flung open, the dead who had been pressed against the other side, fell into the room. George and Danny brought their makeshift shields down on the back of their skulls, causing a stereo of bone cracks to sound out.

With the pressure eased, the two men lunged forward, standing on top of the fallen, pressing their putrid bodies down onto the floor. The two shields blocked the doorway, the men behind began to stab and spear at the new ranks of bloodied mouths and sundered faces as they appeared in sight.

It was tough work, having forced their way into the corridor, George and Danny turned to the left, towards the main doors which were at the end. Thirty feet or so to safety, but every inch of that was taken up by decomposing flesh and clacking jaws. Owen took care of a couple of stragglers, exposed to the right-hand side when the front pair had made their turn, gunshots reduced skulls to open bowls of shattered bone and offal.

Slowly, but surely, they inched further down the corridor. With the shield bearers up front, Todd and a couple of men behind lancing anything they could see, it left Sam and Will in the middle. Owen and Richard brought up the rear.

Then, when it seemed as though the tide had turned, an ungodly scream rang out from within the living. Richard put an arm across Owen's chest, and held him back, as Sam was pinned to the wall. Will, now in control of his limbs, had latched onto Sam's neck with his teeth, they ground and bit deeper, before tearing a chunk of skin and flesh off in one go. Sam sunk to the floor, a hand clamped over ruptured vein and artery, trying to press the blood back into his body. Will idly chewed on the morsel, before falling to his knees, ice-cold fingers raked Sam's face, before finding purchase in the soft eye cavities.

Howling like an animal caught in a trap, Sam was trapped between fighting off the attacker and staunching the horrific blood loss. He did neither, as Will hooked his fingers underneath Sam's eyeballs and plucked them from the sockets, before shoving them in his mouth and chewing on them. Even as he did so, his fingers were already foraging within the bloody craters, eager to pry out more of the warm meat from within. Chaos began to reign. Todd, distracted by the sounds of feasting behind him, missed with a wild stab, and caught Danny in the shoulder. Sagging from the impact, Berman stumbled, the previously impenetrable blockade stuttered, before parting completely.

The throng of dead pushed into the gap, turning it from a fissure into a chasm in mere seconds, the men struggled to push them back, to create some space to counter attack. Clammy hands, sticky with blood, clamoured over their prey, teeth snapped, and the survivors struggled to bring their weapons to bear.

Owen went to move forward to help Sam, even though it was clear that he was beyond salvation, Richard pulled him back, "Come on now, we can't do nothing to help these people, but we can still save ourselves."

Struggling against the barrier, Owen relented, "What do you mean?"

"Come with me, son, I know another way," Richard pulled on Owen's arm, "come on now, don't be silly, let them go, let's save ourselves."

"But I—"

Richard slapped Owen, "Goddammit, fucking follow me, *now*, or so help me God…"

"Help me!! George shouted, before he disappeared into the undead swarm.

"See, it's too late for them, but we still have a chance,"

Richard pulled on Owen's arm, leading him back to the studio.

Owen covered his mouth, before he nodded reluctantly. The two men turned tail and jogged back to the doorway, managing one last look behind, the undead were completely in control, either feasting on steaming flesh, or shuffling towards the two men. Richard crossed himself, before disappearing back into the studio. Pointing to the ladder leading to the booth, he pushed Owen onwards, "Go on now, get up there."

A low moaning came from the room, the pair turned towards the pile of bodies which had been heaped from the initial assault. From the bottom, Connie crawled free, jagged fingernails trying desperately to grip the floor, her mouth chomped thin air, teeth click clacked against each other.

"Holy shit," Owen shouted, before grabbing hold of the first rung and climbing up to the booth.

At the top, Richard nodded towards a closed door, leading the way through labyrinthian corridors, before finally getting to a set of double doors. From behind them, came nothing but feral moans and growls.

"Wh-what are we doing? George said there's no way out up here," Owen sunk to his knees, panting from the exertion and the adrenalin coursing through his veins.

Richard patted the guard on the back, before adjusting his tie, and folding down his jacket lapels, he laughed, "Just wait till you see what's beyond those doors. That's why I needed you. Go on now, take a look-see."

Unsure as to what to think, Owen gripped his revolver tighter and held it down by his side, with one eye on Richard, he edged towards the double doors, "Is this some kind of trick?"

Richard laughed even louder, as the sound of moans joined in from behind him, a monotonal choir, "Not at all, go on, take a look. It's a little present, courtesy of WGON Drive-Time traffic reporting."

A TRIBUTE TO GEORGE A. ROMERO

Owen pushed open the doors and staggered outside, the cold January air hit him like a bat. Unsure as to what to look for, he lurched this way and that, before he turned back to the doors and shrugged.

The triumphalism in Richard's smile faded in an instant, "No, no, no," he shouted. Richard jogged out onto the roof, the double doors slammed shut behind him. He looked across the vast empty expanse, peppered with air conditioning units and vents. "Where the fuck is it? WHERE THE FUCK IS IT?"

Owen stood next to him, looking at the high-rise buildings which stood over the men like grey judging gods, displeased with what they saw, "Where's what?"

Richard sunk to the floor, legs crossed, hands rubbed his bald dome, leaving red marks behind, "It's gone. Someone took it."

"Took what? Tell me goddammit!"

The double doors pushed open as the first of the dead broke through. Richard sat there throughout, Owen emptied the revolver at the oncoming horde. As the first dead hand settled on his throat, he mumbled, "The whirlybird…that flyboy, Stephen…he took the damn helicopter."

STORIES OF THE DEAD

DUNCAN P. BRADSHAW

Formed from a hodge-podge of body parts and random thoughts, Duncan P. Bradshaw is a byproduct of the generation that made do and mend. Why bother throwing something out and buying new, when you could just dig up another cadaver and forage for spare parts? The main side-effect of this is that his brain is a torturous mix of competing thoughts. To keep them all quiet he made them a pact, he'll write down their stories before vanquishing them. This partially explains the genres he teabags in an attempt to make a coherent tale. Go check out his work at www.duncanpbradshaw.co.uk and make up your own damn mind. Now get out of here before I take your hamstrings for my own.

MEMORIES OF ROMERO

I'm ten minutes into a film, and I'm going to be honest with you now, the eight year old me isn't exactly sure what's going on. Some cops, they look like SWAT, have stormed a block of flats and seem a little trigger happy. Oh wait, there's a guy stumbling out of his flat, his face is a little blue but that's cool, he's seen someone he knows. They're hugging, now that, in this maelstrom of madness is pretty-HOLY SHIT HE'S TAKING A BITE OUT OF HER NECK.

That's it right there and then. I'm hooked. I shouldn't be, but I cannot take my eyes off the screen. For the next hour and a half, I'm the silent fifth member of the Monroeville Mall Survivor's Club. What a ride! The rollercoaster of emotions, thinking they're safe, only to have Roger get bit when he gets too wired. The biker attack, but most of all, it's the monsters.

A TRIBUTE TO GEORGE A. ROMERO

I'd never seen their like before, on their own you can take care of them easily enough, but when they swarm you, man, they're borderline unstoppable. They terrified and enthralled me in equal measure. Vampires never did it for me, werewolves neither, but the undead? It wasn't just them you had to be scared of, it was the people left alive too.

Romero didn't just make movies about zombies, they were commentaries on society. The obvious ones are Night and Dawn, but even Diary holds a torch up to the world at that point in time. The beauty with these films were that you could take them at face value, or choose to scratch the surface and find such wonderful hidden treasures.

With his passing, David Owain Hughes contacted me to see if I would be interested in helping him put together an anthology as a tribute to the legend that is George A. Romero. If it were not for Romero and his films, I would never have started writing, so how could I say no?

FUEL
BY
JASON WHITTLE

Peter had given up all hope. There was nothing left for him in this ruined world. Better to accept his fate, end the struggle, end the pain.

He retreated to the back room, watched the doorway and awaited the inevitable. He tried to convince himself he was doing good. After all, every dead head that followed him in here would be one less chasing Francine. He could die with dignity and rest in peace.

However, this would be no serene, dignified passing. Even if a self-inflicted bullet made it quick, he would still be torn apart by teeth and claws. Eaten whole by a ravenous horde.

No. Not today.

Francine needed him. Alone and pregnant, she stood little chance. If he wasn't there to help protect them, then he might as well murder them himself. He had to get to her, and hoped it wasn't too late.

Peter lowered the pistol from his temple and fired at the first zombie through the door. A brother with an afro who might have been a friend in a different world. The bullet tore through his forehead, splattering the wall behind with gore, a good clean shot. As his lifeless body slid down the wall, Peter saw others behind.

They were weak, Peter was determined. He wrestled, punched and pistol-whipped his way through the crowd, knocking the undead aside like tenpins to get to the ladder. If it toppled in the melee, he'd be finished, no question, but there it stood. He scurried up, leaving the zombies grasping at fetid air.

He emerged on the roof, desperately hoping Francine had waited. She had, up to a point, but no longer. The helicopter was taking off. But she noticed him, he was sure of it.

He fought his way towards the hovering chopper, fuelled by genuine hope.

Where the hell did that come from?

When he got to the point where only one of *them* stood between him and salvation, it lunged at him. No, not him. His rifle!

Damn sweet gun, that. The only person who could miss with it was the sucker with the bread to buy it.

Peter allowed it to be taken. Hell, he'd been ready to let *everything* go. The gun-worshipping zombie stared adoringly at its new prize while Peter leapt to grab hold of the helicopter and drag himself in.

He regained his breath and asked, "How much fuel do we have?"

"Not much," replied Francine.

Peter allowed himself a wry smile. "Alright."

Peter looked out the window, trying to find his bearings against the unfamiliar landscape. "So, where we headed,

Fly-Girl?"

"Straight up."

"Really? Feels like a constant altitude to me."

"Straight up on the *map*, that is. Due north. We were on our way to Canada, remember? Before we stopped."

Peter recalled, but damn, it felt like a long time ago. "You know, this thing is probably happening there too. And it's gonna be a long, cold winter."

"Maybe. But we have to go somewhere, and there's no way we'll get enough juice in this bird to make Mexico. Speaking of which, we're going to need more fuel within the next few miles. Unless you intended on swimming across Lake Erie."

"Good. To tell the truth, I was getting airsick anyway. You ever get that nauseous feeling, Fly-Girl?"

"Only four or five times a day. It hurts less when we're in the sky."

"I won't hang about too long, as much as I enjoy having the ground under my feet. Hell, I don't even have a rifle anymore! Dammit Fly-Girl, I should've looked after that gun: any chance we can fly back so I can get it?"

"Peter, we've got enough fuel to get halfway back, maybe. And there's a small handgun back there, plus food and water. I've been ready to leave for weeks."

"Way to plan ahead, Fly-Girl! We should be following 79. There must be plenty of gas stations there."

"Automobile gas? Will this run on that? I thought we were looking for an airfield."

"We might as well try it. It'll be an easier find, and we can keep looking if it doesn't work."

"Peter, don't you get it? This is a one shot deal. Once we touch down, unless we fill up, we're never getting up again."

"Always the crisis, huh? Well, I guess I'd better keep looking real close; this airfield isn't going to find itself."

"I've left a pair of binoculars back there too."

A TRIBUTE TO GEORGE A. ROMERO

"Whoa, slow up, Fly-Girl! I think I've got something."

Francine looked down. "I don't see anything. What, you mean that place? It's an old farm isn't it?"

Peter peered through the binoculars again. "Yeah, it's a farm, but there's definitely a fuel pump. Guy might've had a private plane for crop-dusting or something."

"Or it's a pump for a tractor or ride-on mower."

"True, but I reckon we're out of options. How much fuel do we have?"

"Needle hit E seven miles ago. I never said, because I didn't want to worry you."

"You're all heart, Fly-Girl. Now, let's take her down and see what we find."

Francie touched down right next to the pump. She was so good that you'd never believe she was a novice pilot. However, if the pump was empty, or the contents didn't work, this would be her final flight.

Peter jumped out first and looked around. "I can't see any of them here, but you'd best stay inside to be safe."

"Screw that. I need to stretch my legs. And I'm desperate to pee."

"Then don't wander too far. You can trust me not to look."

Francine got out and went straight to the pump. "I can't go until I know this is okay," she explained.

The pump was unmarked. Peter squeezed out a tiny amount and sniffed at it. "It smells like it's supposed to." He connected it to the helicopter's fuel tank and started feeding it through. "It's flowing nicely, too."

"So am I, nearly," laughed Francine, the strain showing on her face. She'd been able to focus on flying when in the pilot's seat, but now the realisation she'd lost Steve was weighing on her. Maybe that's what she meant by it hurting less when she was in the sky.

Peter wondered how remote their chances were, which were increased by having some fuel, but not by much. Even if they could get to where they wanted, then what? Fly-Girl was going to need a lot of care, and Fly-Baby when it arrived. They weren't going to get anywhere in a hurry until after the birth, even if it went smoothly without a doctor and nurses. They'd need to get settled somewhere and shut the dead out. Someplace secure, with ample food, drink, tools, and medical supplies. They needed another mall. But what were the odds of finding one, and, even if they did, would he be able to clear it and seal it by himself without the help of Roger or Fly-Boy? Dealing with zombies was one thing, but those bastard road warriors had shown that other people were the biggest danger. It was—

Peter's train of thought was derailed by a sudden sharp pain, like a bee sting. He turned to see a teenage girl, dead, reach for the fuel nozzle. She knocked it out of his grasp as if he was stealing her personal supply. She was small and slim, weighing less than a hundred pounds or so. He pushed her away with minimal effort, sending her stumbling a few yards away. She dragged herself up, and Peter got his first real look at her. She was dressed in red: short skirt, knee length socks and a vest style top with the word 'Panthers' written across the chest in black lettering. In the hand she hadn't used to claw at the fuel nozzle, was a dirty, dishevelled pom-pom.

The dead girl lunged forward, attacking one-handed, not wanting to give up her accessory. Ready for her this time, Peter grabbed the back of her neck and slammed her head into the corner of the pump with brute force. And again, and again, never easing up, until her head was a pulpy mush and she'd long since stopped moving and groaning.

She was dead, she was nothing.

What was important was the fuel. When Peter reached

down, he noticed two things. Firstly, the pump had continued to run after being dropped and was now empty. And secondly, the tip of his pinky finger had been bitten half off.

Francine returned from behind the nearby bushes. "Oh shit, we had company?"

"Yeah. And she interrupted the fuelling. We won't get far." Peter held up his bitten finger. "And, er, this happened."

"Oh my God, Peter!"

"Ain't that just my luck? All I've been through and I get killed by a goddam high school cheerleader next to a rotten barn in the middle of nowhere. What was she even doing here? There ain't a school or sports field for miles around."

Francine was sobbing. "Peter... oh, Peter!"

"Don't give up on me yet, Fly-Girl. There's a lot to get done before you can afford to lose me."

"Peter... Peter, you're gonna turn."

"Yes, I am. But not today. And from a little scratch like this, not tomorrow, either. I'm sorry I can't see this whole thing through with you, but there's still time for me to help get you on your way."

He looked back at Francine, but she'd already taken her place in the helicopter. "Shit, Peter," she sighed. "Okay, get in."

Once they were airborne, Peter said, "Look, I know you're in charge now, but I really think we should go back the way we came."

"Back to the mall? Are you crazy?"

"Not the mall. The small airport nearby."

"Peter, we flew over that for a reason – those things were everywhere! It's far too busy to touch down."

"We had too much to lose back then. But now I'm a dead man walking. Might as well take a few risks. And there's so much to gain. We could fill this bird and have spare cans stored back there, and I'm two-hundred-twenty pounds of heavy load you won't have to carry. Fifteen gallons of fuel would be more useful. Plus ten for Steve and about five for Roger. See you soon, guys."

"You sure you wanna do this?"

"I have to, Fran. You also need me to. Fully fueled, you'll be able to go wherever the hell you want. Maybe you'll even find somewhere this isn't happening."

"Yeah, maybe. Okay, here we go. I'm turning around."

"We're nearly there," said Francine, but she didn't need to. The mall was looming into view, dominating the landscape. They flew over it.

"Dammit Fly-Girl, the place is like I remember. Look, that asshole still has my rifle!"

"Don't sound so shocked, Peter; we haven't been gone long."

"Yeah, no shit. Damn."

This time yesterday they'd been a group of three and a half, safely ensconced in an impenetrable fortress, enjoying almost limitless supplies, and set to live as happily ever after as you could in this fucked up world. How things changed.

"Here we are. Hey, look, Peter! It's not that bad."

The zombies were leaving the airport in droves, headed towards the mall. Somehow, in a way that the living could never understand, but Peter might soon, they sensed it was open again; calling them. This was an important place in their lives.

"You ready for this?" asked Francine.

"Yeah, go down towards those pumps, but don't land. Just hover a few feet off the ground so you can get away just like that if you need to. Those hoses stretch out forever, so I'll still be able to fill her up."

A TRIBUTE TO GEORGE A. ROMERO

Francine took the helicopter down to the gas dispensers and saw that the area around them wasn't as crowded as they'd feared, but it was far from clear.

"Get right over 'em," said Peter. "Good job, Fly-Girl!"

Most of the zombies were taken down by the force of the draft, and so Peter picked off those that remained on their feet – the biggest and strongest of them – with well judged head shots from the pistol. Then, leaving it behind because he couldn't risk firing it so close to the pumps, he leapt out of the chopper and onto the tarmac.

The zombies around him reacted to his presence, struggling and crawling towards him once they'd tried and failed to get up. Peter had no intention of giving them another chance, stamping on their heads with his heavy boots until their skulls crushed and their liquified brains oozed out of their ears. He looked around. More were coming, but he'd worry about them when they got here. He had work to do.

Peter removed the hose, which was plenty long enough, and climbed onto the hovering helicopter's foot rail and plugged the nozzle into the tank. It flowed freely, and the pump held all that they needed and more.

Francine looked anxiously at Peter, but he reassured her with a smile and a thumbs up. He then manouevred the nozzle so it would keep pumping even after he let go; it would take a few minutes to fill the tank, which could be better spent than standing around. So he jumped down again and made for the little shop nearby, hoping to find some empty containers for spare fuel.

A little bell tolled to announce his arrival, and it drew the attention of both the zombies in there. The first was close by, so he stopped in the doorway to let it approach, then wrestled it into the doorframe, and slammed the door repeatedly on the zombie's head until it was out of action. The second one had been dead a long time, and was in a bad condition: Peter didn't need any weapons. He grabbed the creature by the head and wrenched, tearing it clean off its ragged shoulders.

He spotted containers on the floor, but when he went to pick them up, he realised they weren't empty. They were filled with fuel.

Damn, they were heavy, though!

He managed to pick up two, one in each hand, and he felt his fingers bend backwards as he bundled through the door, stumbling over the zombie he'd destroyed.

There were more of them gathered around the pump now, staying outside the arc of the rotor blades' downdraft, and with no free hand, Peter was defenceless. He still had power and body weight, and those he shunted into scattered and fell. But he couldn't get them all like that: two of them grabbed hold of him, and one sank its teeth into his shoulder.

Peter grimaced against the pain, shook off the zombie, but knew it didn't matter.

"Lower!" he yelled, trying to make himself heard over the engine.

Francine descended to be almost scraping the ground.

"Some spare for you!" yelled Peter, pushing the sealed fuel cans onto the back seats and reaching in for the gun. "Now, up again, little bit."

Francine elevated to a few feet and Peter stayed at the pump until the tank began to overflow.

Peter dropped the hose and moved round to Francine. "How much fuel do you have?" he asked, grinning.

"Full tank, and more," laughed Francine.

"Damn right, Fly-Girl: we whipped 'em good!"

"Well done! Thanks, Peter: now get in."

Peter shook his head.

"Peter?"

"No, you go – I'm staying here. It's been a pleasure knowing you, Francine. Look after yourself, and your baby."

And with that, before Francine could protest, he jumped down to the ground. She hovered for a moment of indecision, facing Peter. He stood tall and straight, saluting her. She returned it, still a little nervous about flying one handed, and managed to summon a bright smile through her tears. And then she ascended, bound for Canada, and hopefully safety.

On the ground, Peter was surrounded, and with no downdraft to repel the zombies, they closed in. At least he had a gun now, and once again, he found himself holding it against his temple.

But, once again, he had a better idea. "Come on, you stinking motherfuckers!" he hissed through clenched teeth and waited for as many zombies as possible to gather close by. When they were in biting range and gnashing their teeth at him, he pointed the gun. Not at the zombies or himself, but at the pumps.

He pulled the trigger, and ignited the fuel.

STORIES OF THE DEAD

JASON WHITTLE

Jason Whittle is a multi-genre author who lives in (old) Hampshire with his wife and son. He plays guitar and runs marathons, but never at the same time.

He has a variety of self-published titles available, along with the novella *Escaping Firgo* from the BFS award-winning Grimbold Books. His zombie novel *The Dead Shall Feed* is out of print, but a new version is in the pipeline.

MEMORIES OF ROMERO

I can honestly say that had it not been for George A. Romero, I'd never have wanted to be a writer. This in turn means I would never have gone to university, would never have joined Facebook or any writing forums, and would never have gone to any literary conventions or Nanowrimo write-ins. My life would be very different and I would have far fewer friends.

When he passed away it felt I was losing someone close to me. He was an important person in my life. So when Duncan Bradshaw and David Owain Hughes announced they were editing a Romero tribute anthology for charity, I knew I had to write something for it. And it didn't take me long to decide what.

I saw *Dawn of the Dead* by accident, based on a misdiagnosed childhood memory. The film I vaguely remembered seeing the latter stages of, but not catching the title, was in fact *The Omega Man*. But my incomplete yet enthusiastic descriptions led people to recommend *Dawn*.

Thus I was introduced to, in my opinion, the greatest movie ever made. I could write an essay about every scene. Maybe even every shot. And I love the ending, low-key and ambiguous though it is. The hope, resignation, nihilism, pragmatism, loaded into that one little question about how much fuel they have. It takes on a resonance far deeper than the words themselves. It encapsulates their struggle, the perilous vulnerability of their predicament, but also serves as a mission statement. They have no intention of giving up. The fuel levels may fluctuate, but they're going to keep fighting for as long as they can.

I can think of no better analogy for those fighting against cancer.

NOT ANYMORE

BY
RACHEL NUSSBAUM

It's not safe anymore
That's what the radios say
As we barricaded our doors
To keep the monsters away.

We waited all night
Through the gunshots and cries
But when I look through the gaps
I see a dead body rise.

It's not alive anymore
And I'm frozen in fear
It still moans and moves
God, it's coming right here.

It broke its way in
And we ran for the gun
But in the moment we took
It found its way to our son.

A TRIBUTE TO GEORGE A. ROMERO

It's not him anymore
I know he looks the same
His eyes clouded over
It's got control of his brain.

And I know that it's hard
That we loved him so much
But he's dead inside now
And it's him or it's us.

It's not home anymore
Not for a long time
There was nothing left
So we left it behind.

I lost track of how long
It's been since he died
But we venture onward
And try to survive.

It's not murder anymore
And I don't want to kill
But if we don't shoot first
Then the bandits sure will.

And we've tried to reason
They have nothing to say
So line up your sights
And blow them away.

It's not our world anymore
The lights have gone dark
In every city we pass
As we search for a spark.

STORIES OF THE DEAD

Just some sign of life
Something to hold on
But I think we both know
That hope is long gone.

It's not us anymore
We knew it might come
The day where one of us
Couldn't outrun.

I'd made my peace
With the guilt in my head
So oh dear God why
Did it get you instead?

It's not you anymore
Oh dear God please no
I can't do this alone
Can't survive if you go.

But I see your eyes close
And I know it's the end
So like a coward I run
Before they open again.

It's not me anymore
Not after you died
I keep walking on
But I feel nothing inside.

Now I've learned the cost
Of living through hell
You either wind up a corpse
Or you end up a shell.

A TRIBUTE TO GEORGE A. ROMERO

RACHEL NUSSBAUM

Rachel Nussbaum is a writer and artist from the Big Island of Hawaii. Her short stories and poetry have been featured in multiple anthologies, and her favorite genres are horror, science fiction, and urban fantasy. Rachel recently graduated from the University of Hawaii with a BA in English, and plans on pursuing her dream of writing and illustrating her own novels and comic books. Her favorite zombie movies are Pontypool and Shaun of the Dead.

MEMORIES OF ROMERO

"I can't imagine life without the Living Dead," Rachel says on Romero. "Zombies are such a quintessential part of horror and pop culture, it's insane to think that they first entered our films only fifty years ago. George Romero is as iconic as what he created, and it's an honor to be included in this anthology dedicated to his memory."

SAFE ZONE OF THE DEAD

BY
DAVID OWAIN HUGHES

Private Walter Steel eyed the chain-link fence from a safe distance. One hand rested on his holstered .45 ACP pistol. An M16-A1 assault rifle was slung over his back. From where he sat, his free hand parting the foliage in front of him, Steel could see the barrier which enclosed a compound comprised of a helipad, refuelling equipment, and a couple of military vehicles.

He'd been expecting this.

Before he and the others proceeded, he wanted to make sure the surrounding area was secure. He didn't want to get caught out in the wind holding his dick and whistling Dixie. Also, he needed to let Rhodes know he was in position so that someone could open the gates and let him in.

A couple of soldiers roamed the perimeter.

Probably looking for weak spots, he thought, chewing on his cigar. He didn't recognise them.

Steel removed his hand from his pistol and grabbed his walkie-talkie, giving a final scan of the area to see if any dumb fucks were roaming close enough to hear him.

Perspiration beaded his forehead and thin, salt-and-pepper beard.

Sweat stung his eyes.

The Florida heat around this time of year was stifling, and it carried the stench of dead and decaying flesh, smoke, oil, and burning buildings. Most of the smells wafted from off the mainland, but not that of the putrefying meat – that was close by and all around.

Somewhere clear of the fence lay an entrance to an underground bunker. Safety.

Maybe getting the attention of the troopers would be a better idea than using the radio? No, that would mean going out into the open... Steel shook his head. "It's got to be the radio," he said aloud. "Got to be."

Steel turned his peaked hat back to front, which helped keep the heat and mosquitoes off the back of his neck. He pressed the walkie to his ear and hit the squelch button. "Captain Rhodes, come in. Captain Rhodes, do you read me? This is Private Steel. Over."

He released the button and looked about him.

The scant number of dumb fucks continued about their business.

His radio, turned down low, crackled and spat static.

No response.

The only sounds he could hear—other than those coming from his radio and the harsh, raspy breathing of the men at his back—were that of the dumb fucks. Their groans caused his hairs to prickle and his ball sack to wither.

"Captain?" he said from behind clenched teeth. "Do you copy? *Captain?*" Steel tried to keep his voice to a minimum and buried his anger. He hadn't made it this far to die within touching distance of wellbeing.

"They're down pretty deep, Steel," Private Robert Rickles suggested, hanging over Steel's shoulder like a parrot. His dog tags jangled. His voice wavered. "You shouldn't be using names—"

"Shouldn't matter, man," Steel interrupted. "Our equipment's encrypted. Now, be quiet and stay out of sight. We don't want a load of dumb fucks down on our asses." Steel shrugged his shoulder, dislodging Rickles' warm, sweaty hand.

I don't need this shit in my life! he thought, poking his head through the foliage. He looked left, then right, wondering if he could make it to the fence, get the guards' attention, and live long enough to get inside. *Those guys might not have the keys.*

"*Captain?*" He was close to yelling. Steel thumped the ground with his fist.

The dumb fucks' groans intensified, turning into snarls.

Jaws snapped.

Had they heard him?

With caution, Steel parted the bushes again and peered out – a couple of walking pus-bags shambled in his direction.

"Oh, fuck, fuck, fuck... If we fire our weapons, we'll have an army of them down on us."

"What's going on?" Private First Class Howitzer piped.

"We're going to fuckin' die here, man," Private Chambers joined in.

"Shut the fuck up, boot!" Steel snapped. All the while, he kept his eye on the dead walking towards him. His hand lowered from his radio and returned to his handgun. But then a noise from behind the zombies caught their attention and they switched direction, leaving Steel and his small group safe. For now.

"We got to make a move, Steel," Rickles pleaded. "We're sitting ducks, man."

"Don't you think I know that?" Steel said without turning to his friend and colleague. "Rhodes, that cocksucker, won't ans—"

The radio crackled like gunfire.

"Steel, do you read me? This is Captain Rhodes. Over."

"I'm in position with Private Rickles and the others. I need you to open the gate."

"I'm sending someone right now. Is it busy up there?"

"Not just—"

"*Argh!*" Howitzer screamed.

An M16 roared to life at Steel's back. Muzzle flashes lit up his peripheral vision. He whirled his head to look over his shoulder in time to see a gang of zombies crash through the bush they were hiding in and tear off Howitzer's face, chew through his neck, left arm, and Achilles tendon, and claw through his chest and back.

Blood jettisoned into the air and pattered leaves.

One dumb fuck, a fourteen-year-old girl with most of the flesh gone from around her mouth, tore Howitzer's right eyeball out and stuffed it into her gob whilst it was still attached to its cords. When she bit down, pearl-coloured ooze pumped out, spilling down her chin and spattering her bare chest.

It was Rickles who'd opened fire, cutting a male zombie in half.

Steel drew his .45 and drilled a hole through the teen's forehead.

"Let's go. To the gate. Now, now, now!" The veins in Steel's flushed neck protruded. He covered Rickles, Chambers, and Gomez as they smashed through their cover and raced toward the fence.

Bang, bang, bang! Steel's .45 sounded, his rounds finding targets: a rotted head ripped apart, an eyeball collapsed, and a throat tore open. When he squeezed the trigger again, the hammer found an empty casing, and there was no time to get the M16 off his back.

Steel turned and ran. His hulking, six-three frame brushed branches and bushes aside, and he soon caught up with the others.

"They're ripping Howitzer's fucking guts out his nose!" he bellowed. His heart thundered in his chest, making him think it would crack ribs.

STORIES OF THE DEAD

Rickles was first against the gate, which had a sign on it: Seminole County Storage Facility. He slammed the flats of his hands against the fence, gaining the attention of the two patrolling privates, who came rushing when Rickles started yelling.

"Let us the fuck in, jackasses!"

Chambers crashed against the gate next and, like Rickles, started slapping his hands against it. "*Hurry!*"

Gomez and Steel reached Rickles and Chambers at the same time and saw more men, including Rhodes, running towards them.

They came from underground, Steel thought, shaking the fence. "Move your mother-loving asses!" Upon hearing dumb fucks, he turned and removed the M16 from his back. "Come and get it, ya pus-breeding bags of shit." Bullets whizzed out of his assault rifle's barrel like angry bees from a disturbed nest.

Decayed skin was riddled.

Flesh stripped from bone.

One after another, zombies hit the deck.

Rickles joined the gunplay. Gomez, too.

I could be soaking it up, Steel thought, *not battling it out here. Fuck, I could have gone AWOL.*

Yeah, but Tampa is as fucked as the rest of the world. Nowhere's safe...

When shit started hitting the fan, Private Walter Steel out of Camp Blanding Army Base in Stark, Florida, was in South Tampa enjoying a few days' leave and some cold beers. However, he'd had to cut his holiday and drinking short.

Two days before he was due to head back to barracks, Steel decided to blow town after an incident at a beachside

A TRIBUTE TO GEORGE A. ROMERO

bar called Coconuts rattled him.

Steel was enjoying his third ice-cold Coors whilst watching the sun set over Old Tampa Bay. The heat in the dying evening was pleasant and brought with it a light breeze which rippled his short-sleeved Hawaiian shirt depicting swaying palm trees, surfers and horizons.

Bikini-clad girls rolled by on rollerblades, and he wolf-whistled and called after them. Some ignored him; others turned and blew kisses or winked.

Life's good, he thought, *but not as good as their juicy, jiggling asses.*

He laughed, drained his beer and was about to turn and go to the bar when a commotion to his left made him stop and rubberneck.

One of the white-jacketed, shorts-wearing waiters was involved in an argument with a customer. The punter wasn't shouting or gesticulating or swearing at the man holding a tray of brightly-coloured drinks with mini umbrellas and translucent straws sticking out of them. No. He sat there, unmoving.

A small crowd was gathering around them.

Steel decided to investigate.

He removed the cigar from his mouth and inched his way through a throng of people who hadn't noticed the unfolding disturbance. When he got closer to the ruckus, he heard the waiter.

"You pay and get out, sir. Please." The server put his tray down and gave the man a few shoves. "Did you hear me? You're getting blood *everywhere*. You need a hospital. This is the last time I ask nicely. If you aren't gone in five seconds, I'm calling the cops."

The seated man, who had his back to Steel, looked like

a surfer type. He wore a loud 'gnarly dude' shirt, and a straw hat covered the top portion of his dreadlocks, which ran the length of his back.

Steel got within touching distance and saw the bloke wore flip-flops and both his wrists were covered in bracelets made from twine, leather, and beads. Some had pendants shaped like shark teeth and shells hanging from them.

I can smell the ocean on the dude, Steel thought, eyeing a surfboard on the floor next to the man.

"Right, I'm—" The waiter gasped when the man shot an arm out and grabbed his wrist. The surfer jumped from his chair, his hat flying off in the process, his hair trailing in the wind, and clamped his mouth around the attendant's throat. A collective scream tore through the crowd.

Blood squirted.

Tables and chairs were knocked over and sent flying.

A stampede ensued, and a multitude of beer and wine bottles, various glasses, and tumblers were sent crashing to the ground.

Steel was about to intervene, to try and calm the masses, when he was shoved aside, almost toppling as people fled with their arms raised high. Had Steel gone to the ground, he would have been crushed under heel like others around him.

Over the top of the commotion, however, Steel heard the munching, ripping, slurping sounds that came from the surfer as he tore into the waiter's flesh.

The man had long since stopped screaming.

His white jacket was saturated with blood.

Steel covered his mouth and bit down on the rising vomit. With a tear in his eye, he swallowed it and shook his head. "*Ugh!*"

He didn't have time to think of anything else as a weight descended on his back.

More shrieks.

Someone or something snarled in his ear.

A TRIBUTE TO GEORGE A. ROMERO

Teeth clicked together.

Saliva dribbled down his chest as a face appeared over his right shoulder. A snaking, searching tongue licked at his cheek.

"Fuck off!" Steel pumped his meaty elbow backwards, driving it into the guts of the person clinging to him – from the weight, he presumed it was female. A second drilling, shoving elbow blow dislodged them, allowing Steel to turn and see the sprawled figure on the floor.

"The *fuck*?!"

A full-figured girl lay on her back. She was drenched in an orange haze from off the sun. Her red hair matched the spatters mottling her torso. She was topless; her right tit, heavy and swaying, pumped blood from where the nipple should have been. Her left breast was non-existent – it had been replaced by a large, bleeding, cavernous hole. Headphones adorned her head, the cord hanging loose, the tape deck missing. In her hand, she clutched a nametag: Tamra Crow.

The wheels on her skates were spinning, the sound eerie amidst the chaos.

"Holy shit," Steel muttered. "What type of drugs they got down here?"

The girl started to rise off the floor.

"Stay the fuck down, lady, or I won't be responsible for my—"

Her hands snatched at him, with one set of stiff fingers going for his balls; the other, his ankle.

"*Fuck*!" Steel bent and smacked her in the face with his empty beer receptacle. Glass flew. Particles cut his hand, but most of the damage was done to her face, eye, and throat. Some of her teeth rattled along the floor like tossed dice.

She collapsed backwards, but, within a second, she sat bolt upright, her remaining teeth gnashing, face cut to ribbons, eye damaged.

"No, impossible..."

Steel turned to run, but the mêlée erupting all around stopped him in his tracks: waiters, couples, singletons, and passers-by were entangled in a fight with a bunch of crazy, drooling people like the surfer and skater. They had appeared from nowhere.

"I've got to get the fuck out of here."

The skater-girl snarled and snapped. Before Steel fled into the night, he delivered a powerful knee strike to her chin. Her mouth snapped shut, and more teeth broke and fell away.

By the time Steel got back to his apartment and packed, the attack was all over the news, but it wasn't the only reported incident. Dozens of random outbursts involving confrontation and violence had swept along the bay and coastal areas of South Tampa. The images shown on screen, captured by various people with cameras, were that of lunatics setting on people for no apparent reason.

"They look exactly like the skater chick and surfer dude... They're...dead behind the eyes."

He knew that sounded stupid.

Steel didn't bother switching off the TV before grabbing his things and leaving.

He'd managed to bag himself a red-eye flight out of Tampa International back to his barracks in Starke. Even though the wait to fly was uneventful, the news channels playing at the chaotic airport and on his uneasy plane were disturbing, to say the least: the police had become overstretched and the hospitals were filling up. Fast.

Several areas in all directions were without communication and power. In some places, the National Guard had been called in to help reinforce the police.

One newsperson feared that the Army Reserve would need to be called upon if the bizarre situation couldn't be contained within seventy-two hours. "Just what is going on in our beautiful state of Florida?" the same anchor asked. "In an unrelated news story, a Florida man has been eaten by an alligator in his meth lab."

A TRIBUTE TO GEORGE A. ROMERO

Steel stopped listening at that point.

After landing at Keystone Airpark and grabbing a taxi back to base, Steel was relieved to hear from Captain Rhodes that, so far, everything at base was okay, and the situation down in Tampa and surrounding areas seemed to be dying out, thanks to the National Guard.

"They're kicking ass, Steel," Rhodes had informed him.

Then news broke that things were much worse than what they'd been told at Camp Blanding. When Major Cooper addressed Rhodes and his small team of men, his words were shocking.

"I never thought I'd say this, but the Army, its reserves, and every available man has been called up to sort this shit out. The police and National Guard are losing. Their casualties are sky-high."

"What's going on, sir? Is it a coup?" a young private towards the back of the room asked.

"No, son. And it's not escaped lunatics from the local booby hatches either, as some reporters are making out."

"Then what's going on, sir?" Rhodes asked.

"The thing's spread—" Cooper muttered.

"*Thing*, sir?" Steel chirped.

"I've been informed by the lab brains that the reason for people going crazy is caused by a virus. Also—and let me make this very, very clear—if any information is leaked, I'll have your asses slung in jail! This is Top Secret information. By all accounts, the disease is also...*reanimating*...the dead.

"Who laughed, *damn* it?! You think this shit's funny? Well, what you might not find hilarious is the fact it's gone as far as *Maine*; it's swept along the eastern shoreline like some ravenous dog, chewing its way through everyone it comes in contact with. There are rivers of blood on our streets, people! And the eggheads are forecasting by this time tomorrow, if there's no form of control, over fifty percent of the population of the United States is going to have this germ. Christ, by tomorrow evening, we could be bombing our homeland."

A few of the soldiers, including Rhodes, gasped and spoke among themselves.

Cooper continued. "We've lost contact with New York... and I'm told Massachusetts and Pennsylvania have both been hit in a catastrophic way. We're not sure—"

"What about the Carolinas? Georgia?" Rhodes wanted to know.

"It's there, too. So far, thankfully, it's contained in Ohio. Kentucky, Tennessee and Alabama are also unaffected. But that may not last long."

"Are we being deployed to help the troops north, sir?" Rickles asked.

"No, Private. I, Rhodes, and you, his team, will be heading south to a research facility on Sanibel Island. Our orders are to facilitate the job of a scientific team that will be placed in our care, along with one helicopter pilot and a skilled radio operator. Get your gear ready to roll within the next two hours."

"Isn't this a little rushed, Major?" Rhodes questioned.

"We don't have the luxury of time, Captain." Cooper's face was expressionless.

"What about equipment, sir?" Steel asked. "Do we—"

"I'm told the caves are well stocked. Now, enough questions. Get ready to roll on my command – the helicopters will be taking off at oh-seven-hundred hours. Dismissed," Cooper said, turning to leave. "Oh, one other thing: you have to shoot them in the head. It's the only way we've found to stop them."

The war with the sick raged on.

At precisely oh-seven-hundred hours, Rhodes, Steel, Rickles and a dozen or so other men were led to helipads where two Army choppers were waiting. They then broke up into two teams, with Rickles, Steel, Gomez, Howitzer, Chambers and a couple of others in one.

As they flew over war-torn towns and cities, Steel could hardly believe his eyes: explosions rocked their helicopter and sucked them into air pockets, buildings collapsed into mushroom clouds of dust and shrapnel was thrown hundreds of feet into the air.

"Looks like Saigon or some shit down there, Rickles. I can't get my fucking head around it, man. This is the U-S-of-fucking-A."

"Yeah, and Uncle Sam will deal with this crap, you'll see."

"Just God's way of thinning us out, guys," Gomez chirped.

"It's FUBAR, man," Howitzer said.

The pilot came over the airwaves. "Ten minutes from the drop—"

A skull-cracking blast from below shook their chopper again, sending a shudder through the aircraft. "Jesus!" the pilot screamed.

From somewhere up front, an alarm blared.

Red lights flickered.

"Mayday, mayday! We're going down!"

"Holy fuck!" Rickles screamed, placing his head between his legs.

The helicopter zigzagged through the air in a haphazard fashion, before starting to spin. Something blew up. Smoke billowed and someone screamed. Steel raised his head in time to see sparks cough out of the pilot's control panels – an electrical fire burst to life.

"Argh!" the co-pilot bellowed.

Another explosion rocked them, sending the chopper into a barrel roll. The underbelly scraped along something, possibly a car or building, and the noise of metal grating set Steel's teeth on edge.

A few seconds later, the whirlybird hit the deck with an apocalyptic crash. Glass erupted and the rotary blades whined to a death turn.

Steel, not badly injured in the crash, unbuckled himself and grabbed Rickles, who was also relatively unharmed. "We need to get the fuck out, man. Now!"

Gomez, Howitzer, and Chambers were scrambling for the door, along with two other privates, Simms and Higgins, who both had minor cuts about their faces. Simms' uniform had been torn at the sleeve, his elbow bleeding.

"Pilots are dead!" someone called.

Steel could smell fuel. "Get fucking moving," he commanded, hearing electrical equipment spark and chopper discharge splash the ground, "before the whole sorry mess goes up with us inside."

When the side door slid open, the soldiers got out and ran from their downed ride. A minute or so later, a vicious *whoomph* erupted at their backs, producing a deafening roar as the helicopter detonated. They were showered with chunks of debris and shrapnel.

Steel turned to look at the burning wreckage – the flames glowing in his aviators – and stuck a cigar in his mouth. After lighting it, he looked about to see where they were.

"We're goddamn lucky to have landed in a remote area," he said.

"Streets are probably crawling with them fuckers," Gomez surmised.

"Have you got your map, Rickles?" Steel wanted to know. "We need to get to Seminole, pronto."

Rickles nodded. "Yeah, and I can get us there." He produced his map and pinpointed where they needed to be. "Okay, follow me."

"Howitzer, get on the fucking horn and inform Rhodes what's happened and that we'll be there as soon as we can."

"Got it." Howitzer unclipped his radio and raised Rhodes.

"Let's roll," Steel commanded. "Try and conserve your ammunition, boys."

"Okay, from what I can gather, we're not far from the Sanibel Causeway," Rickles informed them.

A TRIBUTE TO GEORGE A. ROMERO

Steel smiled, rolling his cigar from one side of his mouth to the other. "Cool, so we're close."

"Yeah, only the Causeway is close to three fucking miles long! However, the good news is the research facility is practically on the other side, so once we get there we should be home and dry."

"I've informed Rhodes of our situation, Steel."

"Good, Howitzer. Now, everyone shut the fuck up and follow Rickles. Stay low."

They passed Athena Charters' boat hires and the BarHopp'R Kayak and Flats Boat Fishing, before making it onto the Causeway, which was littered with burnt-out wrecks and dead bodies.

Up ahead, beyond a flaming tanker, Steel spotted a pack of people shuffling towards them. From this distance, he couldn't tell if they were friend or foe. He dropped to his knees behind a ruined car, signalling the others to do the same.

"Could be dumb fucks at twelve o'clock, guys." He kept his voice low. "If that's the case, we're going to have to deal with them."

Rickles nodded and flipped the rifle's safety to fire.

The others followed suit.

"Let's break off into two columns and flank them from both sides. Rickles, Howitzer, you're with me."

They followed Steel's lead and kept to a crouch.

As soon as they cleared the car they'd hidden behind, the troops broke off into two groups, snaking their way around abandoned vehicles and hopping over decaying bodies entrenched with buzzing flies.

The stench of rotting flesh in the Florida heat was overpowering.

When Steel reached an overturned Humvee, he got down on his knees, hearing groans coming from the other side. This confirmed his suspicion.

Rickles and Howitzer did the same.

Steel poked his head around the huge tailgate of the

vehicle and saw the other men were in position. He gave them orders via hand signals before turning back to Howitzer and Rickles. "On three, we attack... One, two, *three*! Open fire!" Steel picked out a target: an old man still clutching his walking stick with a Panama on his head. His face was a rotten mess and his jaw hung off its hinges. Steel's shot tore through the man's temple and exited the other side. Blood, bone, and brain matter ejected.

Rickles' and Howitzer's M16s roared to life by his side.

Bodies were shredded.

Heads ripped apart. Arms and legs blew off.

Bullets pinged off metal and obliterated windshields.

"Ceeeeeeease fire!" Steel ordered. Over the silence that fell, Steel heard the moans of the dead that were down but not out. The smell of cordite hung thick in the air. "Affix bayonets and stab their skulls. Conserve your ammo."

They went from body to body, staving in the heads of those still moving, snarling or twitching.

"Come on, keep moving – we ain't got all day, ladies." Steel waved them forward, failing to spot his old friend as he moved beyond a VW Beetle with its roof cut off and its bonnet rumpled.

"Ugh-*argh*!" Simms cried.

Steel turned and saw the skater-girl from South Tampa attacking the private, whose M16 was pointing skyward, his finger pressing the trigger and firing wasted rounds into the air.

"Can't be..."

She held one of her skates in her left hand, which she used to smack Simms about the skull and face, whilst the fingers of her free hand went in search of his bollocks. She tore through his toughened fatigues, ripped his balls free and stuffed them into her mouth.

Simms' screech caused Steel to wince.

When the dying soldier hit the deck, blood pissing from his ruptured crotch, he curled into a ball and rocked back and forth.

"*Mommy!*" he sobbed.

Tamra Crow, Steel remembered as the bitch hobbled towards him. For the first time, he noticed she wore knee-length multi-coloured pop socks, and her hair was fashioned into pigtails. She reached her hands out and collapsed onto him. "*Shit!*"

He kept her mouth at bay by shoving at her forehead.

Bloody saliva drooled from her mouth, forcing Steel to press his lips together as tight as possible.

"Get... this... bitch..."

The crack of gunfire startled Steel. A hole the size of a dime appeared in Tamra's forehead. Blood spilt out of it, pooling in her eyes and mouth. Her tongue lolled.

"Fucking *whore!*" Steel kicked the dead woman in her ribs before picking her up and throwing her off the Causeway. Her body dropped through the air at speed and hit the water with a ferocious splash – her corpse came apart at the seams, her arms and legs floating off in different directions.

Once Steel had regained his breath, steadied his nerves and ended the life of the suffering Simms by putting a bullet through his brain, they'd moved on.

Seeing the way ahead was clear, they picked up their pace to a steady jog and made it to the other side of the Causeway with minimum effort, having only to dispatch the odd dumb fuck here and there.

"Okay, we're within touching distance," Rickles informed them.

"*How* far, Rickles?" Steel wanted to know precisely. Sweat stung his eyes.

"Less than half a mile, man, and the area around it should be pretty secluded, too."

"Fuck, ain't much out here but palm trees and bush anyway," Gomez informed them.

Danger drifted on the air all around them.

"Come on, Rickles. Get us there." Steel pushed the

smaller man to get him going.

They continued at a jog, their gear rattling.

A lighthouse came into view, surrounded by the threat. The six men huddled into a circle.

"Shit, you mean we have to get through *that* lot?" Howitzer asked.

"Fuckers are four deep!" Chambers added.

"We're going to be *balls* deep, you mean," Gomez said, laughing.

"Look, we've enough rounds left to carry us through," Steel said, trying to calm them. "Once we're inside the compound, we'll be fine." He looked at the men's faces one at a time. They were sweaty and ashen. "This is the last push, guys. Let's fucking show 'em what Uncle Sam's all about."

"Fuckin' A," Rickles said.

"Same as before, Steel?" Chambers wanted to know.

"Two-by-two? You bet. Everybody, ammo check."

The men ejected their mags – those who had a full one reinserted it while others counted their rounds and reloaded their side arms.

Once finished, Steel led his men into the open and fanned them out. Rickles stayed with him.

They inched their way around a bullet-hole-riddled building with its roof and windows missing and peeked around the corner closest to the lighthouse.

"Look." Rickles pointed with his bayoneted rifle, hair still stuck to the blood near the base.

"What?"

"Just after the lighthouse – see it? There's a compound. That's where we need to be."

"So fucking near." Steel watched as the other men moved in, flanking the thirty or so dumb fucks that were corralled close to the striped boat-guiding structure. "We could try slippin' by 'em, Rickles? They're so fucking slow."

"I'm game. We could shoot and move, move and

shoot."

"That's what I'm thinking." Steel gave Howitzer, Gomez, Chambers, and Higgins fresh commands via hand gestures. "Get ready to move, Rickles," Steel said, looking back at his friend.

"You bet."

Steel poked his head out again. "Their numbers are pretty low on the left. If we push through there, we'll make it."

"Let's do it."

"Okay. Follow me."

Steel weaved this way and that, keeping his head low and using buildings and cars as camouflage. Then he flat-out ran, calling the others to follow suit. Gunfire emitted behind him, but he didn't stop to look, as he shoulder-charged drooling, snarling threats out of his way to get to the greenery on the other side of the lighthouse.

"Help!" Higgins screamed.

Steel stopped and turned, clear of the confrontation. Rickles was closing in on him, as were Gomez, Chambers and Howitzer. "Oh, no…" Steel could only watch as the mass of dead washed over Higgins like the Red Sea, his screams cut short.

"Come on, Steel, there's nothing we can do!" Rickles slapped Steel's shoulder as he ran past him.

The gates at their backs opened.

"Get the fuck in here, Steel!" Rhodes yelled.

Steel stopped firing and sprinted through the opening, taking Rickles with him.

The pack from around the lighthouse had caught up with them, and was inches from the chain-link fence; they were in danger of crashing through and getting to Rhodes and the others.

"Close the fucking gates," Rhodes demanded.

"Wait!" Gomez pleaded, making a dash for it.

Chambers tried to break away, but he was swept up by a few zombies and pulled to the ground. They ripped through his clothes and punched into his stomach. Chambers screamed as his insides were ripped out and scoffed down before succumbing.

Gomez was halfway through the opening but tripped over a searching hand. Before he could get to his feet or raise his arm in a bid for help, he was pulled out into the feeding frenzy.

"Steel!" he screamed, before his tongue was ripped from his mouth, his shirt and trousers pulled asunder.

Steel turned away when he saw probing fingers enter Gomez's anus, knowing the man's shrill squeal alone would haunt his dreams for years to come.

"What took you so long?" Rhodes asked with a smirk. "Come on, let's get you below. This one belongs to them. It's—"

"The day of the dead," Steel interjected.

A TRIBUTE TO GEORGE A. ROMERO

DAVID OWAIN HUGHES

David Owain Hughes is a horror freak! He grew up on ninja, pirate and horror movies from the age of five, which helped rapidly instil in him a vivid imagination. When he grows up, he wishes to be a serial killer with a part-time job in women's lingerie…He's had multiple short stories published in various online magazines and anthologies, along with articles, reviews and interviews. He's written for This Is Horror, Blood Magazine, and Horror Geeks Magazine. He's the author of the popular novels "Walled In" (2014), "Wind-Up Toy" (2016), "Man-Eating Fucks" (2016), and "The Rack & Cue" (2017) along with his short story collections "White Walls and Straitjackets" (2015) and "Choice Cuts" (2015). He's also written three novellas – "Granville" (2016), "Wind-Up Toy: Broken Plaything & Chaos Rising" (2016).

https://www.facebook.com/DOHughesAuthor/?ref=hl

http://www.amazon.co.uk/David-Owain-Hughes/e/B00L708P2M/

http://david-owain-hughes.wix.com/horrorwriter

https://www.goodreads.com/author/show/4877205.David_Owain_Hughes

https://twitter.com/DOHUGHES32

MEMORIES OF ROMERO

George A. Romero. AKA: The Godfather of the Dead and Father of the Zombie Films. Or, quite simply put, Legend.

STORIES OF THE DEAD

My first encounter with a Romero film, although I didn't know it at the time, was when I was around six years old. My brother, Richard, who is ten years older than me, was babysitting and had rented a copy of *Day of the Dead* from our local video shop. I was in my element. My passion for horror and all things blood-soaked had been implanted the year prior with the viewing of *Evil Dead* and *The Howling II*. And, for those who remember the old VHS cover of DotD, the image of the green ghoulish faces intrigued me and has stuck with me ever since.

Sadly, I never got to see the movie, nor did Richard, because our mother caught him with it and made him take it back to the shop; he also got a clip round the ear and a rollicking.

It would be sometime later before I actually got to watch my first Romero zombie flick, which started with *Night of the Living Dead* at some point in the nineties. Still, I'll never forget that night with my brother...

LAST OF THE DAY

BY
CHAD A. CLARK

"CHOKE ON 'EM!"

The things are in the corridor, right below me. He's yelled that a few times already but now it sounds like he's the one choking. Probably on his own blood. What a son of a bitch. I can hear something tearing. Sounds like fabric but somehow I doubt it's his uniform alone.

I can't dwell on it. There's nothing I can do to help and it isn't like I'm going to shed tears for that asshole. Captain Rhodes deserves whatever deep, dark hole he's falling into right now. He brought all this on us because he had to control everything, had to do what he wanted instead of listening to people who knew better. Now our facility is overrun by the dead. We're all food for those things, now.

And they're making a feast out of that guy, for sure. Even with as much moaning and shifting around, I can still hear that dammed slurping sound. It's like they're sharing a Big Gulp filled with tomato soup. Rhodes has got to be long gone by now. Lucky bastard. I'm sure I'll be seeing him again soon enough...

STORIES OF THE DEAD

They can't get to me up here. Or at least I don't think they can. Regardless, I need to keep quiet and not give them a reason to try. Eventually, they have to clear out of here, right? They wouldn't perpetually take over this place, waiting me out until I showed myself. I was able to get up here into the duct system before they were on top of me. Nearly tore my fucking finger off getting that panel open. I'm worried about that. It feels like it's still bleeding and that can't be good.

What the hell am I supposed to do, now?

None of this was supposed to happen.

We had them under control. This facility was keeping them that way. Doctor Logan was making progress, I thought. Then that fucking Rhodes had to go and kill him. Real smart move. Knock off the one guy who could actually help us. And how the hell did all those monsters get in here? It's like someone just let them in but why the hell would they do that? I don't understand.

I guess we're never really in control, are we?

Finally risked coming down to the corridor. Couldn't stay up there forever. Still can't believe the things didn't find me by following the stench from my hand. I'm going to have to take care of that. The wound on my finger isn't bleeding but it's caked and black. It smells like them. There's got to be something in Doctor Logan's lab I can use.

Gonna hurt like a son of a bitch.

I found Private Steel. Or what was left of him, anyway. Score one more for the monsters. They managed to take out the one guy who was a bigger asshole than Rhodes. I guess pretty much everyone here is dead, though. I'm probably the only one left. The dead finally moved on to find their food elsewhere. And I have no idea what I'm supposed to do, now.

Part of me thinks I should stay here. But it's a bad idea. Those things are gone now but no reason why they couldn't circle around or another pack could come stumbling along. I could seal myself in. I found the entrance wide open. Either someone fucked up or did it on purpose. I could close it again and be safe. But would locking myself a tomb be any better than wandering around in a bigger one up there? At least outside, I'd have fresh air and options. The only choice down here would be to go insane.

I can hack it up there. Right? What choice do I have?

It's always been like this. I get shuffled around from one assignment to the next and hardly anyone ever takes note of me. I hadn't been here that long, just assigned to Major Cooper as an aide. I don't think anyone knew I existed, let alone that I was still alive after Cooper was killed. I'm not surprised no one ever bothered to try and track me down after that. Chances are guys like Rhodes and Steel forgot I was here.

I'd be safe here.

I still can't convince myself to stay, though. It's worse on the outside but I'd rather be out there than in here. I'd rather die outside where I can see the sky, than in the depths, underground with no one and nothing to hold on to. I want to get out of this place because it isn't a choice between surviving down here and dying up there. Survival isn't relevant anymore.

We're all going to die, in the end.

How does it come to this? It's not like I thought I was going to make four star General but how did I end up here, having to do this?

The finger must go. The cut is too deep and I can tell it's getting infected. I can't stitch it up and even though there are probably antibiotics lying around, who the hell knows where they are? Better to remove this than let it slow me down up there.

All I could find was this paper cutter.

At least the thing's heavy. I won't have to put too much backbone behind it. It should only take one shot. I've got a blowtorch I found in one of the lockers and I'm heating up the blade. Maybe the thing will be a little sanitary and also, I'm pretty sure I'm going to pass out when I do this so maybe the hot metal will cauterize the wound. Can't go through this to bleed out while I'm asleep.

This thing is hotter than a bastard. I can't put this off any longer. Got to do it, put it behind me and move on. It's not going to get any hotter and the longer I stand here staring at it like an idiot, it's going to cool off. I need to do it, my finger is ready on the block like it's some kind of God dammed guillotine. Do it.

I don't want to. God dammit, this is going...no, it'll be fine, I'll leave it and it'll be...fuck...I'm doing it.

Wow, that was...my finger is free, on the board and I'm not sure if I even felt...what is that? I don't know if there was enough time, I...wait...shit...I'm starting to feel some...holy fuck—

I'm on the floor and I'm sobbing. I woke up crying. I feel like Andre the Giant is standing on my hand. I'm afraid to look at it but I need too make sure it's okay.

Seems like the metal was hot enough. It cut through the finger cleanly and the stump is scorched black. I don't care about that, as long as it isn't bleeding or oozing anymore. I'm going to need to get some bandages out of Logan's bathroom. God dammit, I have never felt anything like this pain. My hand is throbbing in time with my heart. I guess I'd better stay away from coffee for a while. I'll get something to dress this.

A TRIBUTE TO GEORGE A. ROMERO

It's time to move on.

I don't know how long it's been. I don't keep track. What's the point, after all? It isn't like I have appointments to uphold. It's just me for the most part and this road. This part of the country seems to be pretty isolated. Not many people out here to bother me, living or otherwise.

Of course as soon as I say that, I come across one of them. It's a couple hundred yards off but they aren't hard to spot. No human walks in such a way, stumbling as though drunk, head tilted to the side at a crazy angle. It's like they're napping and strolling at the same time. Plus, they looked like they've just stood up and ambled away from colliding with a bus. At least when they're alone, it's easier to avoid them. You don't get the pack mentality that might come along with huge crowds. It's the mobs that force you to hide under dumpsters for hours. The other week, I hide in one of those porto-potties. Good thing the smell of shit was still present. Probably kept them from smelling me.

That thing is still a long ways off so I've got plenty of time to hide.

I know, it's just one. Why don't I off the thing?

I still haven't been able to bring myself to kill one. It isn't like I don't want to. I don't have the balls. Sounds crazy, right? I mean I'm a soldier, after all. Be all you can be. You'd think I'd be up for this kind of thing but the truth is I've never been this scared and I don't know if, when the time comes, I'll even be able to do it. I'd like to think that survival instinct takes over but will that actually be true? Do I even have it? What could I possibly do to those things?

My life is about scrounging and scraping. I lurk around

the world, trying to stay away from the monsters and I live in spaces I hope no one can see. I eat hardly anything, just what I can find along the way. I don't know how much weight I've lost but it's a lot.

Here we go. There's a phone booth here that's been mostly spray-painted. That'll be good enough to hide in.

It isn't long before I can hear the thing staggering past out there. Sometimes, I like to make up lives for these monsters. You got to pass the time, you know? I think this one was a vacuum salesman. The kind of guy who comes to your house and demonstrates his product on a little piece of sample carpet he has with him. Watch while I clean up coffee, soda and tomato sauce stains. Maybe he goes home at night and hits his wife a few times before getting drunk and dwindling out the night screaming at Dan Rather and Johnny Carson about the Communists.

Now that guy is a drooling corpse who hasn't figured out that he's dead.

The footsteps have been gone for some time. I could probably make it out now, get clear before that thing could double back. Assuming it was even here in the first place. That's the other thing. I don't really trust my senses so much anymore. Did I just imagine all that?

How much longer do I have before I'm not able to run and I have to fight? What happens, then? How much longer before all this comes crashing down around me? How long before the last man alive becomes the last man to die?

How much longer?

I wish I had someone here. I want someone to talk to instead of festering all day long. I had a cousin not far from here who was a security guard at a shopping mall. No idea what happened to him but I'm sure he's dead. What would the odds be that both of us could have survived this long?

Slim and none. That's what kind of odds there are.

I've seen more people as I move west. Real people. And it isn't like I actually thought I was the last person alive but some of the assholes out here are making me wish I was. They're almost as bad as the real monsters. You cross paths with the wrong person at the wrong time of day and you're likely to end up dead. Then you can wind up being just another freak stumbling around inside rags of rotting skin.

There's nowhere I can go, where I can feel safe. I keep walking as if there was somewhere I was actually going but my brain knows better. It knows how full of shit I am. It does make me think, down deep, am I really any better than the freaks walking the world now? What makes me so different? The fact that I can quote from Hamlet? That I know how to make alfredo sauce? Or change the oil in my car? Does any of that help me? In this place? On a basic level, aren't I the same as all the other hollow shells? Shuffling and grunting, doing things simply in imitation of living people? Just because I don't feed on the dead, does that make me any less departed myself?

Who cares?

The only reason I'm still here is because I'm too much of a chicken shit to do myself in. And I'm too terrified of those things to lay down on the road and let them take me, limb from limb.

I'm too scared.

I don't know why I'm bothering anymore. Where am I going? What am I trying to accomplish? My whole career in the Army was defined by going after things, by knowing what I wanted and going seeking it. Now? I can't even bring myself to take down a monster who, by all rights, isn't even alive. It's like I'm regressing back to being five years old again. Thunderstorms scare the shit out of me. I huddle up in an outhouse and all I can hear is thunder, rain and things walking around outside.

Something has to change. I don't know how I'm going to make it but I need something to be different. I have to be willing to defend myself. Eventually, I'm not going to be able to avoid conflict and I need to be prepared. I can't ignore this. The longer I wait, the worse off I'm going to be when something does happen. I have the skills I need. I went through basic training. It isn't like I'm completely worthless. I just need to remember I have the ability needed. I just have to do it.

I'm weak.

This morning, I was crying when I woke up. I can't even start the day feeling good about myself. I stagger around, waiting for something to either kill me or give me the fucking strength to exist. I need something to happen. I need help. I never thought I'd hear myself say it but I wouldn't even mind having Rhodes around right now. Anyone who could help me figure this out. Whoever thought that killing monsters would be this hard?

I don't know what's going to happen to me.

Well, this is about as bad as it could get. This house is three stories and seemed like the kind of place I might actually find some stuff. It looked like it hadn't been picked over so of course, as I walked up to the second floor, two other guys came in behind me. I can hear them stomping around downstairs but there's also something upstairs, above and below. But there's one thing about upstairs.

I'm pretty sure it's one of them.

I can smell it. After being around them at the facility, you get pretty sensitive to it. I can pick up that stench a mile away, it seems. Kind of surprised the guys downstairs aren't noticing it. Doesn't matter to my situation. Can't go up. Can't go down. There isn't even a porch or something I could get to from climbing out a window. What the hell am I supposed to do?

"Come on, you little bastard. Come on out here!"

Sounds like they came up to the second floor. All I can do is keep quiet. Maybe if I'm lucky the y'll hear the thing upstairs and think it's me.

"Come on, we just want to talk with you, buddy!" That voice sounds different, must be the other one. "Why don't you come out and we can see what's what?"

Right. Not a chance I'm going to stumble out there and hope things turn out for the best. I haven't been surviving out here for this long to be that stupid. The way I stay alive is I don't trust anyone I come across, I—

God dammit.

They're banging on the door. Guess I'm lucky this closet had a lock on it. I don't think I've ever seen that before but I'm sure as hell not complaining now. If it slows them down just a little, I'm happy.

"Get the hell out of there!" That was the first one again and now they're actually hitting the door with something heavy, a baseball bat or something. The wood is starting to splinter and crack. They're putting me to the decision, the moment where I have to act, where I can't do anything else but step forward and meet them head on.

The other one is talking now. "Hey, wait a second, I think I hear—"

"Shut the hell up, the guy's here in the closet. Ain't no one else around."

"How do you know?"

"Because we watched him come in here by himself, dumb ass. He's alone. Now shut up and help me get—"

They're screaming now. Whatever is going on out there isn't going so well for my friends. Blood is oozing in under the door.

Before I can do anything else, the door comes crashing in and the dead thing is pulling me out through the hole. All I can hear is the hollow clicking of the things teeth as it's lunging for me. I'm sandwiched between the two dead assholes on the floor as the thing falls on top off me. I push up to keep it away from me and the teeth flash out. Pain lances across my arm and I can barely hold it up. I have to risk transferring the weight of the thing to one arm as I reach down for the hunting knife sticking out of asshole number one's pants. The fucking thing on top of me is almost on me as I bring the blade up and into its mouth.

Blood spurts out and I turn away, clamping my mouth shut to keep fluids out. It's thrashing around but after a few seconds, it goes still and rolls off aside. I'm alone again.

My arm.

Now I'm panicking. I jump to my feet, slipping on blood as I do so, nearly falling back down. I can hear groaning coming from the assholes. They're already starting to stir back to life. There's no time to be creative or subtle. Taking the knife, I drive it into the head, up through the chin of its former owner, all the way to the handle. The body jerks once and is then still. Withdrawing the blade, I turn and do the same to his friend, this time down through the top. I close my eyes and other than the hot splash of blood, it almost sounds like a melon. Leaving them behind, I sprint for the bathroom.

There's blood on it but I don't know for sure where it came from. As I run it under the faucet, I start to cry as I scrub the area with a half-bar of soap.

It looks like the teeth didn't break the skin. There's a

A TRIBUTE TO GEORGE A. ROMERO

scratch, but nothing else. I'm starting to breathe a little easier but now I'm hearing moaning from outside. Going to the window, I pull aside the curtains and look out.

"Son of a bitch."

There's at least ten of the things. I can't see clearly so there's no way to know for sure with my limited line of sight. I can't shoot them all, not before they'd get up here.

I don't have time to think about it. I need to flee. I search the guys in the hall quickly for other weapons. One of them has a gun and I take it. Running for the master bedroom, I start going through the clothes. The best I can come up with are a few sweatshirts and some jeans. Not ideal but I suppose it's better than nothing. Gives me some padding. I'm either going to make it through this or die horribly.

A gun and a knife. Nothing but great odds for me, here.

As I run out onto the porch, there's already three of them hanging around the bottom step. One shot each takes them down. That leaves seven more, coming in my direction. I produce the knife and walk forward with the gun and the knife out, ready to take action. They're spaced apart pretty well so I don't want to rush them. Let them stay like that. Two of them are staggering forward a little faster than the rest and I reward them with head shots, two rounds each. Those bullets were the last and I toss it aside and approach the next two. I stab out with the knife, driving it between the things eyes as another is grabbing my arm, lunging with bared teeth, I pull the knife free and stab it the top of its head.

Three left now. They're circling me, stumbling closer with each step. All I've got is this knife but somehow I think it'll be enough.

All that time I was worried that I wouldn't be up for this?

Turns out I was more prepared than I thought.

STORIES OF THE DEAD

I shouldn't have survived that day. My life just keeps going and all I keep adding are more days and stories.

Time?

I don't know. I said I'm not keeping track. It's been a long time. Sometimes I have people with me and sometimes I'm alone. There are good people out here and there are assholes. Really, in some ways it isn't a whole lot different than before. The stakes are higher now.

Last week, I came across a parking lot for a big shopping market. I don't know if I've ever seen so many of the dead things in one place. It looked like hundreds. I heard real people in there screaming. I knew they weren't the monsters because they don't scream. Not like that, anyway. This was fucking despair. So clearly the things were feeding on something. Someone. Regardless, it was enough to keep them off of me.

I feel like a shell. I need more than this. Surviving isn't enough anymore. I need to find people. To feel like I'm a part of a real community, not just a rung on the food chain.

And for once, I actually have a goal I can strive for. Somewhere to go. Who would have guessed I'd be pushing this hard to get to Pittsburgh? Still, I've heard from some people on the road that a major outpost is being set up there. The city has a huge natural border with the river that should keep the dead out. Supposedly, they're building a huge electric fence to keep the people inside safe.

I keep hearing the same name. Paul Kaufman. He's building a community in one of the high rises in the city, a place for people to be together and safe. People say he has the resources to make it work, for folk like me who are unaffected to stay in relative peace and comfort. That's what I need, to get away from this endless wandering. This may be my last chance at something normal, to be in a place where people actually take care of each other.

I need to get to Pittsburgh.

STORIES OF THE DEAD

CHAD A. CLARK

Chad A. Clark is an author of dark-leaning fiction, born and raised in the middle of the United States. His road began in Illinois, along the banks of the Mississippi and from there he moved to Iowa, where he has lived ever since. From an early age, he was brined in the glory that is science fiction and horror, from the fantastical of George Lucas, Gene Roddenberry and Steven Spielberg to the dark and gritty tales of Stephen King and George Romero. The way from there to here has been littered with no shortage of books and movies, all of which have and continue to inform his narrative style to this day.

Find more about Chad A. Clark at www.cclarkfiction.net

MEMORIES OF ROMERO

The intense realism of Romero's films were particularly vital to Clark's development in the early days of writing. This was the glorious days of practical special effects, where if you wanted to see something on the screen, you had to figure out how to make that happen. This was a time of passion and of drive. George Romero was there during the birthing process for an entire genre. George Romero made movies about inhuman monsters in order to tell impactful stories about human characters. It is this that Clark attempts to infuse in his writing, every day. And if the landscape of our culture not been blessed with a George Romero, the world today would be a far different and less interesting place.

BY
EMMA DEHANEY

The dead never stayed buried in New Orleans. The rich built houses to store their cold ones when the end came, to stop the tide of bones. But, of course, not everyone can afford a mausoleum. The poor had to place their dead lovingly into the damp earth. Bodies interred below sea level had a habit of reappearing whenever Lake Pontchartrain flooded. Coffins would poke through the sodden earth and embalming fluid flowed through the streets like blood.

No, the dead *never* stayed buried in New Orleans.

Sunday...

Low Jenkins hammered the last nail into the ply-board and stood back to admire his handiwork. The storm wasn't due to hit land until four that afternoon, but it felt like all the air had been sucked out of the swamp bowl city he called home. The sky was offensively blue and it was hot. Damn hot. He wiped a thick forearm across his brow, flinging sweat droplets sizzling onto the pavement. Anyone with enough sense or money had already left town. The only ones left were the sick and lonely, the old, the poor and a small band of party animals and jazz fiends who thought they could sit out the worst hurricane in fifty years in a downtown bar.

Eddie's Sports Bar and Grill had been the haunt for singers, writers, junkies and winos since the 50s. No-one could remember if there ever had been an Eddie. It wasn't important. What was crucial to the patrons of Eddie's was that the bar never closed. Not on Thanksgiving. Not on Christmas. Not when the owners were sick. And certainly not because of something as commonplace as the weather.

"Low? Low! Get yo' ass in here and help me with these bottles, y'hear! I got customers to serve," Maybelle Jenkins yelled at her husband from inside, a crate of Dixie Beers in her arms. To a stranger, her voice would have seemed like a nag, but the barflies at Eddie's knew that shouting was how Maybelle Jenkins showed her love. Low ducked inside, welcoming the cool darkness after the soul draining humidity outside. He saw two of his regulars perched on stools, munching their way through a bowl of salted pork rinds. He nodded at them as he passed on his way upstairs to the cramped storeroom.

"*Bonjour*, Low! Hey, not frightened of *un peu de* wind are ya? We in need of refreshments." Frankie Thoreaux, swamp-fisherman and constant cognac companion, shook his empty glass in Low's direction. His friend, Louis 'The Thump' Mason, tipped Low a silent greeting with the battered trilby that stayed permanently fixed to his head. Low asked him once if he wore it in bed. The Thump just smiled a gummy smile and said nothing. He had been a great saxophonist in his day, but a forty-five year heroin addiction robbed him of everything, including most of his teeth.

Up in the storeroom, the air was dead, and so stifling

A TRIBUTE TO GEORGE A. ROMERO

Low couldn't feel himself breathing. The oxygen in his lungs was the same temperature as his body, making it impossible to feel it going in or out. His head started to spin and he staggered against a stack of soda crates. The bottles shuddered. Low's ass bumped on the bare boards. In his confusion, the shadows in the corner of the room seemed to reach for him. He shook his head, but he still saw figures all around, black, looming.

Then he passed out.

Maybelle's voice drifted up through the floor.

"Now fellas, what'll it be?"

Low heard the muffled baritone of The Thump ordering another round. He reasoned he couldn't have been on the floor for more than a few seconds. He stood on shaky legs, brushed himself down and grabbed a box of mixed spirits under each arm, balancing packets of peanuts and napkins on top of each. Low Jenkins had no desire to return here in a hurry. Those shadows looked hungry.

Back in the bar, the hurricane party was in full swing. Maybelle had served the boys their drinks, and Frankie was trying to convince Thump to come out of retirement and play one last show. Jake Petrie was sat in his usual booth at the back, nursing a Dixie with a bourbon chaser. His wife was up at the old jukebox, bopping her hip to the beat. Corrine had been a dancer back in the day, but a motorcycle accident left her partially paralysed in one leg and in constant pain in the other. What with her medical bills, and Jake losing his job, they couldn't afford to get out of the city, so they had left their rundown shotgun for the relative safety of Eddie's.

"Hey Corrine, you'd better be careful. With moves like those, I might be forced to join in." Low knocked her a wink as he set his cargo down at the end of the bar.

Corrine held her walking stick down at arm's length and started to twirl around it gracefully on her good leg.

"You ain't even seen my moves yet, Low Jenkins," she said, before wobbling slightly and falling into the front of the juke. Frankie, Thump and Maybelle all looked round in concern. Jake leapt up and tenderly took his wife's arm.

"You need to sit down, *cherie*."

Low held his breath.

"You know what I need, Jakey? Another drink."

A chorus of whoops erupted from the bar as a gust of wind banged the door shut.

"Drinks all round!" Maybelle yelled, ringing the bell behind the bar. For some reason, Low didn't feel like celebrating.

When the wind started to scream through the gaps in the windows, they turned the music up and poured more shots.

When the jet-engine roar had been battering at the nails for over an hour, finally pulling the boards loose and leaving rain to batter the glass, they all cheered and drained their bottles.

When that same glass exploded in glittering bullets, they downed their drinks before taking refuge in the back of the bar.

When the storm surge began to force water under the doors and through the windows, they danced on the tables, holding their liquor clear of the rising flood.

And when the brute force of the storm broke down the door, and they found themselves knee deep in branches, hubcaps and strange sea-creatures that had been ripped from their homes by the typhoon, the realisation finally hit.

This wasn't weather.

This was apocalypse.

"Upstairs, *now*!"

Low herded the frightened group to the stairway. They followed Maybelle up the narrow steps to the storeroom, scrabbling over each other in drunken panic as the water formed a solid wall behind them. Corrine lost her stick in the swirling blackness and Jake had to drag her up by her arms. Low was up to his waist at the bottom of the stairs when the lights flickered and the bar plunged into darkness.

"*Low!*" Maybelle screamed, her voice drowned by the raging water.

"Keep going,' he shouted. "Get everyone up top, I'll follow."

Arms out in front, unnamed detritus snaking and clawing at his skin, Low pushed upwards into the black. He slipped, his head colliding with the steps, his shoulder crashing onto a leg with a sickening crunch. He and the owner of the limb both yelped and tumbled onto the floor of the storeroom in a mass of wet bodies. The thundering rain and wind was even louder up here and Low's voice burned to be heard over it.

"We all here? We alright? May? You okay?"

"I'm here Low, I'm here."

He reached out his hands.

"That's me," said a deep voice.

"Thump? You got Frankie?"

"*Oui*, I'm here. Jake? Corrine?"

"We're here," they yelled in unison.

Cold water rushed over Low's feet.

"We gotta get higher. Stand up everyone, the water's still coming."

Huddled together in the dark, water lapping at their ankles, they waited for the storm to pass.

Monday morning...

Grey sunlight started to filter into the storeroom through tiny cracks in the walls. How the structure was still standing after the storm was a miracle, but they'd clearly lost many of the roof shingles. This allowed more weak morning light in, as well as the rain that had only just stopped falling on the shivering group as they cowered from the power of the hurricane. Low began to make out faces, hair plastered against foreheads, blood and dirt on skin. His temples were pounding. The scream of the storm still whistled behind his eardrums.

"Low, oh Low honey," Maybelle cooed. "You're bleeding." She gripped hold of his hand, her fingers icy.

"I'm fine, just a little bump on the head is all. It's Frankie I'm concerned about. How ya doing, buddy?"

It turned out Frankie was the owner of the leg that Low had so violently crashed into. Thump had propped his friend against the wall to see the night through, convinced his leg was broken.

"It hurts man, hurts real bad."

"Here," Low reached into a cardboard box, now disintegrating with damp. "Drink some of this." He handed Frankie a bottle of Chivas Regal. "It won't fix your leg, but you sure won't give a damn until we can get you to a hospital."

"Uh, Low," Jake said slowly. "The water's still at the top step. How we gonna get down?"

Low looked at the murky brown water filling the narrow stairwell. In the dappled light, he swore he saw a face bob towards the surface before sinking into the silt. Could have been a grocery bag. Could have been a leaf. Could have been a lot of things.

"If we can't go down, we'll have to go up," Maybelle said resolutely.

Corrine, clinging onto Jake for balance, looked up into the rafters.

"How the hell am I gonna get up there?"

"It's OK, *cherie*," Jake stroked her hair. "You ladies can stay here. We'll go get help."

"The hell I am," Maybelle barked, moving a storage crate aside. "We're all getting out of here together. They'll be sending helicopters and shit soon. We have to get up onto the roof."

She turned round triumphantly, a three-foot fire axe in hand. "I knew this was here somewhere. Been thinking about it all night. Remember that retirement party, Low? For the fire department guy? One of these bad boys got left behind. So, who's gonna give a lady a hand smashing us the fuck out of here?"

Low had taken charge of the axe after Maybelle tried to swing it in the small space, nearly decapitating Jake. They busied themselves building a sturdy stack of crates that they could climb up on while Low stood on a chair and took chunks out of the weakest looking part of the roof. Corrine and Frankie were slumped together on a broken table. He sipped steadily on the Chivas, his face taking on a greenish hue as the sun fully rose. His trousers were dark with blood, and his left foot protruded the cuff at an odd angle that made Low wince every time he saw it.

"Between the two of us, we got a fully functioning pair of legs," Corrine joked half-heartedly. Frankie laughed, winced and offered her the bottle.

"No thanks, I'm good," she said. Corrine's hand strayed to her jeans pocket without her noticing. Thump, who had been silent since they'd got up here, speaking only to confirm his presence, saw her involuntary gesture but said nothing.

With a final solid whack and a tumble of sodden wood, Low broke a hole big enough to pull himself through. He put his arms up, testing the strength of the surface, found enough tension, and hoisted himself out of the storeroom and into daylight. He squinted, his eyes blurry and blind as he got enough purchase to pull his legs out of the hole in the roof. Then, he sat up, rubbing his eyes, and looked out to see...

Water.

Eddie's Sports Bar and Grill had been picked up and dropped into the middle of the ocean. Roofs poked out here and there, some two-storey buildings you could see the second floor surrounded by water. The tops of trees dotted about, and a few points which he assumed were telegraph and electricity poles, now naked wooden fingers pointing at the sky that had rained down this destruction. There were no roads, cars, bridges, or street signs. Just water.

"How's it looking up there," Jake called.

"You'd better come see for yourself," Low shouted back, his voice sticking in his throat. His mouth suddenly dry, his tongue cracking.

Jake's hands appeared through the hole, then his head and shoulders. Once up, he stared out at the 360 degree sea-scape, his jaw hanging.

"What...what happened?"

The men stood in silence for a while, their sleep deprived brains struggling to take it all in.

"The levees must have broken," Jake said.

"Or they was flooded on purpose."

Jake and Low jumped, unaware they'd been joined on the roof by a third member of the group. They turned to see The Thump hauling himself through the gap, hat still firmly on his head.

'Jus' like '27. They dynamited the levees and flooded the Ninth. Killed the po' folk. Killed the black folk. Jus' to keep the rich city white-folk dry.'

This was the most Low had heard Thump say since the storm hit, and was getting on for the most he had ever heard him say in one go.

As the men stood on the roof, Low spotted movement in the water, what would have been a block over from the bar.

"Hey! Hey, over here," he yelled, waving his arms. It looked like someone was swimming in the filthy brown soup that had swallowed the land. The longer they stared, the more it was clear it was a man, splashing in the water in a jerky appropriation of doggy paddle.

"He must be hurt," said Jake. "Come on buddy, you

A TRIBUTE TO GEORGE A. ROMERO

can do it, swim to that roof."

They all began shouting encouragement at the man who, as he got nearer, they could see was not very well at all. His skin was bone white and he had cuts about his head, which would be sure to get infected with all the waterborne bacteria and filth. He finally made it to the closest roof and began to scramble awkwardly onto the tiles. Low, Jake and Thump clapped with joy. He was going to be OK. They would all get rescued soon, and everything was going to be...

Splash.

The scissor-snap of an alligator's mouth broke from the water and clamped around the man's ankle. The gator thrashed and rolled, biting the man's leg clean off.

Jake released a string of curses. Thump closed his eyes and remained silent. Low fell to his knees, watching the alligator slip back into the water with its prize. Expecting the poor man to scream, fall down, bleed out or cry for help, he instead bellowed a guttural moan and plunged into the water after the gator, jumping onto its back.

"What the—"

They watched as the now one-legged man wrestled on the surface with the alligator, a mass of pale skin and thrashing scales. At one point they saw the man raise his head out of the water and chomp his mouth down onto the tail of the animal, but the gator got the better of him, flipped round and bit the man clean in two, before gliding away, leaving floating body parts in its wake.

"What's going on up there? I heard shouting."

Low dragged his eyes away to see Maybelle's head pop up through the gap in the roof. Jake shook his head furiously. They didn't need to know.

"Nothing, darlin'. Go on back down. We could all do with a bit of breakfast, hmm?' Food was the last thing Low could think about after what he'd witnessed, but wanted to take his mind off it, plus they would need all the strength they could muster if they were going to get up onto that roof. Jake climbed down. Low beckoned Thump to follow him.

"Y'all go on," he growled. "I'm gon' stay up here. I needs the air."

Once back down in the oppressive heat of the damp storeroom, Low understood why the old sax player wanted to stay put. Nevertheless, he dished out some packs of potato chips and bottles of grape Ne-Hi. He reckoned they had enough supplies up here to last a day or two, maybe more if they were careful. He was hoping they wouldn't need to find out. Halfway through his soda, Low realised another reason why he might have wanted to stay up top. Confident Thump would have had time to do his business, Low headed up to answer his own call of nature. As his eyes came level with the roof, he saw Thump laid out flat on the few remaining tiles, eyes closed, looking to the world like he was sunbathing. Low opened his mouth to make a joke, when he saw Thump's grimy shirtsleeve rolled up exposing his arm, tied off with a belt and stuck with a needle.

"Oh, Thump," he said softly.

He opened his eyes lazily and looked at Low with pupils like matchheads.

"I couldn't wait anymore."

"Don't you think poor old Frankie could have used a bit of painkilling, with his leg the way it is? I thought he was your friend."

"I only had one shot. Didn't think the storm would be this bad. Figured I'd be home by morning. Now I ain't got a home to go back to. And you know what, right at this particular moment, I don't care. That's junk for ya."

Too exhausted to be angry, Low took a seat next to Thump. "You can't stay up here on your own being high, we've got to work out how we're gonna get ourselves out of here. There might be more gators."

Worse than that, thought Low, *there might be half a man still paddling around in there, looking for his legs.*

A TRIBUTE TO GEORGE A. ROMERO

Monday afternoon...

By the time the sun hit its peak, the whole crew had managed to make it onto the roof. It was a struggle getting Corrine up there, and although Frankie was strong enough to hoist himself through the gap, he was so drunk on Chivas Regal and pain, that he slipped a few times, falling on his broken ankle with sickening screams.

"Mad dogs and Englishmen," Jake Petrie murmured.

"What'sat now?" Maybelle asked, fanning herself with an old bar menu.

"Mad dogs and Englishmen go out in the midday sun. It's a song."

"Well, I sure as shit ain't no English man, and I don't see no dogs neither."

They all sat, sweating, but more comfortable than they had been below. The air was at least breathable, if already starting to take on the stink of stagnant ponds.

"I wonder what happened to them..." Corrine said suddenly.

"Happened to who?"

"All the dogs. And cats. All of everybody's pets."

An unexpected breeze blew across the rooftop, bringing with it the stench of death and raw sewage.

They all knew what happened to the pets.

The whomp whomp of faraway helicopter blades broke the maudlin silence. Low leapt to his feet, waving his hands. Jake and Maybelle jumped up too, and soon they were all screaming and flailing their arms in the air, not knowing which direction the chopper was coming from. It circled over nearby trees, skitting round in the sky until it was facing them. Sunlight bounced off the glass, blinding them and protecting whoever was inside from view. It hovered for a few moments before pulling up and away.

"Noooooo!"

"Come back, hey! Come back!"

STORIES OF THE DEAD

They all shouted, in vain. The helicopter was gone. Only Thump was sitting in calm quiet, still riding the opiate wave. He pushed his hat up with a finger and said to no-one in particular, "Jus' like '27, man. Flood the bowl, save the rich folk."

Save them from what? Low almost asked out loud. Then he remembered the pale man's clawing hands and face as he chomped down on the gator's tail.

Monday. Dark…

After a dinner of peanuts and beef jerky, they watched the sun set, and for the first time, saw the night sky over the city without the diluting glare of streetlights.

"This is what it looks like out in the bayous," Frankie slurred. "Just me and the stars." He winced and nudged Maybelle on the arm. "Hey darlin', you got another bottle of that Chivas? My leg is hurtin' something awful."

"Hey, Maybelle," Jake shouted. "While you're down there, fancy bringing up another bottle of soda. Corrine needs to take her meds."

"*Meds?*" Frankie whipped his head around, needling Corrine with bloodshot eyes. "You got painkillers? Pills? Shit, I'm dying here."

Corrine turned away, looking up at Jake.

"They're for Corrine, for her leg…"

"Her goddamned leg don't even fucking work!" Frankie raged, leaning over to try and snatch at Corrine's pocket.

Jake jumped to defend his wife, smacking Frankie's hand away. Overestimating the distance, foot slipping on a loose roof tile, his weight shifted too far and he lost balance. His eyes widened in fear as he tumbled over the edge. Frankie reached out to grab Jake's hand, but his fingers clutched air. Corrine screamed for her husband as they heard the splash.

"Quick Low! Get him! Save him, Low!" she shouted.

Low ran to the corner of the roof, guided by the sounds of Jake in the water. He skidded to a stop, confronted by endless black. Bloated limbs and gator grins flashed before his eyes.

"Help!" Jake gargled.

Not wanting to impale himself on a tree concealed beneath the water line, Low crouched and eased himself into the stinking flood, feet first.

"I'm here, Jake. Swim towards my voice."

Low held his arms out, strafing the water, feeling for movement.

The splashing came closer.

All around was black and cold.

Ripples lapped against his chest, forcing slimy liquid towards his mouth. Keeping his lips clamped shut, Low started to swim further from the safety of the roof. His fingers brushed against something soft. He imagined skin coming away with his touch, waterlogged flesh putrefying in his hands.

"That you Low?"

"Yeah, it's me, buddy. Grab on, you're almost there."

Jake gripped Low's wrist and the two men bobbed their way back to the roof. Low's hand bumped brickwork, skinning his knuckles.

"That's it, we're here. Hold on to the edge. I'll climb up and pull you on."

Starlight illuminated Jake's face, floating in the dark, blood oozing from a deep wound on his cheek. Low reached down and heaved his weight up onto the roof, struggling to get purchase, his shoes slippery with greasy water. He heard Corrine babbling behind him, but he blocked the noise out, concentrating all his efforts on dragging Jake free from the flood. Laid down on the tiles, feet jammed against the guttering, Low knew one final pull would get the injured man to safety. He gritted his teeth in determination. Jake gave a weak smile, as a white orb burst through the water next to his face. Low jumped back in shock, losing his grip on Jake's hand. Teeth clamped onto Jake's cheek, hands emerged from the black, gripping his shoulders. Rotten skin covered the orb in patches, tufts of wet hair plastered to what Low could now see was a head. The head shook violently, until it came away with the sound of ripping cotton sheets. A bloody chunk of meat hung from the mouth of the creature.

Not meat, thought Low. *Jake. A chunk of Jake.*

The creature pushed Jake from him, his agonised screams turning to weak gurgles as something, or someone, dragged him under. Noise from all around invaded Low's ears, panicked shouts, yelling, high pitched wails and bellowed warnings. He scrabbled backwards, up the tiles, away from the thing chewing on the lump of cheek, its fingers clawing at the edge of the building. Bone protruded from the end of each digit, and above all the commotion and screaming coming from behind him, somehow Low could hear the scritching-scratching of dead hands as they clamped onto the gutter by his feet. Opal eyes stared at nothing from deep sockets. Its teeth could be seen clearly chomping up and down inside its mouth through a ragged hole in the side of its face. A white scythe of decomposing arm raked through the air and missed Low's foot by an inch. He yanked his leg back, as steel glinted in moonlight. The axe swung down on the thing's skull with a crunch. Its fingers splayed out sharply, then curled under. Its arms jerked. Maybelle hefted the axe high in the air and swung again, this time separating head from neck. The body slid silently into the water. The head rolled along the gutter before plopping into the flood with a splash.

Tuesday. Sunrise…

The rest of the night had seen the survivors huddled together in the middle of the roof, as far from the waters as possible. No-one could speak. No-one knew what they had witnessed, and if they talked about it, it would become real. Every ear listened out for a splash in the dark, for scraping on roof tiles. Corrine sobbed into Maybelle's shoulder, shivering in shock. Frankie couldn't look anyone in the eye, knowing Jake's death was his fault. The pain from his ankle was no longer dulled by alcohol, and he deserved it. Nerve bullets pulsed up and down his leg in rhythm with his heartbeat, each stab of agony like an accusation. Thump had his back to the group, facing the location of Jake's demise. Low saw him fumbling about under his jacket, felt him tense up and then relax. Of course he had more than one shot. Junkies always lie.

The sun finally broke cover, the morning light reflecting off the oil-slicked waters, creating a swirling eddy of rainbows.

"It's almost beautiful," Maybelle whispered in her husband's ear. Corrine had fallen into a fitful sleep an hour or so ago, after swallowing a handful of pain meds. She had taken Frankie's hand, opened his palm and placed some tablets on there, before curling his fingers back round with a small nod, and he too was managing to get some much needed sleep. Thump was passed out, no doubt having hazy junk dreams.

"What are we gonna do, Low? If more come?"

"I don't know."

His voice was flat. He had no fight. He was drained to his marrow. Those things in the water were impossible. They could not be. But they had all seen them. Corpses floating on a tide of industrial waste with blind, dead eyes. Grasping hands and biting teeth. Bile burned his throat as he thought of Jake's living flesh being torn from his face.

"We just have to stay here until the choppers come back. We'll be rescued soon darlin', don't worry."

It wasn't only junkies that lied.

Tuesday. Sometime before dark...

The foetid stench was now a solid mass filling their nostrils with death and abandonment. No-one was coming. No boats. No helicopters. Their homes were gone. Their businesses. Their family. Their friends. There was no way of knowing who had survived, and if there was anything worth surviving for.

But still the human body called for sustenance. Low's stomach growled and churned, turning itself inside out. He opened a bag of chips, nudging his wife to wake up and give some to Corrine. The women ate in silence, Corrine's eyes red-rimmed and dozy with painkiller sleep. Frankie had woken a while ago, but shook his head at the offer of food, still punishing himself. He prodded Thump firmly on the arm, not understanding how he could have slept so long. Still he slumbered on.

"Wake up, you lazy *connard*!" he shouted, dragging his battered leg behind him to shake his pal by the shoulders. The old man's eyes were open. The trilby slipped from his head. His skin was cold.

"He's gone," Low said firmly in Frankie's ear. "One last shot."

Frankie shook his head and slumped on the roof next to Thump's lifeless body.

"Ya know what, Low?" he sobbed. "Right about now, I wish it was me lyin' there. No more pain. No more dead people tryin' to get us. And no more fucking water."

Night…

Not wanting to sacrifice another member of the crew to the poisonous waters, Low dragged Thump's body to the far edge of the roof, out of sight. Flies were already buzzing around him, looking for dead crevices to lay their eggs in. It wouldn't be long before the stink of rotting meat forced his hand, but for now, Thump could stay where he was.

Before night had fallen, Maybelle had gone down into

the storeroom and gathered the last of the snack supplies. She also dragged up the wooden legs of the broken table and started chopping them into splinters with her axe. Once she had amassed a satisfying pile, she stacked them onto a tin drinks tray and set fire to them with a box of damp but miraculously functional matches.

"I can't stand another night in the dark, Low," she admitted, sitting next to Corrine, who was staring into the flames. She hadn't said a word since they lost Jake to…whatever it was they lost him to. Maybelle held tight to the axe, her eyes darting all around.

Low opened bottles of soda and passed them between the group. He was handing the last one to Frankie when movement behind the flickering flames caught his eye. Corrine snapped her attention away from the fire, pointing into the shadows. Maybelle stood, axe at the ready.

Frankie shouted, "Wait! It's Thump."

The old saxophonist lurched across the roof, the light from the fire jumping over his face, shifting his features into a rigid death mask. Milky blankness shone in his eyes.

"He's dead, Frankie. That ain't Thump anymore." Low ran towards the lumbering ex-Thump, barging into him with the strength and skill of an NFL quarterback. He carried on running as teeth snapped the air next to his ear, and gave the walking corpse a mighty shove into the inky waters of the Mississippi. Knowing it wouldn't be long before the splash attracted more of them, Low spun round, desperate for a way to fight them off. Maybelle was already there, flaming table leg raised overhead.

"Let the fuckers burn," she said, and tossed the torch into the water. The multi-coloured oil slicks, so hypnotically beautiful in the daylight, bloomed into walls of fire with a whoosh. The blaze encircled the building, creating a floating barrier against the dark.

"What do we do now?" asked Frankie. Corrine and Maybelle looked at Low. Low looked into the flames.

"We wait."

STORIES OF THE DEAD

Fires burned all over the city. People hid on rooftops and balconies and tried to stay alive. Bloated corpses feasted on their loved ones. Children cried and parents screamed. Bones snapped and teeth chewed through sinew.

The dead never stayed buried in New Orleans.

A TRIBUTE TO GEORGE A. ROMERO

EMMA DEHANEY

Em Dehaney is a mother of two, a writer of fantasy and a drinker of tea. By night she is The Black Nun, editor and whip-cracker at Burdizzo Books. By day you can always find her at http://www.emdehaney.com/ or lurking about on Facebook posting pictures of witches https://www.facebook.com/emdehaney/ You can also follow Em on Twitter @emdehaney. Her debut short fiction collection Food Of The Gods is available now on Amazon:

A perfect corpse floats forever in a watery grave. A gang member takes a terrifying trip to the seaside. A deserted cross-channel ferry that serves only the finest Slovakian wines. Nothing is quite what it seems, but everything is delicious. This is Food Of The Gods. hyperurl.co/oc1tjo

MEMORIES OF ROMERO

"To be part of a tribute to the George A. Romero is a huge honour. Without his unique vision there would be no zombie pop culture, none of the films, TV shows, books, graphic novels and video games enjoyed by millions all over the world in the last 30 years, myself included. The horror world is forever in his debt."

BY
TONY EARNSHAW

Ada Partridge had been dead for four minutes. Understandably the last thing Mark expected was for her to sit bolt upright.

As she did so the blanket slipped from her face. Mark saw that her eyes were open. Then, ever so slowly, her head moved until her face was looking at his. Her glassy eyes seemed to shake off the glaze of death and focused on him with an intensity that was hypnotic.

Mark gaped. His lips mouthed unheard words, making movements that might have been an attempt at speech. He was frozen in shock. Then, quite suddenly, and with frightening speed, sweet old Mrs Partridge lunged forward and attempted to sink her teeth into his cheek.

Mark yelped, slapping the woman's face hard. She fell back onto the stretcher, her false teeth going flying onto the floor of the ambulance.

In the driver's seat Carole strained to see what was going on behind. Within seconds, the elderly woman who she thought had just shuffled off this mortal coil was flailing her bony arms at Mark, who was defending himself and yelling. Her emaciated legs were kicking beneath the blanket.

"Christ!" he yelled. "*Christ!*"

"What is it? What are you doing?"

Mrs Partridge made strange screeching noises. Her gummy mouth was wide, her eyes blazing and fixed on the stunned paramedic, as he fought to keep his balance in the moving vehicle. There was power in her now. No longer was she the frail octogenarian they had collected from her room in the sheltered housing block twenty minutes before.

When Ada was found in her room close to death, staff dialled 999. An ambulance arrived. Carole and Mark attended the old lady in her bed, assessed her quickly and moved her via trolley to the rear of their vehicle. Then, siren wailing, they headed for the local infirmary.

But Ada had not the strength to carry on. Her eyes flickered behind closed lids; her breathing slowed and her body seemed to sink into the cushion beneath the blanket that covered her. Mark gently placed an oxygen mask over her nose and mouth.

"Come on, Ada. Breathe. Just breathe for me. Come on, love."

He was willing her to live. It wasn't even nine in the morning. On a Monday morning. He didn't want to start the day with a death. He stroked the elderly woman's forehead, trying to provide comfort, passing his strength to her.

"Come on, love," he repeated.

Ada's eyes opened fluttered. He caught a glimpse of

pale blue irises. But the eyeballs rolled back and the lids closed. Her breathing was barely audible. Her chest rose and fell, rose and fell, a little lower each time.

He held her tiny hand, pressing his palm against hers. Was there just a hint of a response? The ambulance was moving too quickly; he couldn't tell. And the only sound he could hear clearly was the ululating noise of the siren: woooo-ooo, woooo-ooo....

"How's she doing?" Carole's voice, steady and measured, came from the cab a few feet away.

"She's going." He felt a jolt of pain as he looked down into the woman's lined face. He searched for her pulse. Barely there. "How far?" Mark glanced up to look through the windscreen at their route.

"Ten minutes."

Carole was overtaking cars, buses and trucks at speed. Most pulled aside. Some were stuck in lines of traffic and despite the approaching blue lights and siren, struggled to shift out of the way. Little delays, but crucial ones. In Ada's case, it probably wouldn't matter.

He turned his attention back to the patient. She was fading. The throb in her wrist weaker still. Then, without fanfare, she died.

Mark tested her wrist pulse again, then felt for the same in her neck.

Nothing.

It was 8.52am.

"Kill the siren. She's gone." Monday morning. A new shift. A fresh week. Another corpse. Mark shook his head. He placed Ada's hand beneath the blanket, removed the mask and covered her face.

Shit.

Carole slowed to forty miles per hour, observing the speed limit on the road that led to the hospital. No rush now their their passenger had popped off. No urgency. She flicked off the siren.

For a few moments neither paramedic spoke. Then Carole radioed through to control.

"What the—?"

Directly in front of the ambulance a mother with a pushchair was running from a man chasing her into the middle of the road. Carole swerved to avoid them and stole a glance in her wing mirror as the staggering man caught up with the young woman and dragged her to the ground. He was set on by passers-by. The pushchair tipped over and was clipped by a car.

"Oh my God!"

Mark moved into the passenger seat. Through the windscreen he saw more people than usual on the pavements and in the road. Several were running towards the ambulance.

"*Jesus!*"

They were five hundred yards from the hospital entrance. They'd head through the car park and drop off Mrs Partridge at A&E. But something wasn't right.

The running figures – ordinary folk, shoppers, mums with children – headed past the ambulance. As they neared the hospital entry Carole and Mark found people were sprinting from it and flooding out of the car park onto the main road.

Carole reached for the radio. Mark climbed into the back, ready to strap in Mrs Partridge's body.

Then it happened.

Mark overbalanced as Carole swerved to avoid an

oncoming car that was travelling at speed from the car park. The ambulance veered left, then jerked right, pitching Mark backwards and then violently forwards.

Mrs Partridge fell onto his chest. Her fingers clawed at his face, her toothless maw just centimetres from his eyes. She was making low gurgling noises – part snarl, part growl – and saliva drooled from her lips.

Seconds later the two bodies, ambulanceman and corpse, were entwined together in the narrow space between stretcher and equipment. Mark began to panic.

"Carole!" he yelled, his voice high and strident. "Carole, help me!"

But Carole was navigating a route through a car park thronged with vehicles and people dashing in all directions. Her mind was attempting to process the scene before her.

There was smoke billowing from one of the upper floors. The hospital was on fire. Patients and visitors were fleeing a blaze.

Close to the entrance she saw something that caused the blood to drain from her face. Four young men were kicking out at a figure on the ground. It was wearing a doctor's white coat and black trousers and was rolling around, flailing its arms, seemingly unaffected by the ferocity of the blows that rained down upon it.

Her attention shifted to the slope that led down to the ambulance point outside A&E. A small crowd was gathered there. In its midst she saw Shirley Talbot, one of the admins.

She fired up the siren and gave it a quick blast. Shirley turned and immediately began waving her arms madly. Carole couldn't make out her words over the cacophony outside the ambulance and from behind as Mark pummelled the writhing Mrs Partridge.

Then Shirley went down as she was attacked by two women who raked her eyes and used her long hair as a means of dragging her to the paving stones. What happened next almost made Carole crash: one of the women bit Shirley's throat, tearing out a sliver of flesh that caused a spout of blood to erupt all over them. Both Shirley and Carole screamed, one in agony, the other in horror. Then Shirley disappeared beneath her assailants.

Carole manoeuvred the ambulance down the slope, towards the milling throng. She made to open her door… and then looked through the window straight into the bloodied face of a middle-aged man in a hospital gown. His eyes were weirdly opaque. With deliberate movement, his hands reached for the window and began to scrabble at the glass.

Behind her Mark was beating Mrs Partridge with a fire extinguisher. He hit her in the centre of her face with the flat base, smashing her nose and eyes with manic violence. The old lady fell backwards from the force of Mark's assault, her upper body lying on the trolley.

Mark fought to stay upright. He swung the heavy metal cylinder at the woman's head. It smashed against her temple, spattering the interior of the ambulance with blood. Then, as she lay stunned, he raised it overhead and brought it down with all his strength. It shattered Mrs Partridge's skull, sending a gruesome split through the thin skin that covered her forehead, opening a gash that exposed bone. Her right eye socket exploded, leaving the eyeball dangling over her cheek. Then she was still.

Mark grabbed a yellow bar above the stretcher and held onto it, breathing hard. He looked down at the bloodied corpse of the woman they had picked up less than 20 minutes before and tried telling himself that she really *had* died before waking up to attack him.

What on earth had he just done?

Before he could ask himself any more questions Carole screamed from the cab.

"We need to go! Go!"

She jammed her foot on the accelerator and slammed the vehicle into gear, barely managing to avoid stalling. Mark clung on as the ambulance hiccupped forward. He looked through the windscreen at a scene of utter mayhem. His mouth hung open.

There were people running and fighting everywhere, with what seemed like dozens fleeing from all and any door at the hospital. The ambulance became a focus for those seeking sanctuary, and Mark cowered as what sounded like a thousand baseball bats hammered on its sides.

Carole drove forward madly, trying to avoid colliding with the figures that crowded her path. She serpentined, flinging the ambulance this way and that, staring in terror at a succession of strange, lurching figures as they emerged from the hospital. One ambled towards her, its eyes fixed on the vehicle. She made a vague attempt to skirt it but struck it anyway. As she drove on she saw it climb to its feet and head off to attack an old man.

"The radio!" shouted Mark.

Carole fought to reach the handset as she sped up the exit ramp and through the car park. All around her was chaos.

Mark's knuckles were white as his hands gripped the back of Carole's chair. His mind raced. People were running, flailing, falling, fighting. It was a scene of madness the like of which he had never before witnessed. Mass hysteria. Mass violence.

He decided to lock the doors. Then he noticed Mrs Partridge. The old woman was sitting up on the stretcher, her bloodied and shattered head weaving from side to side. Her one good eye seemed to burn into him. She attempted to stand.

He brought his left knee up and knocked her to the floor. Hurdling her, he flung open the doors... and saw hell.

The hospital was an inferno. People could be seen at the windows. Some were on the flat roof of the reception block. One man was punching another who was attempting to climb out of a window. And all around him were moving bodies. Some ran. Others shuffled with purpose. Like Mrs Partridge.

He grabbed the old woman and bundled her out of the ambulance, kicking her dentures after her. Then he closed the door. And locked it.

Carole was driving like a maniac.

"Where to?" she gasped

"Anywhere but here."

They fled.

STORIES OF THE DEAD

TONY EARNSHAW

Known primarily as a journalist and award-winning writer specialising in the cinema, Tony Earnshaw is a relative newcomer to horror fiction. His debut short story "Flies" appeared in *The Eleventh Black Book of Horror* (Mortbury Press, 2015) and was described as "foul, grisly and unutterably sad". He has since written a clutch of other tales focusing on zombies, cannibals, werewolves, evil fairies and other creatures of shadow and darkness. His books include studies of Peter Cushing, Jacques Tourneur's *Night of the Demon* and Tobe Hooper's *Salem's Lot*. His work has been nominated for four Rondo Hatton Classic Horror Awards.

MEMORIES OF ROMERO

I met George A. Romero just once, back in 2005 when he was back on the interview circuit promoting *Land of the Dead*. I was 39, but I could have been 15 again, such was my unbridled excitement. I was vibrating in my boots.

I'm sad that Romero is gone. It's fully 36 years since I was introduced to his work via a screening of *Zombies: Dawn of the Dead* at an event at the University of Manchester Institute of Science & Technology (UMIST). That movie – the first of thousands of times that I have watched it – opened my eyes to mature cinema and spurred me onto a voyage of discovery. George A. Romero dared to do things differently and in doing so made supremely intelligent cinema. That's a rare thing these days.

When we met I shook his hand, asked for his autograph and blurted out that I'd wanted to meet him for 24 years. "Gee," he said, "I hope it was worth the wait."

A TRIBUTE TO GEORGE A. ROMERO

By George, it was.

Once Bitten Twice Die

BY JAMES JOBLING

I know something is wrong as soon as I pull into the driveway. An ambulance is parked across the road – outside Mr Dooley's – and, as I climb out of my van and walk towards the front door, I see two paramedics in the back of the vehicle, pumping his chest. Hardly surprising. Tom Dooley drinks like a fish and smokes like a chimney. It was only a matter of time before his old ticker gave out. Shaking my head, I open the front door and rush inside my house to find out what has happened to my son. Kate greets me in the hallway.

"*Bitten?*" I ask, tossing my keys onto the corner table next to the phone. I hold my arms out, waiting for an explanation. "What do you mean, *bitten*? *Bitten* by whom?"

"John, calm down, okay? Getting worked up isn't going to help matters."

"Then tell me who bit our son, Kate?"

She sighs wearily, running a hand through her long black hair, staring at the battered oilcloth of the kitchen floor with dog-tired eyes. I know why she's reluctant to tell me who attacked our son. She knows what I'll do.

It doesn't take much for me and that arsehole next-door to come to blows. Since the Sinclair lot moved in six months ago, Frank (the joint-smoking, beer-guzzling, work-dodging lout who somehow managed to father *five* feral kids) and I have had numerous arguments; kicking off on a few occasions. Noise. Mess. Late-night to-dos between Frank and his missus. Loud parties. His eldest son's insistency on parking across my drive. Oh, yeah, and the most regular thing that sees us butting heads – his little girl bullying my son.

"It was Imelda, wasn't it?" Without thinking, I make for the front door, livid the little bitch has hurt my son again. "I've had enough of that madam. Somebody needs to teach her a lesson."

"And that somebody is going to be you, is it?"

"Maybe."

Kate barges past me, blocking the front door with her body, crucifying her arms to the sides of the jamb. "Don't be stupid, John. You'll get arrested."

"Get out of my way."

"Where are you going?"

"Where the bloody hell do you *think*?" I bellow. A siren screams to life and blues-and-twos light up the hallway as the ambulance carts Mr Dooley off to the hospital. "I'm going next-door to tell Frank that he'd better keep his bloody kids under control or—"

"*Or?*"

I open my mouth to reply, then realise I don't *have* one. Promptly closing it, I look down at the threadbare carpet beneath my boots.

"John, I know you're upset, but leave it for me to deal with, okay?"

"You?" I snigger. Arrogant. Sarcastic. Unmerited.

Kate nods. "Let me talk to Stella. I promise if the bullying continues after, then you can handle it whichever way you want. But please, for the moment, leave it to me."

I fumigate my nostrils with a furious sigh and, against my better judgment, turn from the front door. "Okay. I'll do it for you. But I'm getting sick of *his* daughter kicking the shit out of *my* son whenever the mood takes her. It needs dealing with. Now."

"I'll nip over after dinner and speak to Stella. In the meantime, go check on *our* son. He's not himself."

I ascend the creaky staircase and rap my knuckles against Matthew's bedroom door. No reply. I crank the handle and shoulder the door open an inch.

My son is fast asleep on the bed.

Stripped down to just underpants and vest, the sight of his clammy body causes niggling pain in my fast-throbbing heart. No sheets cover him and, as I creep forward, I notice his entire body is beaded with sweat. His eyes are twitching restlessly behind sealed lids, as if he is suffering from a nightmare. My first thought is to wake him, but Kate once told me that sudden shock can cause him to have a seizure. Matthew was diagnosed with epilepsy at the age of two. His left hand has been wrapped in gauze and kept in place by blue *Finding Nemo* plasters. Streaks of blood stain the back of the bandage.

"He's been sleeping since he got home from school."

Kate's unexpected whisper causes me to jump. My startled heart skips a galloping beat. Turning, I find my wife leaning against the doorway, arms folded across her heaving chest. Crouching, I gently stroke my son's flustered cheek with the back of my finger.

"Have you called the doctor?"

"Yes, but I can't get through. Lines are jammed."

I curse quietly, kissing the back of Matthew's uninjured hand.

"He was sick on the way home," Kate tells me. "We were stuck in traffic for almost an hour. Poor little blighter had to use a carrier bag to puke in."

I nod. "Took me almost double that to get home after you told me he'd been bitten. Everybody's panicking about

A TRIBUTE TO GEORGE A. ROMERO

that space probe in America. They think it brought back some kind of exotic radiation which is responsible for this new flu. It's madness! People seriously think if they're out of the city, they won't contract it."

"Bloody morons. If they're going to get it, they're going to get it," Kate whispers, gesturing for me to leave our son sleeping.

Together, we go downstairs. I follow Kate into the lounge. Unzipping my Hi-Vis vest, I scrunch it into a ball and toss it on the sofa; eager to turn the news on and hear the latest about the epidemic.

I stayed awake until midnight last night, glued to the news, watching looters and yobs clashing with the police for the third consecutive night of chaotic rioting. Despite the footage now being live, the images are no different from what I witnessed the previous night; hooded fuckwits smashing shop windows and hurtling glass bottles at the police. Shaking my head, I use the remote control to channel hop, but all I find is more destruction and anarchy. One news channel displays the bold headline **CENTER FOR DISEASE CONTROL & PREVENTION DESCRIBE NEW STRAIN OF FLU AS BEING 'AS CLOSE TO THE ZOMBIE APOCALYPSE THAT WE ARE LIKELY TO GET'**. I hit standby and run both hands over my shaved head.

"It's really going off in London," Kate says from her armchair. Her legs are rolled beneath her, and she is on her phone, scrolling through Facebook. I stopped checking my account when it became clogged with people complaining about feeling unwell.

"I know. I've had the news playing in the van all day."

"You've had work on?"

"Not really. But you know what Harry's like. Could be the end of the world and that fat prick would still expect you to pull a shift. He had me clearing the yard all afternoon."

Kate isn't listening to a single word I am saying. "It

says on Sky News' website that the military are being drafted in to deal with the rioting in certain boroughs."

"Good," I grunt. "That ought to teach the idiots for tearing apart their *own* city."

"Apparently, the media are referring to the riots as the 'Uprising'."

"I heard."

"Christ, John," Kate whispers, a tremor in her voice. "It's like something out of a horror movie."

"Look, calm down." I inch my way to the edge of the sofa. "It's just scaremongering. You know what the bloody media's like, Kate. It'll die down soon."

"That's what I'm afraid of."

"Relax, Kate. A couple of months ago it was Ebola. Before that, Swine flu. Remember when HIV and AIDS were discovered? Everybody thought we was going to get wiped off the face of the earth then. But we didn't. We're still here."

"I know, I know," Kate mutters. "I just can't help feeling that something—"

The power goes off.

The TV—already gone—loses the red glow of its stand-by switch, and the screen flashes a death rattle. The corner lamp goes dark and, as I jump to my feet and cross the room, I flip the light switch to find it lifeless, too.

"John? What's going on? Why has the electricity gone off?"

"Don't know," I mutter, trying the lights in the hallway to no avail. "Maybe the circuit box has overpowered."

"If that's the reason, then how come my phone is dead?" She holds it up for me to observe. "It was fully charged."

I crash into the kitchen and, straightaway, the startling quietness makes my ears ping. No hum of the refrigerator. No thrum from boiler. When I cross to the oven and try to ignite the hob, no gas hisses free. Even the *click-click-click* of the sparker is missing. This is weird. This is fucked up.

"John, the landline is down, too!" Kate screams from the hall. "There's no dial-tone!"

We both clash in our haste to reach each other. I give Kate a reassuring cuddle and tell her to stay calm and to check on Matthew.

"Where are you going?"

"I want to see if anybody else has any lights on."

"Of course, they bloody don't!" Kate snaps. "It's only half-six in the evening!"

"Then I'll knock on and ask!"

Fingers curl around the Yale lock. I pull the front door open and rush into the arms of a man wearing Hazmat coveralls. The crinkled plastic overalls are white, and he has yolk-yellow Wellingtons on his feet. A breathing apparatus conceals his face beneath the plastic hood.

Yelping like a mistreated puppy, I stagger from the man who doesn't make a sound or seem fazed in the slightest. The only reaction I get is a disgruntled command of, "Get back! Go in the fucking house! *Now!*" And then, I'm gawking down the yawning muzzle of an assault rifle.

Swallowing hard, I kick the door closed and race down the hallway, screaming for Kate. She staggers out of Matthew's bedroom, and I open my mouth to tell her to come downstairs...when I see blood dribbling from a gouged rupture in her forearm. The fingers on her other hand are trying to clasp the wound closed, but blood is gushing free. Her face is ashen. Waxy. Her body trembling spasmodically.

"Kate?" I wheeze. "What—what's happened?"

Before she can answer, Matthew steps from behind her; blood flowing from his grinding jaws.

"Kate? Kate, are you okay? Is Matthew? Oh, dear God, what's happened?"

She opens her mouth to reply, but the words lodge in her throat, making her look like a fish out of water, drowning on air. She's in shock, and I can't blame her.

Looking from Kate to Matthew, Matthew to Kate, I realise what's happened. And the sickening reality hits me like a sledgehammer to the groin. Matthew has *bitten* her! Matthew has *bitten* his own mother! Staggering from the staircase, I force myself to do something productive.

"Stay there, love? I'll get something to stem the blood," I say, panicking. "You'll be okay, sweetheart. I give you my word."

Racing into the kitchen, I snatch a tea towel from the side and I'm in the throes of returning to my injured wife when the kitchen grows inconceivably gloomy; like rainclouds passing over the sun on a summer's day. I turn towards the window overlooking the driveway, and I'm taken to despair when two Hazmat silhouettes raise a sheet of plywood to the window. Blackness fully consumes the room. A petrifying second later, rounds from a nail gun are heard firing into the window frame.

"No! Help!" I shout. "Help! I need fucking help!" More nails are punched into the plywood, and I scream into my cupped hands.

Lurching drunkenly into the hallway – heart thundering, mouth dry – I open the front door, tossing the PVC partition back on its hinges, only to find the doorway blocked by a length of thick wood.

I shoulder barge it, but my weight's no contest for the stern barrier. Testing the obstruction with my fists proves futile, too. Even kicking the blockage only results in me being forced backwards a few wobbly footsteps. The words CONTAMINATION ZONE: ISOLATE SUBJECTS has been stencilled in black spray paint on the wood, just below a hazard insignia. Screaming in fear, I slam the door closed, but it merely bounces off the towering wood and swings open again, taunting me.

I turn towards Kate. She's half up, half down the stairs. Her injured arm is hanging loosely by her side. The other reaches in front of her, groping at air with long fingers. Her head is cocked to one side. As I watch her struggle to descend the stairs without tumbling, I realise she's using the wall as support, swiping photographs and cherished portraits painted by Matthew's artistic hand off the wall in the process, sending them smashing to the ground.

Her eyes are completely white. No pupils. No scleras. Only the milky whites of a ninety-year-old cataract sufferer. Glancing over her shoulder—at Matthew—I realise my son looks the same. They release groans from throats that sound slick with phlegm. My heart threatens to break with fear and grief. I force myself to run into the front room and close the door behind me.

Grabbing the corner of the sofa, I hoist it behind the door as Kate (or what *used* to be Kate) feebly bashes her fists against the opposite side of the partition. I turn to the backdoor—my only escape—but this has also been sealed by men wearing breathing apparatus with oxygen tanks strapped to their backs. As the final plank of plywood is nailed in front of my living room window—gobbling up the dregs of dying daylight forever—the lounge door is inched open, Matthew shuffles in, mouth wide, underpants streaked with blood and runny excrement.

Kate follows, stumbling on the balls of her feet, eager to reach me, almost colliding with our dead son. Her eyes are lifeless. I swallow hard and take a nervous step forward, knowing that—for me at least—there is nowhere left to run. I can't escape. I can't hide. Besides, even if I could, the thought of a life without my family terrifies me more than anything that's transpired over the last five minutes.

As my arms embrace Kate for a final time, I try not to howl when her teeth sink into the joint of my shoulder. "I love you, Kate," I grunt in pain. "I always will."

Milk teeth tear a huge knot of muscle from my thigh as Matthew tears my leg to pieces. Yet, still, I refuse to scream with the indignity of agony. Not even when he moves up to my testicles. "Matthew," I whisper, tears flooding my eyes, flowing down my flushed cheeks. "I love you, champ… I… love… you… both… so… much…"

I am only able to remain upright and embracing for a few seconds before I feel something moving around inside my chest. I close my eyes and try to smile, thankful that the end is close. We might be nothing more than walking corpses, but at least we'll be together. Forever.

With a final shaky breath, I drift away.

Only to wake up seconds later, famished.

A TRIBUTE TO GEORGE A. ROMERO

JAMES JOBLING

James Jobling has been a rabid fan of anything horror for most of his life, blaming his older brother for leaving a copy of James Herbert's fantastic novel, *The Rats*, lounging around the living room when he was only a child for starting his obsession. A huge fan of the horror book genre, James regards Herbert and David Moody as being his writing heroes.

James lives in Manchester, England, with his world – his beautiful wife, three adorable, sleep-avoiding children, and Nanook, his pet beagle. He can be contacted through Facebook and would be honoured to hear from anybody who might wish to get in touch.

MEMORIES OF ROMERO

I must have been in my hormonal teenage years when I finally lost my Romero cherry and watched *Dawn of the Dead* – arguably the best in the Zombie saga – on a rainy Sunday morning, just before football training, at my best friend's house. Having not seen *Night of the Living Dead*, I was not aware that *Dawn* was a straight-off-the-bat sequel which refused point blankly to rehash the harrowing events of the first film or even attempt to give an explanation as to what had caused the initial outbreak, leaving me just as confused as Peter and Roger. Growing up with two horror-loving brothers, I had of course heard of *Dawn of the Dead*, and thanks to my love of anything *Resident Evil*, I was aware of just what a Zombie was and did. However, I had no idea of how much gory fun the *Dead* series truly was – and remains to this day. All three films – *Night of the Living Dead*, *Dawn of the Dead*, and *Day of the Dead* (yes, I am purposely ignoring anything made after

that) – still stand their own in a genre swamped by the undead… which is a true testament to just how much love and respect George deservedly earns from his ever-growing fans.
Thank you, George.

who they were
BY
RICH HAWKINS

Cowering in a sodden garden, the rain falling about him, Caleb peered between the wooden slats in the garden gate. He watched the shambling dead roam amidst the rusted, begrimed cars on the street.

Some of them meandered, almost hesitant, as if they were trying to remember what became of everything. They moved in small groups or on their own. Socialites or loners. Slack-eyed ghouls with spoiled-meat faces.

On his way back through the streets, he dodged their grasping hands, and they loped after him in their threadbare clothes and meagre rags like the followers of the last prophet in a ruined world.

He reached his home street as daylight began to fade and

slow rain fell on the murky shapes of abandoned vehicles.

He stepped over a jumble of human bones by the kerb.

Arriving at his parents' house, he halted at the garden gate. He'd searched all the houses in the street. Most had been deserted during the first days, his neighbours fleeing to other places deemed safer than the village. Several houses contained mouldering bodies with deep wounds to their skulls. A few dead pets accompanied them.

In some houses he'd encountered the living dead slumped in living rooms or lurking in hallways and kitchens. Some had waited for him in their deathbeds.

And in the end he'd run from them, terrified and witless, clutching the plastic bags he'd hoped to fill with stolen food.

The rain eased off as he opened the garden gate and walked across the ankle-high lawn to the front door of the house his parents had lived in for over forty years.

With the front door locked behind him, Caleb stood in the darkness of the hallway between the living room and the stairs. The curtains were drawn over each downstairs window. The back door was bolted and barricaded. He pushed his mother's prized mahogany cabinet against the front door; a meagre security measure, but better than nothing. He'd been thinking about nailing wooden boards over the windows, just in case, but he was worried that the noise might attract unwanted attention from outside.

He lit a candle. It was the only light he needed. He climbed the stairs, holding onto the banister. The landing was an enclosed space, the walls moving in on him. There were three doors: two to either side of him, one straight ahead. The candle flame flickered and danced in his hand as he stepped to the door of his parents' bedroom. He held his breath and listened, but there was only silence from inside.

He rested his forehead against the door. "I'm home."

He squeezed his eyes shut as his heartbeat rose and fell, spiking louder before fading again. And he opened his eyes when scraping footsteps approached from inside his parents' room. The slow pawing and scratching of hands and fingernails began against their side of the door. He stepped back, blinking, stifling a sharp intake of breath, and looked down at the doorknob as it turned one way then the other. A sudden, irrational panic that he'd never actually locked the door all those months ago made him retreat to the opposite side of the landing. But the door held and his parents did not emerge to welcome him home.

He didn't move for a while, until he heard his parents' shuffling footfalls move away from the door. Then there was silence.

He went downstairs and changed his clothes. Shook off his trainers and placed them near the sofa. He hung his wet jeans, jumper and coat on the washing line he'd hung across the width of the living room.

He fired up the camping stove and emptied a tin of baked beans into a pot he'd scraped clean of congealed food residue, and let them simmer while he checked the downstairs windows. When the rising steam warmed the air and the beans were ready, he ate them in a paper bowl with a plastic spoon and listened to the rain upon the house.

Darkness fell. He spent most of the night reading one of his father's paperback Westerns, sipping a can of cider between chapters and listening for sounds from outside or upstairs. When his eyes grew tired, he put away the book and did a cursory check of his food stocks in the kitchen. After that, when he was fairly certain the house was secure, he grabbed another can of cider and returned to the living room and lay on the sofa with the musty blankets and sheets around him.

The rain was still falling. He looked up at the ceiling beneath his parents' room and pictured them dwelling in darkness. He wondered if they were standing next to each other, if they held hands, or if they were even aware of each other. What remained of all those years of marriage, their life together? Was it all gone from their dead minds?

Did they remember him?

Caleb downed his drink and closed his eyes.

Before.

Dusk approached in a sky smeared with shades of red, yellow and deep orange. The vague outline of a ghost moon over darkening fields.

Caleb let out a deep sigh and tightened his hands on the steering wheel. Next to him, his father sat in silence, staring through the windscreen at the road ahead.

The radio murmured a list of civil disturbances happening in the cities. There were riots in several parts of London, Manchester, Birmingham, Newcastle and Glasgow. Rumours of Army units on the streets. Caleb had heard about armed police storming apartment blocks on council estates. His stomach squirmed with anxiety and a sort of dreaded anticipation he hadn't felt since Mum had first fallen ill. He didn't know what was happening to the country.

"The Prime Minister is due to address the nation within the hour..."

Dad switched the radio off and made a dismissive sound in his throat.

A TRIBUTE TO GEORGE A. ROMERO

Caleb turned the wheel to guide the car around a slight bend in the road, past indistinct hedgerows and overhanging trees. "You okay, Dad?"

"People. It's always something, isn't it?"

"What do you mean? The riots?"

"Do they even know what they're rioting about? It's nonsense, lad. Sometimes people just need something to get angry about. The only bright side of all this is that these things usually blow over. People will forget about it all and return to their distractions, until something else pisses them off and they throw another hissy fit."

"I think it's more than that." Caleb didn't like to contradict his father, but he'd seen too much grainy video footage of staggering figures in dark streets, and people being swarmed by roving gangs.

Dad looked at him, frowning. "You've been spending too much time on the internet, lad. It's got you believing in all sorts of things."

Caleb changed gears through a narrow section of road. The falling sun glared over an open stretch of fields. "I hope you're right."

"It'll be fine," Dad said. A pause. "You look tired."

"Been on early shift this week."

"How's work going?"

"Same old shit."

"That bad, eh?"

Caleb shrugged. "A job's a job."

"I worked for forty years in a factory," said Dad. "I know how you feel. Are you still doing your drawings?"

"Haven't drawn anything in a while."

"Why not?"

"I dunno."

"You've got talent, lad. Always said that."

They arrived at the care home a few minutes later.

Caleb parked outside the front of the building. He turned the engine off. They climbed out and crossed the car park.

The doors were shut. Soft light glowed from within. No one emerged to greet them.

STORIES OF THE DEAD

Caleb wanted to know if they still remembered him.

He stood for hours outside their bedroom door, talking about old memories. He spoke until his voice began to slur. And when they started scratching and pawing at the door, he placed his hand on the other side and said their names.

A sudden silence within the room. Caleb waited, blinking back tears. His throat tightened with grief.

Moments later, he heard his parents' slow footfalls moving away from the door.

After that, nothing.

Before.

They went up the steps and through the main entrance. They stood in reception. The desk was unattended and the door to the manager's office was ajar.

"There's usually someone at the desk," Dad said.

Caleb looked around. "Maybe they're on break." He slowly pushed open the manager's door and stepped inside, but no one welcomed him. The BBC News on the wall-mounted television showed footage of a burning building in central London. The volume was muted.

He turned away and looked down at the pot of pens which had fallen from the desk and spilled across the plush carpet. Upon the desk a standing photo frame showed a middle-aged woman with her teenage daughter. A pile of invoices and documents in a tray. He noticed his dull reflection in the dark monitor screen of the computer.

A TRIBUTE TO GEORGE A. ROMERO

Caleb left the office and led his father down the corridor flanked by the residents' rooms to either side. The overhead lights stung his eyes. Orchestral music, low enough to be barely heard, drifted from beyond the partly-open door of one room. A damp lump clogged his throat. Something like a voice, half-whispered or wheezed from an old mouth, rose from inside another room. Dry clacking and scraping movement. The creak of bedsprings beneath a heavy weight.

There was a slow scratching on the other side of one door, like an injured animal trapped in the room.

"Where's the staff?" Dad said.

They reached Mum's room moments later and entered. Caleb closed the door after checking both ways of the corridor.

Mum didn't move under the blankets upon her bed. The curtains were drawn, and the watery light of the bedside lamp showed the room to them in jaundiced shades. The far wall was burdened with shelves of little trinkets and porcelain figures. Next to the window was a dressing table. A pot of hairbrushes. A bottle of perfume. Lotions and creams. A framed photo of Caleb as a boy.

Dad went to her and spoke softly, hunching over her prone form. With trembling hands, he stroked strands of greying hair from her forehead. Her eyes fluttered open. She was deathly white. She looked at Caleb once, then regarded her husband of fifty-odd years and smiled a smile so frail it was more of a tremble across her lips than anything else. She muttered something only Dad seemed to hear then closed her eyes, and it was as if she'd never awoken at all.

Dad held her hand between his own, and nodded, apparently aware of some terrible resolution, before he looked back at Caleb and told him to fetch someone quickly.

"I'll stay with her. Don't come back until you've found someone, lad."

Caleb left the room and closed the door. He blinked away tears.

The next day, drunk on Strongbow, he climbed the stairs

with a torch and Mum's favourite photo album and unlocked their bedroom door.

Standing there, with his hand on the door handle, he experienced a sudden jolt of lucidity and questioned his actions, but it was soon forgotten as he remembered moments from the good years.

He opened the door and entered the room.

They stood hunched and silent at the foot of the bed, turning to face their son. In the torchlight they regarded him with crumpled faces and dull eyes. He halted one step past the doorway, his chest full of bile and froth, his legs trembling. He stared at them.

They were the occupants of a haunted house, and he a fellow ghost.

Dust motes and the smell of decay stifled the air. The drawn curtains made the room ill-defined and murky. Everything was covered in dust and the carpet was gritty under his trainers.

"Mum. Dad. It's me. It's Caleb."

His mother's mouth moved in a silent opening of shrivelled lips and brown teeth. The nightdress hung like a thin blanket on her emaciated body. His father gave a dusty rasping from a torn throat. His jacket begrimed on the sleeves and at the collar, and darkened with congealed blood.

They loped across the floor, side-by-side, reaching for him, and at first he didn't move and awaited their embrace. But at the last moment, as their fingers brushed against him, he lost his nerve and retreated from the room. He slammed the door and locked it, then stood shaking, speechless and drunk.

His parents scratched at the other side.

"Do you remember me?" he asked, forehead pressed against the door. "Do you remember your son? Do you remember anything at all?"

No answer. Just silence. He imagined his parents standing inches away on the other side of the door,

A TRIBUTE TO GEORGE A. ROMERO

listening to him.

"Do you understand me?" he muttered, voice cracking.

Again, there was no reply.

He turned away.

Before.

Down the corridor and round the corner, he found one of the staff. He stopped, frowning in the harshness of the rectangular light fixtures on the ceiling, squeezing the car keys in one hand. The carer stood with her back to him, head sloping to one side, as if she was listening to some signal in the air that was inaudible to him. Dressed in baggy tracksuit bottoms and a blue apron, she was slightly hunched, arms hanging loose down to her hips. There was a dark patch of damp around her feet on the carpet. A little beyond her and to one side was an open doorway, probably to a store room. Past that, at the end of the corridor, was another door. It was closed.

Something was wrong with her posture, as though her spine was damaged in some way.

Caleb called out to her, and she turned around and showed her face to him. He stared in disbelief and numb horror. He wanted to step back, turn and flee, get out of the building and drive away, but all he could do was let out a low cry that ran out of breath as soon as it left his mouth. He was rooted in place, paralysed by shock and disbelief.

Her name was Cassandra, according to the plastic nametag dangling from the chest of her torn apron. A grievous wound in her stomach glistened. Her hands were red and wet. Blood around her mouth and down her chin; some of it had dripped onto her apron. Her left eye had collapsed into its socket and the flesh around it was gouged and lacerated, as were other parts of her face, particularly her nose, which had been reduced to a knot of gristle and meat. The ripped, weeping skin of her throat hung in glistening flaps, upon which a silver crucifix necklace caught the light. Her right eye strained within her head, bulbous and reddened. When her mouth opened and she uttered a rattling groan, it was all Caleb could do not to cry out. He thought his heart might stop.

The woman came forward on raggedy legs, brushing against the walls as she lurched from one side of the corridor to the other, unable to walk straight due to her hideous injuries. And before Caleb could force himself to move, she was upon him with grasping hands and a mouth stinking of offal juices. She seized his shoulders with her red hands and drew her determined mouth towards his face. She pushed him against the wall, her cold weight pressing against him, arms horribly animated as they tried to gain purchase on his shoulders and bring him closer to her open mouth. Her hair was matted with blood. Dark, stinking fluid bled from the wound in her stomach and made a puddle between them on the carpet.

With all his strength, he shoved her away and her back slammed against the opposite wall. Her mouth had been excruciatingly near to his face. Close enough for him to see the dirty teeth inside her head. And as she reached for him again, Caleb swiped at her with his keys, scoring a shallow line across her left cheek.

She didn't react to the wound. At the same time, Caleb slipped on the wet patch of carpet and fell on his backside. He began to crawl away. The woman lunged for him. He rose from his hands and knees and stumbled forward, towards the open doorway of the store room, but she caught the collar of his t-shirt and started to pull him back. He twisted, knocked her hand away with his flailing arm, and fell back against the wall.

She came at him again, gurgling in her throat. No time to avoid her, so he planted his foot against her stomach and pushed her away. Then she came at him again, and he grabbed her cold wrists, keeping away from her horrid mouth, and jostled her through the doorway and into the storeroom, where she fell against a shelving rack full of cleaning supplies. Plastic bottles and cardboard boxes dropped from the shelves and hit the floor.

The woman was already staggering towards him when he closed the door and turned the lock, trapping her inside the storeroom. She stared at him through the little window in the door, her busy mouth working at the glass, smearing reddish saliva and grime ravaged lips and face.

"Oh, do fuck off," Caleb said, wearily.

She turned the handle, but the lock held. Caleb stepped back and eyed her, his heartbeat tolling in his ears, bile and froth mixing in his airless chest. Nausea soured the back of his mouth. He put one hand to his lips and stifled a sickly burp. He couldn't feel his legs. He wanted to cry.

"What happened to you?" he muttered. "What happened here?"

He turned away as the woman started banging at the door.

Two hours later, after a few more cans of cider, he went back upstairs with the photo album. He swayed upon the landing, clicked the torch on, and entered his parents' room.

Again, when the torch beam swept over them, they were found standing together, this time in the far corner.

They approached him on shuffling feet. Reaching for him.

He opened the photo album. He was trembling all over. He stepped back and showed them the photo of their wedding day back in the Seventies, when they were young.

They kept moving towards him.

When he showed them a photo of himself as a boy on his old BMX, he could have sworn Mum slowed a bit, but it wasn't enough and they went for him as he turned and fled. In his sudden panic as their bony hands grasped for him, he dropped the photo album. He barely got the door shut this time, and locked it with shaking hands.

He went back downstairs and drank some more.

STORIES OF THE DEAD

Before.

He opened the door at the end of the corridor and stepped into the common room.

And tripped on something damp and heavy on the floor.

He righted himself by placing his hand against the wall and looked down at the body of an old man revealed in the soft glow of a lamp on a nearby table. He turned away, but he'd already seen the man's ransacked stomach and ruined face. The curls of grey intestine and drying shapes of blood on the floor. Some of the blood had been smeared on the linoleum. The stink of offal almost brought him to his knees, and he stepped away with one hand at his face, looking into the main area of the common room ahead of him.

On the wall at the far end of the common room, a flat-screen television showed the Prime Minister addressing the nation from outside 10 Downing Street. He looked exhausted; haggard and gaunt, like he'd lost weight in the last few days of turmoil. His tie was loose around his neck and there were creases in his suit. His throat worked between barely audible words.

And in the light of the television in the darkened room, the shapes of bodies were revealed to him. He stepped back and clenched the keys in his hand until the little grooves of metal pinched into his palm.

Several residents and nurses knelt or crouched on the floor, gnawing at the scattered human remains around them. They held scraps of flesh and bits of skin to their chewing mouths. They pulled apart ransacked bodies and wrenched skin, muscle and meat from angles of bone. A man with a bald head and blood over his face, chest and shoulders, used his fretting teeth to strip the flesh from a pelvic girdle. The carpet was waterlogged with blood.

Dead people slumped in old fashioned armchairs; parts torn away, eyes open to the ceiling, mouths agape. Violent deaths. The smell of butchery and slaughter induced tears in his eyes and made it

A TRIBUTE TO GEORGE A. ROMERO

hard to arrange his thoughts. He put one hand over his nose and mouth and swallowed a sob that scraped at the inside of his throat.

A woman, her black wig askew on her head, sat crumpled and soft over a chessboard of scattered pieces and pawns on a Formica table. The back of her cardigan had been torn open, as was the skin underneath, and the dull white of her spine and stacked vertebrae was exposed. A short man in a stained dressing gown, his movements jerky and awkward, crawled over to her body and buried his face in the plumpness of her lower back. Animalistic and savage, he ate as if he'd been starved for days.

Caleb watched the cannibals. He couldn't close his eyes.

The care home manager lay pinned to the floor by the hands of a nurse and two residents. Her three attackers seemed to be wounded, their bodies covered in cuts and what looked like bite marks. Their mouths worked at her stomach. She spluttered from her trembling mouth and gasped at the air as she stared at Caleb. Bloody froth covered her lips and chin. Her eyes implored Caleb, and she tried to reach out to him until the nurse sank her teeth into her face. She didn't scream.

"Remain calm," the Prime Minister said. "Do not panic. The situation is under control."

Something cold and rigid grabbed his leg from behind, and he looked down to see the old man – who he'd tripped over upon first entering the common room, and had presumed to be dead – on the floor gripping his ankle. The old man's grey eyes regarded Caleb with desperation and hungry pleading. His mouth opened and close, rasping lowly, and the pressure of his gnarled hand sent jags of pain through Caleb's ankle and foot.

Crying out, Caleb kicked the man away and stepped back, but lost his shoe in the escape, as the man pawed and flailed and tried to bite at the back of his thigh.

He fled, leaving his shoe behind.

STORIES OF THE DEAD

Caleb passed out for a while, and when he woke, he went into their room to retrieve the photo album.

His parents stood by the window, heads bowed, jaws snapping at the air. They slowly raised their heads to appraise him as he realised that one of them had picked up the photo album and placed it on the bed. That shouldn't have been possible. That wasn't supposed to happen.

And it was almost as though they allowed Caleb to take the photo album before lunging for him with their grasping hands.

He escaped and locked the door.

Before.

When he burst back into his mother's room, Dad was sitting at her bedside, still holding her hand. Caleb sagged against the wall, struggling for words, panting and trying to regain his breath.

Dad's face was wet with tears. Confusion widened his tired eyes as he noticed the blood on Caleb's t-shirt. "What's happening, lad?"

Caleb managed to gather some air into his chest. "We have to go."

"Your mother needs medical help."

"We won't find any here."

His father frowned; face bloodless and tight with fear. "I've heard such horrible sounds in the last few minutes. From the other rooms."

Caleb went to his mother and wrapped the blankets around her and picked her up from the bed. She was frail and sagging in his arms. His father looked at him.

"What are you doing?"

"We haven't got much time before they get here."

"What are you talking about?"

"Trust me, Dad. Get the door. We're taking Mum home."

A TRIBUTE TO GEORGE A. ROMERO

The shambling things were on their heels as they fled the care home. They emerged to a night sky. Caleb blinked in the glare of the security light at the front of the building, hobbling as he carried his mother. He winced every time the grit and loose stones in the car park found the sole of his shoeless foot.

Behind them, the people of the care home groaned in the starkly-lit corridors.

They reached the car. A helicopter passed high overhead, unseen except for its blinking red light. Dad grabbed the keys and unlocked the car. Caleb laid his mother across the backseat then climbed behind the steering wheel and started the engine. Dad sat with Mum and cradled her head on his lap. Her eyes remained closed. She muttered something inaudible as the cannibals reached for the car, their faces agape with desperate, ravenous hunger.

Caleb revved the engine and lifted his foot from the clutch, and the car screamed away in a spray of grit and clouding dust. His hands were rigid on the steering wheel as they left their pursuers behind.

The next day, while looking through the photo album, he found that one of the pictures was missing. He returned to the room and when he saw in his mother's right hand the photo of himself as a child, it was almost enough to stop his heart.

They approached him, but slowly and with some hesitation. He almost let them get near enough to bite him, but he turned away and left the room.

As he shut the door, he realised they hadn't chased him. And that night, confused and muddled by thoughts and memories and more cider, he went back to the top of the stairs and found that the picture of young Caleb had been pushed under the door of his parents' room.

He smiled for a long while. And then he sat down on the top step and laughed to himself, hugging the photo

STORIES OF THE DEAD

and the half-empty can of Strongbow.

Before.

He only remembered to switch on the headlights once the care home had receded in the distance. He kept his eyes straight ahead and made sure not to look at his father's face in the rear view mirror. An ambulance raced past, flashing blue lights leaving blurred shapes upon his vision.

Dad was talking to Mum about the places they'd visit once she recovered. He reminisced about the good years. His voice dipped into a sob. He said her name, but she didn't respond.

"She's barely breathing," Dad said.

Caleb stared ahead. "We're nearly home, Dad. Just stay with her. It won't be long now."

They reached the village much later than expected, after getting caught in several traffic jams. The streets were deserted. Curtains were drawn against the night. Streetlights flickered.

He parked outside their house and killed the engine. Dad had left the kitchen light on. A dog was barking from a nearby back garden.

"She's gone," Dad said. His voice was flat.
Caleb nodded, said nothing.

In his dreams during the night, he relived a memory of when he was a boy and he locked his parents in the back shed. A summer day. The lawn freshly-mown. Sunlight dappled upon the surface of the goldfish pond.

196

A TRIBUTE TO GEORGE A. ROMERO

When he had released them from the shed, they tickled him until he was in hysterics on the ground, and then they hugged him and everything was fine.

That day. That childhood day.

Such a day burned into memory, to be recalled and held close to his heart.

Caleb woke and knew what he had to do. They would show him love, just like on that summer's day.

Before.

They carried her body inside the house and laid her across the sofa. Wiping his eyes, Dad pulled up a chair and sat beside her, while Caleb went into the kitchen and splashed his face with water from the cold tap. He poured a tumbler and sank its contents in seconds. Then he put the glass down and stood with his hands on both sides of the sink and lowered his head to his chest. He stifled a sob and closed his eyes.

His heartbeat was the only sound, growing louder until it was hammering at the inside of his skull. Slow tears seeped from under his eyelids and ran down his face.

He opened his eyes when Dad screamed, followed by a heavy thud and the shifting of what sounded like Mum's blankets being cast aside.

"Dad?"

There was no answer. And when Caleb hurried to the living room, he found Dad on the floor and Mum kneeling over him with her busy hands buried up to the wrists in the gaping rent of his chest. She moved jerkily, a ghastly figure, ghost-white and bloodied around the mouth and down the front of her nightdress. Her waxen face was without emotion, her eyes dark and dull and undeniably dead.

Caleb halted in the doorway. The walls seemed to compress and creak as his vision narrowed to the two figures on the living room floor.

Dad's face was preserved in the last moment of terror and confusion before his death. Blood spray flecked his throat. His left hand rested on Mum's right knee. Mum's hands rooted within the broken chest cavity, forcing apart bone and dank tissue with awful cracking and snaps. Liquid sounds. When she pulled her hands free, all red-slick and glistening, she held the lumpen shape of Dad's heart. Ventricles and rubbery tubes dripped fluids. She looked up at Caleb, wheezing and bleating in her throat, cradling her husband's heart in her hands before she raised it towards the bared teeth in her crooked mouth.

He climbed the stairs in some sort of daze and unlocked the door to his parents' room. He stood on the landing and called out to them, then returned downstairs and opened a fresh can of cider.

Moments later, he heard the door open, and he smiled. He had made their armchairs ready for them, for when they wanted to sit down and rest. There was plenty of food for them.

Shuffling, scraping footfalls grew louder on the upstairs floor.

He walked to the foot of the stairs. Two murky figures stood upon the landing, swaying gently.

Caleb told his parents to come down. It was time to be a family again.

A TRIBUTE TO GEORGE A. ROMERO

RICH HAWKINS

Rich Hawkins hails from the depths of Somerset, England, where a childhood of science fiction and horror films set him on the path to writing his own stories. He credits his love of horror and all things weird to his first viewing of John Carpenter's THE THING back in the early Nineties. His debut novel THE LAST PLAGUE was nominated for a British Fantasy Award for Best Horror Novel in 2015.

MEMORIES OF ROMERO

I discovered the genius of George A. Romero at some point in the early Nineties when late one night I happened upon a film on Channel 4 called DAWN OF THE DEAD. As a young teenager whose horror education consisted mainly of the Hammer classics and not-so-classics, DAWN blew my mind and scared me in a way I can remember even now.

After that, I was hooked. I managed to get hold of NIGHT OF THE LIVING DEAD and DAY OF THE DEAD, and they both had the same impact on me as DAWN. They inspired a love of zombies and 'end of the world' stories that still burns bright today. Hell, they're part of the reason I write apocalyptic horror. So when I was asked if I'd be interested in submitting to this anthology, I had to. It was as simple as that.

How could I turn down the King of the Zombies?

His influence will be felt upon filmmaking and cinema for a long, long time. His memory lives on and will inspire generations to come.

Thank you, George.

hopelessly devoted

BY KELLY GOULD

Under normal circumstances, this room on the fifth floor of the one-hundred-year-old hotel would have cost close to three hundred dollars a night. They'd been in there for two weeks and hadn't paid a single dime. Nobody from the hotel had asked them for money and now, for all they knew, there might not be a single living soul left in the building besides them residing in room 519.

The two room suite was spacious enough to comfortably coexist for a night or long weekend. It was never meant for such an extended stay. The longer they were trapped, the smaller it seemed.

The two queen beds sat empty. It was early afternoon and the sun shone through the open curtains. They were kept open during the day ever since the power turned off. At night it was so dark you could pretend you were somewhere else. Daylight brought a break from the blackness but was also a reminder. In the bathroom the tub was half-filled with cold water. Next to the toilet was a

A TRIBUTE TO GEORGE A. ROMERO

small plastic garbage can with an old newspaper set on top to cover it.

Emily and Bobby sat at the small table in the living room. Technically, they were adults; both were in their early twenties. Neither of them felt very grown-up right now. Grown-ups always knew what to do, but they were apprehensive and unsure. It was little comfort to know that no amount of life experience could have prepared them for what they were facing.

Their clothes were dirty and getting worse by the day. Most of them had already been worn once when they arrived at the hotel. By now, each item had been reused multiple times without washing. Emily's long dark hair was pulled back in a ponytail. She had stopped brushing it a few days before and was getting used to the greasy feeling.

Every once in a while they would hear something moving out in the hallway. Bobby always motioned for her to be quiet. Then, he would tiptoe over and press his ear to the door before looking out the peephole. Sometimes he would stay there, watching and listening, for several minutes. Emily couldn't take her eyes off of him. He was her protector and would take care of her. Bobby was the head of their little household.

When he was satisfied that whatever had been outside was gone he would sit back down. Emily reached out to run her hand through his beautiful blond hair. Even now, as dirty as it was, it was gorgeous. Like before, he pulled away, moving beyond her reach.

They had flown back to Portland after spending a long weekend in Montana for her sister's wedding. Emily's mother had fawned over Bobby the whole time, even calling him her future son-in-law on more than one occasion.

"Bobby stared at you during the ceremony," her mother told her at the reception after a couple of glasses of wine. "If you ask me, I think he's going to propose. He has that look. Maybe this weekend?"

"Oh, Mom, you're being ridiculous," Emily smiled.

Later that evening, back in the room, she spent half an hour writing 'Mrs. Emily Sutton' in different styles on the hotel stationary. She even practiced her faux surprise reaction in the mirror in case her mother was right.

Her mother was wrong. Bobby didn't propose.

He hardly spoke on the flight back to Oregon. That wasn't like him. Emily could tell something was on his mind but she didn't think it was anything she'd done. She assumed he was tired and a little grumpy from having to deal with her family. Bobby was such a great guy but her parents and siblings could test anyone's patience.

Their flight from Missoula, normally ninety minutes or so, took more than three hours. Most of that time was spent in the crowded skies over Portland, circling and waiting for a runway to open for them. Emily could see several planes doing the same thing from her window seat.

When they finally landed, the captain came over the intercom offering apologies but no explanation for the delay. The airport itself was chaos. Frantic, angry people crowded around big screens as, one by one, the posted flights changed from *delayed* to *cancelled*. Bobby and Emily watched helplessly as their connecting flight—the short hop that would take them home to Irvington—joined that disappointing list.

"Dammit," Bobby yelled. Emily clutched his arm and laid her head on his shoulder. Bobby hardly cursed and never yelled. Now they were stuck more than a hundred miles from home with no way to get there.

The bad news kept coming as they elbowed their way through the throng. Word spread that there were no rental cars available. The counters were all closed and unmanned.

Then word came that Governor Foley had ordered the closure of the major highways leading out of the city.

"I've lived here all my life and that's never happened. Not once," said a nearby woman. She wasn't speaking to anyone in particular but enough people around heard her. The woman, along with other people in the airport, was outraged but powerless. Rumors spread through like a virus. News reports, heard from a friend of a friend, began to trickle in of riots, infections, looting, and medicine shortages. Speculation was the word of the day; nobody knew anything concrete. Fear followed the rumors, replacing anger and frustration.

Bobby took the lead like always. Grabbing Emily by the hand, he maneuvered through the crowd towards baggage claim. "Stay right here. Pick up our luggage and I'll meet you back here," he said.

"OK, babe."

Emily watched him head out into the night air. She bit her lip and tapped her foot. Waiting for both bags and Bobby made her anxious. Others around her looked the same as she felt – tired and frazzled, not knowing what was going on or what they should do about it. Some people paced, some cried, others held their loved ones. Emily knew she had one advantage over them. She had Bobby, they didn't. That was the difference between being anxious and completely losing her shit.

She dialed her mom back in Montana but got dead air. The same thing with her friend Kayla in Irvington. Trying to get anywhere online was as disappointing.

"They've shut the grid down! Shut it *all* down!" A man in a rumpled suit screamed from inside the doors Bobby had exited. His tie was undone and hung loosely around his neck. "They don't want us to communicate. Keeping us in the dark and themselves safe. Knowledge is power!"

"Shut the hell up, you crazy fuck," came a reply from the other side of baggage claim.

The carousel started, dumping suitcases and backpacks

one at a time. Emily spotted their bags as soon as they appeared. She had them in hand before they'd gone a quarter of the way around the oval.

Bobby grabbed her by the shoulder as she struggled with the suitcases.

"C'mon, Em. I got us a way out of here but we gotta go now."

He took his luggage from her and led her from the airport. Thirty feet outside the doors, with two of its tires parked up on the median, was their ride. A modified passenger bus, painted black with tinted windows and PARTEEZ 2 GO stenciled on the side, waited with the engine running.

"Thanks, man." Bobby reached through the passenger window and handed the driver a small stack of folded bills.

"No prob. Just hurry it up. Train's leaving the station."

It was already standing room only in the diminutive bus when Bobby and Emily got on. A black light partially illuminated the haggard faces onboard.

"Hang on back there. Gonna be a bit bumpy." He put the bus in gear and aimed it at the path with the least amount of traffic. Emily fell into Bobby as the bus went fully up onto the curb and across the sidewalk. It weaved around vehicles and pedestrians.

"Outta the way, outta the way," the driver yelled and laid on the horn.

Emily cringed and shut her eyes tight at the near misses. They passed several fender benders and small groups walking along the sidewalk with luggage in tow. The driver maneuvered the bus expertly but with little regard for anyone in their way. Primarily using bike lanes and sidewalks, he quickly put distance between them and the airport.

Traffic thinned slightly the further they got. Normal driving habits and rules slowly returned.

"Where are we going, Bobby?" asked Emily.

"I don't know. Just needed to get out of there. We're

not getting another flight so we need to find another way."

"I'm only going as far as downtown," the driver shouted back to his passengers as he drove. "The highways leaving town are all closed. There might be some back roads open. As for me, I'm gonna head home and hunker down until this thing blows over."

A man spoke up from the back. "Until *what* blows over? What's going on? Why did they cancel the flights and close the roads?"

"I don't know, man. Riots, plague, or some goddamn alien invasion. I just know it ain't good."

The bus rolled on, passing emergency vehicles with lights flashing seemingly every other block. Some streets had police cars manning barricades, others, ambulances with EMT's tending to the injured. One building—a convenience store on a corner—had smoke pouring from its doors and windows. A dozen people stood outside watching it burn.

"Shit," said the driver. Up ahead the traffic had stopped altogether. Cars were bumper to bumper and people were yelling at each other. With no way around, the bus slowed to a halt.

Bobby took a deep breath. "I have an idea, Em." He turned to the driver and said, "This is the end of the line for us. Thanks, buddy."

"Good luck." The door slid open. Bobby and Emily hopped out. Bobby looked around, getting his bearings.

"This way," he said, heading down a side street away from the traffic jam. Emily followed him at a half walk, half jog. A block down the road he stopped and looked up at a lit sign that read Historic Eagleton Hotel. "It's worth a shot," he shrugged.

STORIES OF THE DEAD

The lobby of the Eagleton Hotel was impressively large and opulent. It was easy to picture it as a ballroom hosting a gala complete with jazz band and champagne. The young woman at the front desk was pleasant but not very helpful. The hotel had no vacancies. The best she could do, she told them, was offer to let them wait in the lobby. Not everyone had checked in and, "With all the current troubles," maybe they'd have a no-show.

Emily collapsed onto a nearby sofa. They'd been traveling most of the day. Bobby tried repeatedly to get through to someone on his phone. Sometimes he got a busy signal, others he got no signal whatsoever. He became more frustrated with each failure.

"I'm sure your parents are fine, baby." Emily tried to sound reassuring. Bobby nodded and dialed again.

She managed a quick nap on the sofa as they waited. Bobby couldn't sleep. He alternated between pacing, cursing under his breath, and cracking his knuckles.

"Mr. Sutton?" The woman at the front desk called Bobby over. Whatever magical time she had been waiting for had passed. Vacant rooms could now be rented out and she had one for them on the fifth floor.

As soon as they reached the room, Bobby turned on the television. He hoped to get any news about what exactly was happening out there. The TV flared to life. Onscreen was a thirty-something male reporter in a windbreaker speaking into the camera.

"What we have here, April, is different to what we at Channel 9 News reported earlier." The graphic below the reporter identified him as Allan Hill, covering live from Monroeville, Pennsylvania. "Here in Monroeville, about ten miles east of Pittsburgh, I have spoken to dozens of witnesses who have contradicted the official statement coming from the White House. These people, mostly fleeing from Pittsburgh, told me what they saw there. The stories they shared are disturbing and, quite frankly, unbelievable. People somehow standing and moving under their own power after sustaining injuries that, under normal circumstances, should have left them incapacitated...or even dead."

Emily walked to the other side of the room and opened the curtains to one of the two windows there. Behind her, the reporter answered questions from the anchor.

The view from the window wasn't exactly breathtaking. Two floors below, she could see the roof of what had to be the lobby. Across that roof rose another tower of rooms, mirroring the one they were in. If she leaned far enough over, she could see a sliver of city street off to her right. From her vantage point, Emily could look directly into many of the rooms across from her. A handful had lights on and only one had curtains open.

On the third floor, below and to her left, there was a girl sitting on the bed near the window. Emily thought she looked sixteen or so but couldn't be sure. The distance was too great. The girl had bright red hair that cascaded down her shoulders. She sat cross-legged, her attention on an object on her lap. Was it a book? Maybe a phone? Emily wanted to wave but she wouldn't look up.

"Jesus Christ," Bobby blurted, drawing her from the window. "Em, this guy they're interviewing says he got bit by some random dude. Chomped into his bicep like an apple. They showed his arm. You could still see the teeth marks and everything."

The rest of the news was more of the same. Initial reports of civil unrest had severely underestimated the crisis. Now authorities were playing catch up – trying to figure out what was going on and what could be done.

Flipping through the channels, Bobby watched as hundreds of people were shown leaving Pittsburgh like refugees. Parts of San Francisco were on fire and the National Guard had been called out to assist in fifteen states. The crawl at the bottom of the screen warned the residents of Portland and other outlying areas that, effective immediately, a curfew was in effect. If you were not already inside, get in as soon as possible. Do not call 911 in the event of an emergency. Current activity levels prohibit emergency personnel from responding.

"What the fuck does that mean? Don't call 911? That's the goddamn emergency number." Bobby shook his head.

"The whole city is an emergency, baby," Emily offered.

"I guess."

As if on cue, the sound of sirens drifted in from outside.

"Better close the curtain, Em. Those sounded a little too close for comfort."

Breaking news kept coming in throughout that first night. All of it bad. Neither of them could reach anyone on their phones so the only contact with the world was through that flat screen. Eventually, Bobby took a break from the barrage of constant information and decided to take a shower. Emily took over remote control duties.

"What you are about to see is extremely disturbing." She stopped channel surfing when she heard the newsman's somber tone. What was the warning for? Everything being broadcast tonight was disturbing. "Younger viewers should be asked to leave the room."

The scene on the television shifted to a darkened street in Salem, Oregon, The video quality was poor, most likely shot by a bystander with a camera phone. Two police officers stood behind a parked patrol car with flashing red and blues. Their guns were drawn and they were yelling at a solitary man shuffling at them – like he was drunk. In one hand he carried what looked to be a portion of a severed arm.

Emily couldn't make out what the officers were shouting but their intent couldn't be clearer. The man kept coming. He reached the patrol car, mere feet from them, when they opened fire. A rapid succession of close range shots knocked the man onto his back.

There was a small crowd shouting from somewhere out of camera. The officers, weapons still drawn, carefully approached the downed man. The shouting turned to screaming as the man rolled onto his side and began to stand.

The rest of the video didn't show much except the amateur cameraman's feet as he ran from the scene as fast as he could. The talking heads of the news desk took over again, trying their best to explain what they'd seen. The video played silently on a loop in the background as theories of body armor and PCP were advanced as possibilities.

"Babe, you need to see this. They have Salem on." There was no response from the bathroom except the running water. Emily stood, intending on interrupting Bobby's shower. She stopped when she saw his phone on the nearby table. In the dark room the lit screen shone like a spotlight. The message on the screen made Emily's heart beat faster with excitement. Bobby had a voicemail.

"Who's Jennifer?" asked Emily. She pointed the phone at him accusingly. Bobby stood in the hallway with wet hair, wearing nothing but a towel.

"What? Jennifer who?"

"Jennifer. She's just Jennifer in your phone. No last

name. She left a voicemail for you." She about kept herself from calling the girl she'd never met a bitch.

"The phones work? That's awesome." His face lit up and he reached out to take the phone. "Did you get—"

"The phones are still down. I don't know *how* she got through. Doesn't really matter. I deleted it. Her message."

"What, why?"

She had listened to the short recording close to ten times before erasing it forever. It was full of static and the voice on the other end came through intermittently. Emily pictured her as a perky blonde with perfect teeth and a short skirt.

"Bobby, it's Jen," had been the clearest part of the entire recording. "Where are…the roads b…so scared…call…" After that there was a long pause—long enough that Emily thought the call had been dropped—before the voice came back a final time.

"Love you," came through clearly.

Bobby snatched the phone from her and swiped the screen desperately. It only took a few seconds to confirm she was telling the truth, there was no voicemail. He looked at her with anger in his eyes like she had never seen before.

"Why the fuck did you do that, Emily?" He didn't yell. She almost wished he would. His words, spoken quietly through gritted teeth, affected her greater. "We haven't been able to reach anyone and you throw away the only contact we've had."

"No, don't you turn this around on me. This is on you." Unlike Bobby, Emily had no problem with yelling. "She said she loved you, Bobby. Who is she?"

Bobby closed his eyes and sighed heavily. Emily was crying before he even started to speak. "I was planning on telling you after the wedding. It was just never the right time. This…us…it isn't working. I can't do it anymore."

A TRIBUTE TO GEORGE A. ROMERO

They slept in separate beds that night. Emily went to bed first and was disappointed, but not surprised, when he climbed into the other one.

"Do you love her?" she asked softly. He didn't answer. Maybe he was already asleep.

The next morning, Bobby was up and dressed by the time Emily awoke.

"Roads are still closed." He sat, again scanning the news channels, not even looking at her. "I went downstairs. Wanted to see if anyone there could help. They're as clueless as us. Cops and soldiers everywhere outside. They were all headed somewhere real fast."

Emily didn't say anything. She shuffled into the bathroom and turned on the shower. There was no hot water but she didn't care. The running water hid the sound of her crying.

The hotel had even more vacancies the next night so Bobby was able to book the room again. He also brought up an armload of food from the continental breakfast in the lobby. They shouldn't go out, he explained, unless they absolutely had to. It looked sketchy out there.

Emily picked at her food and nodded absently when Bobby talked. Whatever he wanted to do is what they'd do.

The TV channels all blended together in a morass of crisis and panic. The Salem video was replaced with a similar one from Green River, Wyoming. Then another, from New York, that trumped Wyoming's. They had completely lost contact with Pittsburgh. In short order other cities—Bismarck, Reno, Richmond—were added to that list.

Emily could tell Bobby was getting nervous. She'd seen it before. His bouncing knee when he sat, the way he continually sighed, and the way he ran his hand through his hair were all dead giveaways. His need to do something, anything, was threatening to override the little voice telling him that doing nothing is sometimes the best thing to do. Like when you're lost and all of your senses are telling you to move but staying right where you are, doing nothing, makes it easier for others to find you.

The sleeping arrangements stayed the same the next night. Bobby again rose before Emily and took another morning trip to the lobby. This time, when he returned, he didn't come bearing food. He didn't look nervous anymore, he looked scared.

When he got to the lobby, he told Emily, there was no one there. The front desk, where they'd checked in less than forty-eight hours before, was deserted. He waited for a time, hoping someone would show up, that a hotel employee was taking a break or in the bathroom. Nobody came. Bobby walked behind the desk to the employees only areas, opening and closing doors. "Is anyone here?" he shouted. There was no response.

"They took off, Em. Left and ran off without a word."

They tried the TV. A solid glowing blue filled the screen on every channel. While they slept, the cable had gone out, leaving them isolated.

Bobby went back out, long enough to pick up as many items as he could from the vending machine from down the hall. He piled the snack food, mostly nuts, candy, and chips, on the couch. There would have been more but he had run out of cash. Even with the two of them in such a dire predicament, he hadn't so much as thought about breaking the machine and stealing.

Next, he filled the bath tub to the brim. "We'll be ready if we lose water and power," he told Emily. She managed a brief smile. Bobby always thought of everything.

From what they could tell, the world outside their suite continued to spiral. The unmistakable sound of gunfire became frequent. Sometimes only a single shot would ring out. Other times it sounded like a full-on gun battle, like downtown Portland had turned into a war zone.

It took less than a day for Bobby's foresight to prove beneficial. It was still early in the morning when the lights turned off along with the TV. With the power gone, their phones died, becoming nothing more than expensive paperweights.

Bobby ventured out the day after the power outage. He said he was going to look for anyone that might have stayed in the hotel like they had. There was strength in numbers, he reasoned. Emily became worried when he was gone for more than two hours. When he finally returned, knocking frantically but quietly, he was a mess. His shirt was torn and his arm was bleeding from a cut near his shoulder.

Bobby wouldn't say how he'd been injured. He just assured Emily that there was nobody else in the building and they should stay right where they were for as long as they could.

The plan, if you could call it that, was simple. They would ration the food and water, stay inside, and wait for help to arrive. Surely, this anarchy couldn't last. Order would be restored and things would return to normal. It might take a while but they could be patient and cautious.

Bobby and Emily settled in. He stayed up keeping watch at night. She took the days. Neither of them slept much. Every sound, especially anything that sounded like it was coming from their floor, put them on edge. Personal hygiene suffered without the luxury of running water. Baths consisted of damp washcloths and a bar of soap. It was better than nothing. Depending on the direction of the wind, the smell of smoke from nearby fires would fill the suite if they left a window open. The lack of view made it impossible to tell what was ablaze, they just knew it wasn't the Eagleton. At least they had that going for them.

Hope dwindled as the days passed without rescue. No cavalry showed up to save the day. Emily found herself wishing the sirens or even the gunfire would return. At least then they'd know there were other people around. Isolated as they were, it was easy to imagine they were the last people on Earth.

Bobby hardly spoke to her and the silence was becoming impossible. She wanted this to be over. She wanted to return home, she really did, but deep down she knew that, once that happened, Bobby would leave her.

"I had a dream last night."

Emily stared out the window as a light rain started to fall. Bobby sat on the sofa blocking the door, head back, looking at the ceiling. A brief glance in her direction was the only indication he'd heard what she said.

"We were walking in the park," she continued unbidden. "You remember Steel Creek Park, where we had the picnic that time?"

She kept watching the rain. He didn't respond.

"You were holding my hand and the sun was shining. A beautiful day." Her smile was tightlipped as tears shimmered in her eyes. "We sat underneath that big tree. The one by the river? I laid my head on your chest and you held me."

Bobby sighed and folded his hands on top of his head.

A TRIBUTE TO GEORGE A. ROMERO

He turned his gaze to Emily.

"You know," she said, "hundreds of years ago they said it was the Sun that revolved around the Earth. It took a long time but they figured out that wasn't true. Still, though, they said that Earth was the only planet. We were still special, just not *as* special."

Bobby stood and began pacing. Emily slowly examined each of the windows across from them. There were dozens of them. None showed any signs of life.

"Then they said, 'Oh, look, there are other planets but our solar system is the only one.' Pretty soon they looked around and found others, enough to make up a galaxy. Ours was the only galaxy, though. There were no others. Nobody could comprehend anything bigger than the Milky Way."

The rain fell harder, covering the window and distorting the view.

"Now they say they know there are other galaxies, billions of them. But just this one universe. This universe that contains everything there is or ever will be."

Bobby stopped pacing long enough to open the window next to where Emily was sitting. It opened out from the bottom and only for a few inches. The smell of smoke and death wafted into the room through the rain. Bobby quickly closed it.

"I think they're wrong. There are other universes out there. That will be their next discovery. Some of them will be completely different from ours, maybe even unrecognizable to us. Some will be the same with a few subtle differences."

She put her fingertips on the window and slowly ran them down the glass, leaving faint trails behind them.

"That's what I think dreams are. Windows into those other places. They're not just pictures in our head while we sleep. We can see, if only for a brief moment, what might have been."

"What...the hell...are you talking about?" Bobby

asked. His arms folded across his chest and his face flushed with irritation.

Emily turned and looked at him with a pitiful smile. A tear ran down her cheek.

"Don't you see? It means that somewhere out there, we're still together. Together and happy."

Mouth open, he shook his head in disbelief. "Jesus Christ." His voice was low but harsh. "The world is ending and you're worried about us breaking up? What the fuck is wrong with you?"

Emily's smile faded. She looked away from him and back to the window. Bobby stormed into the bedroom. When he came back out he was holding his jacket. Within a few moments he had moved the couch and unblocked the door. He stopped long enough to look back at Emily. She sat almost perfectly still, staring out the window, searching for any sign of hope.

"Make sure you lock the door behind me," he said. He opened it and stuck his head out into the hallway. He looked right, then left. He stepped out and closed the door behind him.

Emily thought she could hear Bobby's footsteps recede down the hall. She got up and walked to the door. She locked the deadbolt and pushed the couch back into its position, barricading the door, just like Bobby had told her.

Bobby was gone. Emily was alone. She started to lay down on the couch but stopped herself. Piled on the cushions were the bags and boxes of crackers, chips, and candy they'd been living on. He hadn't taken any of the meager rations that remained.

"I know you left these for me, Bobby," she said to the

empty room. "But I'm going to save them and you can eat when you get back. You're not the only one who can sacrifice for the ones you love."

Emily gathered the pile in her arms and removed them to the bedroom. She dumped them on what had been Bobby's bed before falling onto her own. Sleep found her quickly.

Time passed. How much, she wasn't sure. The sun rose and fell. Emily slept with no regard for the time of day. Going to bed only when it was night was something she had done in a different life. When it was light out, she opened the curtains and windows as far as she could. The smell from outside hardly bothered her anymore. From the table by the window, she kept watch on the rooms across the way, looking for life. The bed by that third floor window was still there but the red-headed girl was long gone.

The food stayed untouched on Bobby's bed. Emily's dirty clothes hung a little looser on her with each passing day. She allowed herself a mouthful of water—sometimes two—but the food was for him.

Sometimes she could hear something moving in the hallway outside. There were never any words spoken. It could have been someone looking for help or simply searching for another living human being. She doubted it though. The uneven shuffle of footsteps accompanied by awkward thumps against the walls was enough to convince Emily she shouldn't open the door. It wasn't fear that held her back, she was somewhere beyond that. She never seriously considered leaving the room. It wasn't so bad here. At least she had a roof over her head. God only knew what she would find outside. Besides, Bobby knew where she was. He would get help and come back. He was her prince and would rescue her.

The knocks at the door roused her from a light sleep. Judging from the way the sun lit the room, it was still morning. They weren't exactly knocks, more like a slow pounding by someone using the side of their fist. With sunken, bleary eyes, Emily stumbled stiffly out of the bedroom. She stood, staring at the door, not quite believing what she was hearing. That couldn't be her door, could it?

She had to stand on the couch to see through the peephole. Looking out, she squealed at what she saw. Given her body's current weakened state, it took Emily minutes instead of seconds to push the couch from the door. Breathing heavy, she undid the locks and flung it open.

Bobby stood in the doorway. He stopped his pounding, dropped his arms to his sides, and regarded the woman in front of him. Emily held her hands folded in front of her face.

"I knew you really loved me, no matter what you said. I knew you'd come back."

Bobby's mouth hung open and he tilted his head as Emily spoke. His blond hair was filthy, like his clothes. Behind drooping eyelids were the same gorgeous green eyes she saw every time she fell asleep. The dark circles under them suggested he hadn't slept in years.

Above the neckline of his shirt, a fist-sized chunk of flesh was missing from his neck, exposing the muscle beneath. His shirt was one big reddish-brown stain but the wound itself no longer bled. His stomach had been ripped open and his intestines spilled out and ran halfway down his thigh.

"Welcome home, baby," Emily said. She held her arms out to him.

Bobby put his hands on Emily's shoulders and pulled her to him. She leaned in to kiss him as he brought his

A TRIBUTE TO GEORGE A. ROMERO

mouth towards hers.

STORIES OF THE DEAD

KELLY GOULD

Kelly Gould lives and writes in Oregon with his wife and children. His most recent story *Shmoo* was included in Aphotic Realm #3. Other anthologies he has been a part of include The Book of Blasphemous Words (from A Murder of Storytellers), Campfire Tales Book One (from Deadman's Tome), Grey Matter Monsters (from Lycan Valley Press), and Weirdbook #36.

When he isn't writing he is usually enjoying good whiskey and bad horror movies.

MEMORIES OF ROMERO

I was a fan of George Romero before I even knew who he was. As a kid, I didn't pay much attention to who wrote or directed the movies I watched, I just knew what I liked. I grew up in the 80's and, even though I was way too young to watch such things, I saw Night of the Living Dead, Dawn of the Dead, and Creepshow many times. Dawn of the Dead is still the best. It was as I got older that I began to appreciate the man who created those movies. In the midst of the Cold War, nuclear apocalypse was a real childhood fear of mine. George Romero fascinated me with his tales of a different sort of apocalypse. He still does to this day.

I jumped at the opportunity to be a part of this project and I wrote this story specifically for this anthology. I hope you enjoyed it.

DEAD HARBOR

BY
PATRICK LOVELAND

A shallow valley rested in silence, parallel manmade riverbeds of solid blacktop winding through its base. These had once been known as California State Route 163, and this stretch loosely bisected the western third of San Diego's Balboa Park area.

Abandoned cars sat in the road and at its edges, birds, rats, and other small animals having made nests in those whose former owners had left their vehicle's windows rolled down or doors opened. Wasps buzzed and flitted in and around a station wagon they'd made a fortress hive of.

Animals and insects all around scattered or hid as a low growling sound rose out of the silence from the north.

A rusted extended panel cargo van cruised down the southbound side of the 163, all of its windows latticed with welded rebar and three long ladders secured lengthwise on its roof. Its cargo interior was hollow except for empty metal racks lining the insides, and a couple of makeshift jumper seats welded over the rear wheel wells—which each held two people. The van's driver and five passengers all wore coveralls with added layers of protective cloth sewn in; thin, tough gloves tucked into those; and boots with added straps from the coverall leg bottoms under the arches to keep them secured similar to how spats would.

Arroyo drove while Lehrer checked an AR-15, a final time, she'd chosen for this mission. Their camp's semi-official armorer, Pritchard, only provided semi-auto rifles and pistols for scavenging runs like this, reserving full-auto, burst, and shot weapons for camp defense. Arroyo and the others in the back of the van had Mini-14s, Mini-30s, and AR-15s. Lehrer knew the logic was to force them to pick their shots carefully and not waste ammo—if they had to go 'loud' at all, which was of course actively and enthusiastically avoided—and she agreed. Hammers, clubs, and bats made far less noise and didn't run out of bullets. At least Pritchard let them take longer magazines and all the suppressors that could be spared in their weapon category.

Lehrer stowed her rifle and watched the Cabrillo Bridge loom steadily larger as they approached its arch bases that flanked the road. Lehrer had come to think of the structure as a gate to Hell, or at least a neighborhood in it.

"Alright, squad—get focused. This is mostly a medical supply run, but anything that fits in your duffels that's as useful as meds is cleared too. Any questions, you ask. Selby, you're with Arroyo—Haynes, you're on me."

"Is Selby up for this? She's—"

"Fuck *you*, Arroyo."

"Hey, I just thought you might want to rest your swollen ankles or be near a toilet maybe."

Lehrer looked over at Arroyo.

"Stow it."

Haynes said, "Yeah, shut your mouth."

"Maybe you both should've stayed back, seeing as how you're the proud—"

"Just... *drive*, Arroyo," Lehrer said.

She eyed the rear-view mirror. Vance and the new guy,

Novak, shared the back jumper seats with Haynes and Selby. She'd been meaning to ask the camp leaders more about Novak. All she knew was he'd stumbled into their night watch lights two weeks before, and was bloody and raggedy enough to have almost been shot.

"Vance—you and Novak try to siphon something useful out of the vehicles in the parking lot across the street. You'll probably just get sludgy crap not good enough to fuel a lawnmower, but if it's not totally gone, Pritchard says he's got a cocktail to make it usable again for a while—at least in the lighter scout cars."

"Yes ma'am," Vance replied but Novak just nodded affirmative, maybe aware that Lehrer was watching in the mirror.

"Ma'am?"

"Yeah, Haynes?"

"What level of... *presence* are we expecting?"

"Should be pretty minimal—the heatwave's finally breaking, but big groups of dead stumbling around out in the open should've been decomposing badly at this point. Whatever keeps their damn brains active doesn't seem to apply to the rest of them. Short of the health center we're starting at being somehow wall to wall with 'em inside, should be a cakewalk."

"Wish the heatwave was further behind us, since we gotta wear these stupid suits. Sweatin' like a bitch."

Vance scoffed and said, "Hey, the first time one of those dead motherfuckers tries to bite a chunk out of you and can't, you'll be fine with sweating."

Arroyo eased them onto the 4th Avenue/5 North exit, following its curve to the west.

Lehrer said, "Speaking of... hoods and eyewear on."

All of them other than Arroyo pulled reinforced hoods like padded balaclavas over their heads, tucked them into their coverall collars, zipped them up, and secured cushioned guards around their necks. Then each put Paulson style bubble goggle 'eyewear' on last. Each head covering had a mouth cover patch for closer, arms-reach encounters, but for now those stayed velcroed to one side of the mask so they could breathe easier.

They drove along the off ramp that merged with the 5 North, passing under the bridges for 6th Avenue and 5th before ascending to the surface of 4th, taking a right onto it.

"Hey, that's a one-way street, Arroyo…" Vance said and chuckled.

Selby shook her head.

"You're gonna make that joke every time, aren't you?"

"Prob'ly, yeah."

"*Hey*—I said focus, not *say stupider shit*."

Lehrer scanned the area for signs of the dead in large numbers, but saw only scattered crawlers and shaky, almost skeletal upright shamblers. One of the stumbling, cloudy-eyed bastards a couple blocks down seemed to notice them driving along and turn toward them, but Lehrer wasn't worried. It still amazed her how relatively harmless the dead were one on one and in small groups—but how quickly that changed the more of them there were.

"Radio check."

They all switched on consumer handheld ham radio receivers on their coverall utility belts, which had wires running to headsets sewn into their hoods.

"Check, check…"

"Roger."

"Loud and clear."

Arroyo took a left onto Elm and followed it down a few mostly clear blocks before turning up 2nd, then pulled the van over close to a long, locked rear entry gate at the street level of the medical center building they'd arrived at. He stopped the van and started securing his hood and bubble goggles while the others slung big, empty duffle bags and got ready to open their doors. Arroyo pictured their ragtag 'squad' as bank robbers from some movie and chuckled.

Lehrer got out and scanned the street and intersections to the north, rifle in a low-ready position. Arroyo hopped out on his side and slid along between the van and entry gate, then took up a southward watch position as Novak and Vance popped out the van's back doors, each with two five-gallon Jerry cans with hoses attached.

Selby and Haynes slid open the van's side door and used installed metal rung steps on the vehicle's side to climb onto its roof. They detached one of the long ladders and helped each other heft it over the medical center gate, then secured it with karabiners on straps into eyelets on the van roof.

Haynes unslung his rifle and scanned the center's back shipping and parking area as Selby descended the ladder into it. Once down, Selby readied her rifle and scanned around before giving an 'okay' sign with her hand, shouldering the rifle, and taking out a suppressed revolver. Haynes made a whistling sound to her and she re-holstered her pistol and took a cut down baseball bat from a sheath on her coverall back.

Lehrer watched Vance and Novak sucking and spitting old gas from cars in a lot across the street. Arroyo looked down the van's length at her and she gave him a thumbs up. He slung his rifle, walked to the van's side rungs, and ascended. Haynes covered him as he climbed down the ladder and joined Selby. Arroyo took out a thick club and they sneaked to the center entry doors and looked inside as they held position.

Satisfied the big guys were clear to continue their siphoning, Lehrer climbed the van rungs one-handed with rifle pointed high, then patted Haynes on the shoulder as she took overwatch. Haynes took the cue and climbed down, then produced a short bat of his own.

Lehrer scanned the area around Vance and Novak again, then once more. Low over comms she said, "Okay, we're going in. Watch yourselves…"

Vance raised a hand off his current Jerry can and gave an 'okay' sign from across the street.

-We got this, ma'am.-

Lehrer returned the okay, slung her rifle, and moved down the ladder to Haynes. She retrieved her close quarters weapon of choice—it was either an authentic Native American ball-tipped 'war' club or a great replica, whichever it was, it was solid and had busted many shambler skulls since she'd found it while scavenging in an antique shop about a year before.

-Looks clear,- Selby whispered over comms from across the back lot.

"Okay, you two get in, clear the first floor and grab what you can. We'll take the second and leap frog up."

-Wilco.-

Selby and Arroyo pried the powerless automatic doors open and made entry. Lehrer and Haynes followed them in and looked for the nearest stairwell, melee weapons ready and flashlights sweeping the dusty corridor.

Vance hated siphoning duty but knew complaining wouldn't do any good. As he listened to Lehrer and the rest search the medical center over comms, he went from vehicle to vehicle popping gas caps, sucking on a hose to prime it with vacuum, and transfer it into one of his Jerry cans after getting as little as possible in his mouth.

-No... shit. Hey, check this out, Arroyo,- Selby said over comms.

Vance stopped pulling the hose from a car and listened while watching the medical center building.

Arroyo said, -What the fuck is that?-

There was a shuffling sound but Vance wasn't sure it was on comms or Novak still dicking around on his side of

A TRIBUTE TO GEORGE A. ROMERO

the lot.

Lehrer broke in, -What have you got, Selby?-

-Ma'am, there's something in the harbor...-

The shuffling was getting louder and Vance could barely hear over it. He turned his headset down and turned...

"Novak, what the fu—"

...just as the source of the shuffling started moaning.

It had probably once been a woman, but now it was desiccated to the point where you couldn't even call it rotten. Stringy patches of dangling hair from the head, layers of dried blood on its face and hands, cloudy eyes, and cracked, jagged teeth—and almost within arm's reach.

Vance stumbled back, fumbling for his pistol, and knocked over a Jerry can he'd sealed—it came down with a sloshing liquid thud and clang.

"Shit..."

Vance got his pistol free and raised it—

"*Don't.*"

Novak rushed up behind the undead creature and raised a one-handed mini-sledgehammer—bringing it down with incredible force, crushing the braincase and dropping the frail human form like a sack of rocks and branches.

"Th-thanks, man—"

Novak brought his knee up and kicked down into the creature's skull twice, smashing and cracking it flat into the asphalt. He looked up at Vance with his eyes but didn't raise his head. He looked furious behind his bubble goggles.

"You really needed a gun for that one? That *one*."

-This is Lehrer. Are you done with the siphoning?-

Vance waited for Novak to rat him out but he didn't.

"Yes, m-ma'am."

-Lovely. Get that shit stowed in the van and meet us on the medical center roof. Arroyo can guide you if you get lost. And grab the binoculars—the big ones.-

Novak narrowed his eyes and Vance thought it looked more like curiosity than anger toward him.

Novak said, "Wilco."

Arroyo lowered the binoculars Vance had brought and handed them back to Lehrer. He shook his head and exhaled.

"How have we never seen this?"

Lehrer took the binoculars and looked through them.

"Couldn't say… but it's there."

Looking west from the medical center roof, they had an unobstructed view of the hooked northern curve of San Diego Bay as it ran between North Island Naval Air Station to the south and two odd peninsulas—Lehrer had always thought of them as windshield wipers when she saw them on maps, as they jutted from the main bay coast and ran parallel to the bay's curve like thick sandbars, also creating narrow marinas in-between the main shore and their shore-side lengths—and the Liberty Station and Point Loma areas, then out to sea.

In the middle of the water expanse between one of those peninsulas—the strangely named Harbor 'Island'—and the northern coastal curve of North Island Station, there rested a Nimitz class Aircraft Carrier. Anchored, still—just *waiting*, it felt like to Lehrer.

The flight deck had been cleared of airplanes and there were Quonset huts and fences across its surface—like a relief camp, Lehrer realized. There were also two helipads cleared near the port end of the deck but only one chopper, and it looked halfway through some kind of major overhaul.

At the water surface there were makeshift docks attached to the carrier with dozens of small boats and dinghies moored to them, shining in the sun as the wind and water rocked them. There were even paddleboards, surfboards, and a few windsurfing boards mixed in and pulled up onto the docks.

Lehrer said, "At some point, people really wanted on that big raft…"

Selby had attached a scope to her rifle and was scanning. She pointed toward the San Diego International Airport, just north of Harbor Island.

"I think I know what they did with the planes."

Lehrer aimed the binoculars at the airfield. Sure enough, fighter jets and other sleek military planes sat in neat groupings on the airstrip's apron near its southeastern terminal.

Haynes sighed.

"And there's not a person in sight. Why isn't anyone talking about that?"

"Living *or* dead, though. Which could make it easier," Arroyo said.

"Make *what* easier?"

Lehrer lowered the binoculars.

"When we stroll over there and ransack their sweet ass military goodies."

Arroyo laughed loudly and they all looked at him. He stifled it and mock waved down at a few oblivious shamblers they could see in the street to the west.

"Sorry… But yeah, let's do it."

Vance frowned.

"That's not really our mission here, though, is it?"

Lehrer's head snapped toward Vance.

"We're here on camp business, and we've been presented with a golden opportunity—rations, tools, weapons, ammunition, better meds than even this place had, special equipment we might not even be aware of. Not to mention how much Pritchard will owe us if we get him some nice, new toys. Higher ups too."

Arroyo chuckled.

"Yeah, they'd be pissed if we didn't check it out."

"Exactly. This isn't a war anymore. It's a waiting game. We have to survive long enough for these things to die off or get fragile to mow down in larger numbers. Anything that can help us last is worth the risk. Understood?"

"Shit, okay. I'm sorry. Yes, ma'am."

Lehrer looked through the binoculars.

"Also, Vance…"

"Ma'am?"

"If you question my authority again, I'll shoot you in the fucking face."

They drove along North Harbor Drive toward the airport on their right and the Island on their left. Other than crawlers and shamblers lurking, all they saw were signs of desperate struggle, mass exodus, or final moments.

Arroyo was struck with a realization that other than the stand out things—crashed cars and trucks; burnt, crumbling buildings here and there; the odd abandoned military vehicle; faded old bloodstains and roughly picked over human skeletons, etc.—vast areas of the city and surrounding areas didn't seem that different. Quieter, emptier… but not *that* different, he thought. He honestly didn't know how to feel about it, but it unsettled him.

"Hey, you cool?"

Arroyo looked over and saw Lehrer with a guarded but concerned expression.

"Yes, ma'am," he said and turned his head enough to wink that only she could see.

"It'll be worth it."

"I trust you."

Vance couldn't tell what Lehrer and Arroyo were talking about up front over the rumbling, creaking, and shuddering of the van—and all the medical supplies and fuel they'd stowed shifting around in their respective racks and securing straps—but he wasn't okay with this deviation. If they did succeed and grab some great kit from this, he'd ask for a transfer out of Lehrer's bullshit unit. If they didn't, he'd make sure the camp leaders had her head on a fucking pike for risking their lives unnecessarily.

He watched Lehrer look away from Arroyo and whistle.

"Shit... Guess that's what happened to the other chopper."

"What do you see?" Novak asked from the back.

Lehrer eyed him in the rearview mirror. He was sitting in a relaxed position, and what she could see of his face and eyes through his hood and bubble goggles lacked expression.

"Military chopper crashed and took out most of a 7-Eleven. It seemed to be flying away from the carrier, by its heading."

Novak chuckled mirthlessly and said, "Magnificent."

Lehrer narrowed her eyes.

"When we return home, we should have a few drinks and trade stories, Novak."

Novak went silent again.

The sun was sinking in the sky as they passed signs for 'Harbor Island Drive' and Arroyo turned left onto it, passing under an airport exit overpass then following a curvy street toward the peninsula's bay shore. He bowed right and followed its western length.

Lehrer scanned the marina on the other side of the neck of land toward the airport.

"There are some small sailboats and such docked over

here…"

Arroyo noticed something and veered toward what would've been the oncoming traffic lane to get closer to the piled boulders on the bay shore side. He eased to a stop overlooking the water.

"Or we could take a couple of these Zodiacs right here."

Lehrer leaned and looked over Arroyo and saw several Navy rubber raiding crafts pulled halfway out of the lolling water. In the failing light of approaching dusk, the slick black surfaces of the large dinghies had a menacing look, as if covered with blood so rich and dark it was indistinguishable from the rubber.

"Hey… Are *you* cool?"

She looked at Arroyo, his face closer than it usually was when they were around others—even if he was wearing the protective hood and bubble goggles—and guarding his own concern now. She swallowed, sat back in her seat, and gave him a wink.

Something caught her attention in the passenger side mirror—a few of the dead had noticed them driving in and were shuffling and stumbling across the street from near a hotel they'd passed on their way in. Slow as they were, these shamblers would never reach them in time to do any damage—and, once again, so few could be easily dispatched—but their inescapable presence in more densely populated city areas never left her mind.

"As a cucumber."

Wind and salty bay water whipped at Lehrer's goggles and the open mouth area of her hood as Arroyo drove the Zodiac they were in with Haynes—Novak, full of surprises, drove another craft expertly behind them while

A TRIBUTE TO GEORGE A. ROMERO

Vance and Selby held on tight. The aircraft carrier loomed larger and larger ahead.

As they got closer, Lehrer noticed that—as a part of the transformation they were ordered to make from ship of war to relief station, she assumed—they'd raised one of the starboard aircraft elevators and installed ladders at the base of the long horizontal capsule shaped opening that had exposed the hangar deck.

With the sun setting, light was dim enough that all Lehrer could see in the hangar deck were the tops of more relief tents and Quonset huts, the rest of the high-ceilinged chamber rapidly becoming awash in thick, inky darkness. She shuddered, but told herself it was the wind and spray.

They reached the docks and moored the Zodiacs.

As Lehrer led the way to the hangar deck ladders, Vance noticed dark stains on the slick makeshift docks and spent shell casings half-rolling out of seams near its edges with the gently rolling waters, only to nestle back in place every time. He shook his head and tried to stop his hands from shaking.

Lehrer started up the nearest ladder while Arroyo crossed to another and followed in parallel. They each took out their melee weapons and covered while the others ascended, Vance last and shaky about it.

When Vance got up, he immediately unslung and readied his rifle.

Arroyo shook his head, pointed at the weapon, and made a slicing motion past his neck.

Vance winced.

"Are you fucking crazy?—"

Lehrer turned smoothly and before Vance could react, her suppressed pistol was safety off and against his forehead. She got in close and spoke soft and precise.

"That's twice you've openly questioned a superior. This might be a horseshit group to you, but we operate as a military body—I've been given authority by literally the *only* people on this fucking planet who know you're alive and half give a shit, to *end* said life if needed to ensure mission success."

"Pl-please don't..."

Lehrer narrowed her eyes, studied Vance's, and sighed hard.

"Even if this place is a total tomb, you start popping off rounds, even with the suppressors... There will be an army of hungry dead falling all over each other on that shore we just left. You know the one—it's where our van's parked."

"I understand. It won't happen again."

"I know it won't—Selby."

Selby took Vance's rifle and slung it over her own, then un-holstered his pistol and tucked it in her empty duffle bag. Vance looked mortified but the weapon against his head held his tongue.

"Okay, you have your club and duffle. Carry your own weight in supplies or I might still shoot you, understood?"

"Yes, ma'am."

Lehrer reengaged her pistol safety and re-holstered it.

"Fantastic. Let's continue..."

Lehrer turned on an angle-head flashlight on her chest and crept deeper into the hangar deck. The squad followed, tucking anything that looked half useful in their duffle bags as they went.

As the sun hid itself behind Point Loma to the west, the boxy and rounded dimming silhouettes of Quonset huts and fenced areas that covered most of the huge hangar deck fell into deeper darkness. Their flashlights soon became the only light.

In those glows they saw torn tents, locked and barricaded fences and Quonset hut doors, breaks in the fencing. Further in they saw shell casings all over, empty, dropped weapons, and dried blood all over in streaks, spray, pools. They passed open hatch doors to upper and lower decks with more bloody smears, and busted equipment visible in the beams of their lights.

Haynes said what they were all thinking.

"Not a single body…"

The deeper they got into the hangar deck the more Lehrer's stomach twisted and sweat soaked into her hood and coveralls, and she wasn't alone.

"I think maybe we should…" Lehrer started but she trailed off when she caught sight of something in her flashlight beam.

Arroyo stopped too. She crossed to a broken hut entrance, then crouch-walked under its busted structure. Arroyo and Novak followed her in while the others waited outside.

Long, clear capsules on gurney-like rolling supports lined both sides of an aisle running down the hut center. There were about thirty of them, by Lehrer's count, and all but one of them contained a re-killed undead human. They'd been dispatched by something like dual pneumatic captive bolt systems—like a slaughterhouse would have for 'stunning' cattle before the actual slaughter—positioned over and behind their heads in the capsules. Lehrer assumed the bolt positions were based on new data collected somehow and—

"Wait… This isn't a relief ship. It's a fucking research lab."

Novak chuckled in his mirthless way.

"Blissful, to peer into the eyes of Hell. Also… misguided."

Arroyo scrunched his face.

"What's that—some shitty haiku?"

There was a thump from the far end of the hut and they aimed their lights in that direction. More pounding, then moaning.

Lehrer advanced and Arroyo and Novak followed as the groaning grew louder.

One of the dead hadn't been fully dispatched and was beating the insides of its capsule while its clouded eyes rolled around, even more vacant than they'd usually be on one of these creatures. The moans were strident now and vibrated the container.

Lehrer searched for the capsule's latches, popped them, and swung it open. She raised her war club and brought it down hard into the creature's already half caved-in head. It fell silent and motionless. Lehrer froze in place, suddenly aware of the noise the creature had made and that she must have, killing it. She and Arroyo shared a concerned look, but Novak almost looked amused.

"Have you heard the stories about the dead seeking out and going dormant in warm places?"

Lehrer pulled her war club free.

"Warm like...?"

Arroyo scoffed.

"What do you even mean, man?"

Novak sighed.

"Nimitz class carrier. Nuclear powered. Power plants—"

"Below decks,"—"Below deck," Lehrer and Arroyo finished.

"Ma'am—we have problems out here," Selby called from the busted hut opening.

As Lehrer, Arroyo, and Novak rushed back to it, they could hear it too—moans. As they crawled out of the hut, the groans grew louder, echoed, and layered. It sounded to Lehrer like hundreds...

Lehrer's eyes darted around in thought.

"We're cut off from the boats. They're swarming up from below... Selby, give Vance his guns back—Vance, if you shoot me, I will haunt the rest of your probably-very-short life and whatever might be after, got me?"

"Y-yes," he said while struggling to holster his pistol, then pulled his rifle's slide back and let go.

The moans were joined by silhouettes of shambling human forms in the distance in both directions, then their clouded, awful eyes started glinting eerily off the squad's lights. The dead stumbled into the periphery of their

A TRIBUTE TO GEORGE A. ROMERO

overlapping glowing beams by the dozens—and these weren't the weak city dwelling dead worn down by exposure. These dead still shambled and stumbled almost blindly, but their strength was obvious and their truly insatiable hunger could be heard and felt in their harrowing moans.

Lehrer readied her rifle.

"Focus every shot!"

Arroyo primed and readied his gun.

"*Every* shot a *head* shot!"

They fired in overlapping cones, dropping one undead creature after another and causing those behind them to trip and collapse onto their fallen—which was the only thing buying the squad time to reload. Dozens came and dozens fell, but even more replaced them.

While reloading a fourth time, Selby's flashlight passed over a metal staircase to their right flank. She pointed that way before firing again.

"Lehrer!"

Lehrer snuck a look in-between shots.

"Yes! Go-go-go!"

Selby fired the last rounds in her just-fresh magazine and reloaded as she bolted for the staircase. Haynes did the same, and their support fire was immediately missed.

"Retreat to stairs but maintain fire by twos!"

Selby and Haynes laid down cover where they could from the stairs while Vance and Novak fell back, still firing. Arroyo and Lehrer took a few swipes to their protective clothing as they shot at close quarters, but nothing penetrated.

Arroyo's rifle jammed. He slung it and took out his pistol and blunt weapon, shooting and striking in quick succession. Lehrer kicked a lunging shambler back, causing just enough domino effect to buy room to cover Arroyo's retreat. Her rifle went dry with no time to reload and she used it as a club, crushing heads and confusing others with hard strikes. Arroyo's pistol emptied and he cleared his rifle while the rest of the squad covered them, firing round after searing round into the writhing, clawing wave of undead monsters.

The squad's combined efforts gave Lehrer enough time to fall back and reload. She grabbed Arroyo's shoulder and pulled him behind her, then pushed him up the stairs.

"Ascend! Ascend!"

They climbed shorter decks lined with ship operations equipment, hounded by more moaning, vile creatures but fought as they retreated upwards to the flight deck—and its deathtrap functionality.

The Quonset huts on the flight deck were all bordered and connected by a network of fenced-off corridors—and the intersections of the corridors had fenced gates. They could see freedom, but chain-link tunnels kept them trapped. Holes in the fences had been clawed open from earlier struggles and undead that had made it up to the flight deck from outside the fence system—or had still been there from before—tried to swipe at the fleeing squad members.

Novak tried to pry the stairwell door away from its open position, but something kept it in place.

"Keep going toward the boats, no matter what!" Lehrer yelled, then she and Arroyo laid down cover on the gaping maw of the stairwell as the dead found their way up.

Selby and Haynes started through the nearest fence tunnel and found its intersection gate locked. Selby fired her rifle at the fence hinges and busted enough of them to bend it away some. She crawled in and yanked Haynes through the tightest part. Vance tried but he was too big. He fired at the other hinges but couldn't pop them all the way.

Novak pulled him away and pointed him toward the retreating Arroyo and Lehrer.

"Cover them."

While Vance started firing with shaking hands on the dead crawling and shuffling up from below, Novak kicked the fence until it was wide enough for them all, then climbed through.

One of the dead clawed at Vance through a break in the enclosure and grabbed him by his coverall chest material. It pulled him close and tore at his protective suit.

Vance panicked and fired wildly, hitting Arroyo in the back of the neck and blood spraying out the front of his suit's neck padding. Arroyo collapsed into the fence wall on the other side, eyes rolling in confusion.

Lehrer screamed and tried to support him—but life was draining from his eyes in time with the blood seeping from his neck padding and soaking his coverall.

"No! *No!*"

The creatures wouldn't rest for her agony. She fired on them as they filled the tunnel wall to wall, straining and trying to pull themselves past each other in the tightening space.

The dead thing pulling at Vance was joined by another and they made short work of his hood and neck protection, piercing the flesh of his neck with their talon-like rotting fingers.

"P-Please! Help—Nhnngk!"

Lehrer pulled her hood off and threw aside, then aimed her rifle at Vance's head and squeezed off a round, busting it open and spraying blood and brains all over her face. She fired a few more shots at the advancing dead before running dry a last time. As she stumbled away from their awkward steps, she pulled a necklace up from within her coverall chest area. She turned toward her three remaining squad members and threw the necklace toward the bent fence junction opening. Haynes leaned through and grabbed it, then pulled himself back.

"Lehrer, come on!"

Lehrer ignored him and took out her war club and pistol, then turned back—she got one clean strike on an undead skull before the advancing mob took her down and started pulling her apart and gorging on her insides.

Novak pulled Haynes and Selby away from the bent cavity and tried to kick it back in place, but it stayed ajar. The tunnels on their left and across from the crooked opening were securely blocked off, but to their right was a broken fence and path leading to one of the Quonset hut openings.

Novak pushed the other two toward the hut door—it was barricaded. They kicked at it and threw their weight into sliding some of the blockade away, then squeezed their way in.

Selby and Novak slammed the door shut and started reforming the obstruction while Haynes searched his coveralls for ammo. He had some loose rounds in a chest pocket and started reloading his last magazine as full as possible

The dead reached the defense and thrust their clawed hands in wherever they could. Novak and Selby kept their weight against it and Novak took his mini-sledgehammer from his belt. He bashed at the groping hands, crushing fingers and metacarpals—but the dead felt no pain and kept grasping at air—

Desperate, hungry fingers clasped Selby's coverall sleeve enough to slow her movements down—and others locked on her arm, tearing at the thick fabric. Then her arm was wrenched out the opening, pulling her against the barricade.

She screamed in fear—then in a different, more desperate way, and Novak knew she'd been bitten.

"Grab her, Novak!"

But instead, Novak raised his hammer and brought it down onto Selby's skull.

"Novak…"

Novak raised his hammer and struck again, crushing and collapsing the young woman's head half in. Her body slumped limply against the barricade.

Haynes fumbled to finish reloading his rifle in a sick rage. Before he could finish, Novak flung his hammer

back-handed—

It struck Haynes in the face, breaking his nose inward and cracking his right ocular cavity, sending him sprawling onto the hut floor.

Novak crossed to him and retrieved his hammer.

"I had hoped I was wrong this time… but you're all so fucking *weak*."

Novak raised his hammer and brought it down several times, busting Haynes's ankles and knees, as he let out tortured cries of more than one kind.

"You can be useful to me, though. Slow them down just a bit, yeah?"

Novak went through Haynes's pockets and found the necklace Lehrer had thrown—her spare keys to the van.

Before narrowly escaping the flight deck, Novak had been able to set it ablaze thanks to a stash of special grenades he'd found in one of the huts he'd been rushing through. It only took a few to really get the fires going, so he had most of a case of them left over as reward for his former squad's misguided trip into the aircraft carrier. The grenades had even stayed secured in their case after the dive he'd had to make off the flight deck.

As he drove a Zodiac away from the carrier's makeshift docks, he watched flame-engulfed undead walk and crawl off the flight deck, falling to the water below and being extinguished like snuffed out matches.

These burning, wretched things were the only lights for miles and miles.

Novak smiled.

"Beautiful…"

PATRICK LOVELAND

PATRICK LOVELAND writes screenplays, novels, and short stories. By day, he works at a state college in Southern California, where he lives with his wife, young daughter, and a cat so black he seems to absorb light. Patrick's stories have appeared in anthologies and periodicals published by April Moon Books, Shadow Work Publishing, Bold Venture Press, Sirens Call Publications, Indie Authors Press, PHANTAXIS, and the award-winning Crime Factory zine. Patrick's first novel, A TEAR IN THE VEIL, was published in June of 2017 by April Moon Books.

Twitter: https://twitter.com/pmloveland
Facebook: https://www.facebook.com/pmloveland/
Amazon: http://www.amazon.com/-/e/B00S78LF9M
Blog: https://patrickloveland.com/

MEMORIES OF ROMERO

George Romero's films hit me at just the right time—film school. Growing up as a budding horror fanatic, I thought zombies as a horror concept/creature were 'fucking stupid'. A roommate in art/film school strongly disagreed and within weeks of moving in with him, I'd seen the "Of-The-Dead" Trilogy (and Savini's (in my opinion, fantastic) 1990 remake of the first one), *The Crazies*, *Creepshow*, and even *Martin* since that friend loved Romero films in general (as I came to). His indoctrination program didn't stop there and we continued on into the *Return of the Living Dead* series, Lucio Fulci's zombie/z-leaning films, *Dellamorte Dellamore* (aka *Cemetery Man*), etc.

But those Romero zombie classics were the foundation of my love of zombies, no question. By the end of my second year at school, I was writing and storyboarding a planned "no budget" zombie film, educating myself on DIY make-up and gore effects (hell yeah, pesticide sprayer squibs!), and shopping for just the right special effects contact lenses.

That epic of amateurish splatter cinema never got out of planning stages, as many don't. But if I think back to those times, it was in a way the beginnings of what became the second screenplay I wrote about ten years ago, which I'm actually in the process of novelizing right now. That story has evolved into a much weirder kind of thing… but the Romero roots are plain to see.

Much love and thanks, Mr. Romero.

ETERNITY
BY
THOMAS VAUGHN

Earl Pickens' decision to kill his wife Gladys was not a rash one. It evolved over decades of slow deliberation. There wasn't one thing in particular that triggered him, but simply her ongoing existence. This resentment had grown over the course of sixty years of marriage and was now all he could think about. At eighty-seven he wasn't getting any younger and if he intended to make good on his plans he needed to execute it. Gladys was eighty-four and Earl realized that, while time had ravaged her, it had been no kinder to him. Other than high blood pressure and bad eyesight she enjoyed relatively good health he despised her for it. The problem was compounded every time she reminded him of his mortality, which happened multiple times a day. She would say "Oh I'll outlive you, Earl. Mark my words." Well today he was going to put a stop to that.

As Earl shuffled down the hallway after another sleepless night of wandering back and forth to the bathroom he muttered "sixty years is too damn long to be married to the same person anyway."

A TRIBUTE TO GEORGE A. ROMERO

"What's that?" Gladys asked from the living room where she was watching TV. He did not reply because ignoring her questions was a long standing custom in their house. It was difficult for either of them to drive so they spent the majority of their time incarcerated in their modest ranch home nestled in a decaying suburb. Here they conducted searches for lost objects and shouted oaths at one another. When he finally managed to traverse the length of the hallway he found her in the recliner wearing a pink robe and slippers. Their terrier, Sparky, was on her lap. Earl glowered first at her, then at the TV.

"I see you're getting your fill of the liberal/Jew media this morning."

"Good grief Earl I'm trying to watch Regis. He's Irish Catholic for Christ's sake. The thing is I can't find my program."

Earl glanced at the screen and saw images of police barricades.

"What is it?"

"Well I don't know, Earl. I just turned it on."

"I'll tell you what it is. It's those liberal, hippy anarchists trying to wipe their asses with the Constitution—to take away our rights. They're probably out there pulling down another Confederate statue. If that Governor had a set of balls he would roll right in on them with tanks. That's what I'd do. And there you sit, piping that trash right into our home."

"Earl, I'm just trying to drink my coffee. I might be able to figure out what they're saying if you'd shut-up long enough for me to listen."

"Well I don't need to hear what they're saying because I've heard it all before. Someone's got their knickers in a twist because there's a few of us God-fearing patriots left in this country." Earl paused and looked at Sparky. "That dog shit yet?"

"No. I told you I just got up."

Earl shambled to the sliding glass door and opened it.

Sparky bolted from Gladys' lap and into the enclosed backyard for a rare moment of distraction from his otherwise dull existence.

"You better eat your breakfast," said Earl as he stepped carefully onto the back patio.

"Since when did you care whether or not I eat breakfast?"

"You want to watch your blood sugar." He closed the door before she had time to complain. The air outside smelled of smoke despite the fact it was the height of summer. Then he realized it wasn't the stench of a fireplace, but a structural fire. That was probably why he'd been hearing sirens all night. Earl scowled at the sun, then looked at the dog while it strained to squeeze out a turd.

"Yep, Sparky... Things are about to change around here." During Earl's uneventful career working for a company that made toilet bowl cleaner he had not garnered much in the way of material possessions, but he had developed knowledge about dangerous chemicals. He stood on the patio and looked through the back window impatiently as Gladys stood unsteadily then navigated toward the kitchen.

"Here we go, Sparky," he whispered. As he watched the drama unfold the sound of rapid gunshots echoed in the distance. Earl glanced in that general direction. "It's a shame what this neighborhood had come to, Sparky. These Mexicans just shoot at each other in broad daylight nowadays. You know what it is? No one's got any respect for anything anymore."

When he turned back to the window he watched Gladys fill her glass with orange juice from the container he had spiked with enough cyanide to kill ten horses during his nocturnal wanderings the previous evening. She had been complaining of her ulcer lately and he was banking that there were some open sores in her stomach to speed things up, though he was prepared to wait. Holding his breath he watched as she took a big gulp—

then another. At first she looked puzzled. After a moment she began massaging her temples. Before long she collapsed and began thrashing on the kitchen floor. Sparky returned to the sliding glass door and barked at the commotion.

"Here now, Sparky. Let nature take its course." He tried to nudge the dog from the door but it was determined to get inside. "All right. Have it your way. But there are going to be some changes around here."

Earl waited about twenty minutes then reentered the house. Sparky dashed to Gladys' prostrate body, then whined and looked up at Earl quizzically. Sitting on a kitchen chair he reached down and checked her pulse and smiled.

"That is what we call a home run," he gloated, then stood and made a sojourn to the bathroom. It was about as good he could have hoped for, though he wished she hadn't vomited so much.

After he squeezed out a few drops of piss he returned to the living room and sat next to the phone that Gladys had always hogged during the day talking to other old ladies that Earl couldn't stand. He knew for a fact that at least two of them voted democrat. As he waited for the phone to ring he rehearsed his lines in his head, but instead of an operator it went to an automated waiting system.

"Ah, what the hell," muttered Earl and redialed. As he listened he saw a video of a policeman shooting a pedestrian between the eyes on the TV. "There you go," he said. "That's what this country needs—a little more law and order." After the fourth try he gave up.

"Now you see Sparky, this is what happens when godless communists take over the phone company." He rose and returned to the kitchen where, much to his shock, he found Gladys standing with her eyes fixed on him. At first Earl wondered if he was hallucinating because he had been pretty sure she was dead. But it would be just like the old bitch to drag this out. Nothing could ever be easy.

"Are you OK?" he asked feigning concern, but even as he spoke she began to move toward him. She reached out as if she were looking for support and he prepared to step aside when she grabbed him. "Gladys! What the hell is wrong with you?" he shouted as they went to the floor in a heap. Gladys began to climb on top of him as pain shot through his lower back. "Damn you woman! I just had that hip replaced last year!" Instead of listening to Earl's protests Gladys clamped down on his arm with her teeth.

"Goddamnit," he screamed while Sparky ran around them in circles, barking. He wrenched his arm from her mouth, ripping her dentures out in the process. "That hurt! Hey, I'm bleeding!" He shook the dentures from his arm and to his horror Gladys continued the assault by gumming him.

"Gladys! Cut that shit out! Now pull yourself together!"

When he realized that she was not listening he began to rock his body until he achieved enough momentum to roll on top of her. With great exertion he pulled free and began crawling up the hallway on all-fours, his breath coming in short gasps. Gladys likewise crawled in pursuit while Sparky cheered them on by racing back and forth and barking. All Earl wanted to do was get to the back bedroom where he kept his pistol. It looked like he would have to shoot the old bag. The race was a close one and Earl just gained the threshold of the bedroom a few seconds ahead of his wife, shutting the door with a foot.

For a while all he could was lay there and catch his breath. His head was swimming from the exertion and his chest hurt. Meanwhile Gladys had regained her feet and was banging at the door. He kept his heel against it before realizing that she was not reaching for the knob. The woman was completely out of her mind. It was not surprising since her whole family had been nuts. As Earl lay there calculating his situation he looked up at his autographed picture of Barry Goldwater and recovered his courage. Then he crawled to a nearby chair and used the technique for standing that the home healthcare person had demonstrated.

When he opened the dresser drawer the gun was missing. "Oh hell, now where did I put that thing?" He thought for a moment. "I had it out to clean. Was that Tuesday? Or maybe it was Thursday? Is it in the kitchen drawer?" His ruminations were disrupted by Gladys' moaning and pounding. To make matters worse Sparky had joined her by barking and pawing.

Earl sat on the bed and tried the phone again. It was now dead. The dizziness was getting worse. The doctor warned him that if he exerted himself he could have a stroke. He was convinced this was one of the reasons Gladys had always aggravated him so much. But today she was outdoing herself.

"All right! Look, Gladys... I am sorry about the cyanide. I won't do it again. Now would you calm the hell down?" Earl had a rule that he never apologized for anything, but all this violation of protocol accomplished was to incite Gladys even more. Earl looked around. This was a problem. There was no way he could get his aged frame out of the window. Finally he realized what he needed to do. He shuffled to the closet and retrieved his Louisville Slugger.

"Okay, Gladys! Is this what you want? You want a fight? Well you've got one! I should have done this a long time ago! I'm gonna bash your damn head in!" As he shouted the moaning and barking reached a crescendo. He grabbed for the knob and turned it. Gladys spilled into the room and Earl went to work on her with the bat as best he could. The problem was she closed in so fast he couldn't get momentum on his swing. Still he cracked her a couple of good ones to the face that seemed to slow her down, but to Earl's dismay she kept coming. His difficulties were heightened when Sparky's protective instinct kicked in and he locked onto Earl's ankle. It's a hard day for a man when his own dog betrays him in his greatest hour of need.

"Damn it, Sparky! Mommy's flipped her lid! Now cut that out!"

Even with her broken nose Gladys surged at him and started in with more gumming. Before he knew it they had toppled over, only this time he felt his hip give. Pain shot down his leg. Earl was not sure how long he struggled against Gladys. She was too weak to inflict any lethal injuries, but kept clamping down on his throat with her bloody mouth as if she were tearing at a steak with a pair of soggy erasers. Suddenly he realized she was trying to eat him. It seemed like a perfect metaphor for their entire marriage.

With one last effort Earl rolled her off and made for the master bathroom, swatting at Sparky as he crawled. Once again he only just made it, closing the door in her face as she lunged for him. This time he knew his strength was at an end. A sharp pain rebounded through his head and he couldn't form words. 'This is it,' he thought. 'Mommy has finally killed me.'

While Earl stared up at the ceiling listening to Gladys' clumsy pounding on the door he found himself contemplating the afterlife. He was, after all, a religious man in his own way and took some comfort in his coming appointment with God. This was the prerogative of men who lived good lives and had nothing to be ashamed of.

At least I went down fighting, he thought. *I'm not dying like some sorry bootlicker.* And so, as the darkness rushed to greet him, he comforted himself that at least he would not have to spend eternity locked in this house with that godawful woman.

A TRIBUTE TO GEORGE A. ROMERO

THOMAS VAUGHN

When Thomas Vaughn is not writing fiction he is a college professor whose research focuses on apocalyptic rhetoric. He is a refugee from the debris field of Madison County Arkansas. After secretly writing fiction over the past few years he started submitting work in 2018 and has been fortunate enough to publish stories in seven different magazines and anthologies. He doesn't know where any of this is going, but is enjoying the ride.

MEMORIES OF ROMERO

I first became aware of George Romero when I saw Gene Shalit give a bad review to *Dawn of the Dead* on the *Today Show*. I was eleven. The preview images of the dead pouring through doorways while outnumbered police and firefighters retreated mesmerized me. They recurred in my mind over and over again. My opportunity to see the film came several years later when I gained access to a VCR. I cannot count how many times I watched the series. Romero displayed our world in all of its dark, claustrophobic splendor. A small group of refugees defy the masses until they are overwhelmed and the survivors take to uncertain flight. I think this vision resonates with the way I see the world. No matter what you do they are going to get you. Your only recourse is to make sure you have an escape plan, and even then you are just prolonging the inevitable.

ROLL CREDITS
BY
KENNETH E. OLSON

Hillary executed two with clean head shots. Those behind pushed through the narrow doorway into the small passageway. Ray put a bullet between the eyes of a third.

This was perfect.

Gary had done an outstanding job scouting this location; an old farmhouse in the middle of practically nowhere. The sun was setting, casting an orange glow over bare trees and the dried autumn grass. The dead shambled across the lawn toward the house. All the scene needed was rising mist. Ray made a mental note to track down some fog machines.

Just within the woods at the edge of the property, Warren huddled, monitoring the cameras affixed to Hillary and Ray's cobbled armor. Three more stand-alone cameras, stationed equidistant from each other along the tree-line, caught the exterior action. Several more of the cheap spycam variety were placed within the farmhouse. Every angle of this operation was covered.

Hillary leveled her pistol at another creature. Ray let her

shoot before putting a hand on her arm.

"Enough. Let them come in."

"Are you insane? They're bottled up. We can pick them off safely."

"We don't want safe. We want television."

"You *are* crazy."

"Probably," Ray said. "Just let a few get near the end of the hall, then we'll take a couple out. Let the rest into the room."

Hillary cocked her weapon and aimed.

"Holster it," Ray said. "Melee combat unless you get in a jam. So keep it handy."

"Makes sense," Hillary shook her head but did as told. She pulled her survival knife instead. "You're going to get me killed."

"If you die, that's on you. How long have you been doing this now?"

"Since the beginning," she said. "Like everyone else."

"I meant alone."

Hillary hesitated, her lower lip pooching out. The deader in the lead was nearly on her, and Ray had a bad feeling he'd asked the wrong question at the wrong time. Then, with a speed that astonished him, she swung the blade upward, driving it through the thing's lower jaw and into its brain. The knife was removed and at the ready before the creature began to fall.

"Long enough," she said without turning. Ray saw the track of a tear roll over her cheek.

He hoped he got that on camera.

Then they were in the thick of it. Ray jammed a nearby creature's mouth shut with the heel of a palm and drove his knife into its skull.

"Hillary," he called out. "The three rules!"

The three rules, the crux of the show, would be splashed across the screen during the intro credits. Despite the location or method of extermination, these three regulations would tie the series together. He'd have Tshirts with them on one day. Once society righted itself.

"Right now?" She grunted, shoving one creature backward while jamming her knife into another. A killing shot. She was amazing.

"I thought we might do it later," Ray said. "Maybe over crumpets and a nice cup of tea."

"Are crumpets a real thing?"

"God, I hope so," Ray said. A coffee mug reading LET'S DISCUSS THE RULES OVER CRUMPETS AND A NICE CUP OF TEA flashed through his mind. "Number one."

"Keep moving." As if to illustrate, she jammed an elbow into an approaching deader, forcing it back. At the same time, she moved away from it to use the knife on another.

"Right. Number two."

"Engage and go."

"E and G," Ray said. "Perfect. If the first shot doesn't take it down, leave it. Get some breathing room and return to it. Three."

"Don't panic." Hillary seemed to be keeping that rule in good standing. Her gaze was steady, eyes focused, her moves deliberate and flowing. It was a ballet with her. Deaders fell at her feet as if in supplication—worshipping their new goddess of death—rather than defeat. Ray honestly couldn't blame them. She was hypnotic. Beautiful.

Clammy arms encircled his neck. Damn himself for becoming distracted. Maybe that should be a fourth rule. His instincts honed, he dislodged the creature with a helmeted head-butt. Following rule number two, he took two quick steps from it, skewered another deader, then returned to original attacker.

It was nearly on top of him. A quick kick to its knee snapped the dry limb and it went to the floor, unable to support itself. Ray brought his foot back for a strike to its face when his nostrils burned with the death stench of another nearby. He swung his knife towards the new threat, catching the thing across the eyes. Not a mortal blow, but at least it was blinded.

Things were getting dense in here.

"Upstairs!" Ray yelled. "Go!"

Hillary finished the deader in front of her. Ray was already three steps up. She moved toward him, then pitched forward. Ray turned when she cried out and saw her flail at the stair's bannister, her gloves slipping slightly from the gore on them before catching purchase. The thing Ray had broken the knee of grasped at her ankles. With a speed belying its level of rot, it bit into her calf.

"Shit! Get off me!"

Ray was at her side in a heartbeat, bringing his boot down on the creature's head. It shattered in a bog of ichor and bone.

He wrapped an arm around Hillary's waist and herded her up. She didn't seem to be limping, but she did stumble, causing Ray to slow slightly to ensure she was with him. He glanced at her face. Her eyes were open, her mouth set in a deep grimace. Whether from pain or anger he couldn't be sure.

They reached the top of the stairs. Ray stopped, grabbing Hillary's arm to keep her from moving down the hall. She turned to him, battle-fire in her eyes.

"Have a seat," Ray said, indicating the top step.

"Are you nuts?"

"We've established that," Ray said, removing his helmet. "Look, they're not getting up here anytime soon. We need a break."

The cigarette he'd placed behind his ear before the altercation began was flatter now and he pulled it free. He frowned at it. It wasn't the shape of the butt, but the fact there was a small spot of blood on it. Some spray had gotten between his helmet and his head.

Damnit.

Sighing, he pitched it over the side of the stairs. It bounced off the forehead of a deader and into another's gaping nasal cavity. He didn't know if smoking their blood could turn somebody, but he wasn't willing to find out.

He looked up at Hillary who stood motionless beside him. He patted the spot next to him.

"Come on. They've gotta relearn how to climb stairs. Funny what they forget and how fast. They had to use the steps to get onto the porch and it's already slipped their minds, so to speak. Once one figures it out, they all will. It's like a hive mind. Fascinating, isn't it?"

"No," Hillary said.

"Roll up your pants. I want to look at you leg. See if it broke the skin."

"It didn't."

"Humor an old man."

"You're not that old."

"I'm a grizzled fifty-three. I've almost got thirty years on you. Respect your elder."

Sighing, Hillary sat next to him. She slipped her helmet off and began to unstrap her gloves.

"No. Leave them on. Only take them off when we get to the zip line on the roof. Clear?"

"I'm going to get deader shit all over my pants," she said.

"You already have a big hole in the back. Stop whining."

Hillary rolled her eyes as she turned her pants leg up. Ray leaned forward.

Beneath the cloth, Hillary wore a thick plastic brace, the type once used to keep ankles from buckling. On the back of the brace, just over the calf, was a large smear of blood and some divots resembling teeth marks. Ray nodded.

"Brace did its job. You're fine."

"I told you that," she said.

"I've had five guys tell me they were fine when they weren't. Forgive me for being over-cautious."

Hillary rolled her pants over the brace and tucked the

hem back into her boot. She leaned forward, her forearms on her thighs, staring down at the things below. At least thirty of them were trying to crawl over each other. None had figured out the mechanics of stepping up yet so there were several who fell, knocking others over like grotesque dominos. More were making their way into the living room and the muffled groans of those still outside almost vibrated the walls.

"How many were on the truck?" Hillary asked.

"I don't know." Ray slipped another cigarette from its pack. Damn saving them. He'd find more. "A hundred? Maybe more? We don't really count them when we lure them into the semi." He lit the cigarette, took a deep drag, and let it roll around his lungs for a moment before expelling it. Hillary waved the offending odor away.

"Those things'll kill you."

"It won't be these that do it."

"Yeah? And what happens to your show if you die during one of these outings?"

Ray grinned. "It'll be one hell of an episode."

"That's horrible." Hillary shook her head. "Wouldn't this be a waste, then? No lead, no show?"

"Not true. We'll have done some damned fine work. Plus, as they say, the show would go on."

"With who?"

"Gary. Warren. Maybe you."

"Me? Why do you think I'd do it?"

Ray blew a plume of smoke over the bannister, away from Hillary.

"Because," he said, "if you get through this, you'll deserve it. Just like me. Just like anybody. We'll have gone through hell and emerged the on other side. We'll have warranted some reward for that."

"So you're doing this for the money?"

"Hell yes!" Ray motioned to the ever-growing horde of deaders. "I'm going to get my due from this, but I'm going to do more than just that. People will need to have a release, a way to curtail the post-traumatic stress that will encompass this planet. People will need to be reminded that it's *over*, that we *won*. We'll be united in our horror and our victory. And they'll do so from the safety of their living rooms every Sunday night at eight."

"You already picked out a time slot."

"Not really. That was for effect."

Hillary narrowed her eyes at him. "What makes you so sure this'll end?"

"Because everything ends. The credits roll on every damned thing in the universe. It will on me. On you. It did on normalcy, and will on this. We just determine whether or not our names appear in the credits."

"Fine. What makes you think it will end in our favor?"

Ray took a drag from his cigarette before answering. He let the smoke roll around his mouth as he considered the question. The red light of the camera on Hillary's chest stared at him. He gazed back, waited a moment.

"Because," he said, "I don't underestimate humanity's ability to survive...and overcome."

Hillary looked at him for a moment, then shook her head.

"Unbelievable. That was for the camera."

Ray grinned.

"Say we do end this," she pressed. "Say we do win. What makes you so damned sure things will click back to 'normal'?"

She crooked her fingers in the air on the last word and glanced toward the bottom of the stairs. Ray had considered her a doom-and-gloom survivor, and she was, but he'd obviously turned a dial in her. She was looking for hope, just like everyone else. She was still so young, yet aged by what she'd been through. There was history in her eyes; things that nobody else knew. Or would ever know, most likely. He supposed they all had that. Some buried it better than others.

"You're too young to remember Nine-Eleven—"

"I know about it," Hillary interrupted with a huff.

"I'm sure you do. But knowing and remembering are two different things. What I'm talking about is the sense of disbelief a nation—hell, a *world*—felt when that second tower was hit. We were suddenly aware there were bigger things than ourselves. The world went silent. We mourned, but we also came together. United in grief. United in terror. United in anger, but *united*. And in that unity was a certain sense of hope. At least for me."

"Did you lose someone? In the attacks?"

"No," Ray said, and that was the truth. "What I lost was my innocence. I'd believed, even after the attacks, that people could change, could become better than what we were. I thought this might signal the beginning of that. But it only took a few months until people were looking out for number one again. Politicians used the tragedy, still horribly fresh in our minds, to argue against those they considered opponents. The thing I thought might ultimately be a glue to keep us together was, instead, used as a crowbar to pry us apart."

"Politics is gone," Hillary said.

"No, it's not. It may be buried right now, but it's not dead. It'll crawl from its grave the moment this is done." He waited for her to say something. When she didn't, he continued. "But that's not my point. My point is that we didn't learn from it. We didn't become better as a society. And we won't this time, either. I think it's already happening. Have you heard of Fiddler's Green?"

"That's an urban legend."

"Maybe," Ray agreed. "Maybe not. Regardless, a lot of people are talking about it. It's the big shining beacon, the lighthouse, of what humanity wants. We want electricity back. Hot water. Internet and television. All the creature comforts. When this is over, we'll reinstate money and the economy because we don't know any other way. We'll moan about our bosses and how life is unfair and we'll drown our sorrows in alcohol, drugs, and fast food and people will make money off it. We won't forget—we'll never forget—but we'll put it behind us. We'll move on."

"But *this* won't end." She motioned to the deaders below. A clot of something vaguely pink and black flew from her glove and slapped the wall. "It won't because people will die. When they die, they'll become them."

"Did you know people used to believe in vampires," Ray asked. "I mean, *really* believed it?"

"What does that have to do—"

He held up a hand, stopping her. "Just listen. To combat it, they changed how they buried people. Some were laid to rest with a brick in their mouth so if they did awake in their graves, they wouldn't be able to open their mouths wide enough to expel it. Others were buried upside down, so they'd dig in the wrong direction. Mourners cut off the heads of some, and planted a stake through the chests of others to keep them pinned to their caskets."

"That's sick."

"Not to them it wasn't. It was reality. Just the belief, the possibility that it could happen, changed the way people said goodbye to their loved ones. The same will happen here. Do you know what a bolt gun is?"

Hillary shook her head.

"They were used on meat farms. It was a gun that shot a steel rod into the forehead of an animal, killing it before carving it up. It was considered humane."

"It doesn't sound humane."

"Not to the animal, no. At any rate, I'm guessing EMT's, nurses, and police will carry bolt guns, or something similar, with them. When somebody dies…" Ray fashioned his fingers into a gun and pointed it at Hillary's head.

"Pop!"

Hillary didn't speak.

"More humane, I suppose, than a bullet. Plus, you could get the bolt back. That's economically sound."

A TRIBUTE TO GEORGE A. ROMERO

"That's horrifying."

"Now it is. Down the road, it'll be reality. Hell, in twenty years they may tell stories of how dumb we were for not doing it."

Ray shrugged and pitched his still-lit cigarette over the banister. He focused on its fall, heard the camera whirr to zoom in on it. Unfortunately, it didn't hit any deaders or fall into any gaping holes. They could probably do a little digital magic, though. Merge this one with the last and have it bounce into that noseless face. Maybe the head could explode into fire which would form the show's title. Something to think about.

Ray stood, slipping his helmet back on.

"Looks like they've unlocked the secret of the stairs. We'd better get—"

A crash from behind caused them to turn. A deader lurched down the hall, emerging from what appeared to be a bedroom. The door hung askew from its upper hinge, as if blown open. Hillary had no time to retrieve her helmet. The creature was on her, grabbing her shoulders and snapping its jaws. She put one hand to its neck, keeping its mouth from the exposed parts of her body. The thing forced her back. Her left foot missed the top step and found only air. She tipped backward.

Ray snagged Hillary's jacket with one hand while putting a bullet in the attacker's head. Blood, brain, and bone hit the wall, splattering across a family photo. The collapsing deader vaguely resembled the father.

He pulled Hillary forward, barely allowing her to get balance before pushing her down the hall away from the horde. Four more deaders, a woman and three children, emerged from the room that the first had crashed through. Ray shoved Hillary toward an open window at the end of the corridor.

"Get on the roof," Ray said. "Zip line is up top to the right."

Hillary didn't waste time arguing. She made the window

and swung out onto the roof. Ray brandished both pistols, putting down one deader after another, giving himself room and time to clamber out.

"Warren!" He thumbed the walkie on as he slipped through the window. "You said the house was clear!"

"Gary said it was! I swear!"

Ray's foot slipped, and he hit the angled roof on his ass. He began to slide. A quick grab at the windowsill stopped his momentum, and a blast from his pistol took out the deader that grabbed his wrist. He got to his feet.

"Next time," he said into the walkie, "go inside and check for yourself! The family was still upstairs!"

"I'm sorry. I didn't know. I—"

"Enough," Ray growled. "We'll be there in a minute. Get ready to blow the house on my mark."

"Right."

Ray looked toward Hillary. She was at the makeshift zip line, a wire that ran from a heavy iron post screwed into the roof and fortified with an anchor on either side. One of her hands was on the first pre-set trolley. The other was removing the clothespin that kept it from racing down the line.

"Hillary," Ray cried out, scrambling up the roof. "Your gloves! Take off your—"

She glanced at him, eyes wide with realization. She tried to pull back, stop the momentum she had leaning forward, but it was too late. She was airborne. The trolley handle dipped slightly on takeoff. It was enough for her right hand, slick with gore, to come free. With all her weight on the left side, the trolley tilted in that direction.

Ray grabbed the iron post and reached for her. His fingertips brushed her shoulder pads.

She didn't make a sound as she went down. A group of wandering dead waited for her. She collided with them, squashing the most rotted with the sound of a dozen fully-loaded sponges being squeezed at once. The machine-gun rattle of breaking bones followed. Knowing that the sounds came more from the deaders than Hillary was not a comfort.

"Did she fall? Oh God, she fell?"

Ray ignored Warren's radio outburst. He stood at the roof's edge, near the zip line, and looked down into the horror. For a moment he couldn't see Hillary, just a mass of dead writhing like maggots. Then her hand exploded from the pile. An elbow crashed into a deader's nose. For a moment Ray thought she might actually survive and was surprised at the jump his heart took. It dropped as quickly when her face emerged, still determined, fighting, but torn and bleeding. Her left cheek was near nonexistent.

Her eyes met his. Her free hand went to her forehead, pointing as if there was a gun in her hand. She cocked her thumb.

Pop!

Ray was way ahead of her, his gun already in hand. He chambered a round, pointed the weapon. She was fighting to keep her face in view, biting her lower lip, sneering as another deader tore a chunk from her neck.

His shot was clean. A neat hole opened in her forehead and her head snapped back. He swore she smiled before the deaders dragged her down.

"Jesus," Warren's voice crackled.

Ray unstrapped his gloves. As he did so, he heard a thump to his left. A deader had managed to make its way out the window head first. It immediately rolled off the slope to join its fellows below. In other circumstances, it might have been humorous. He'd probably still use it as part of the end credits.

Ray shook his head and let his gloves drop. He grabbed his trolley, his grip firm. Still, he tightened it a little more than usual when he launched from the roof, allowing gravity to carry him safely over the horde. The ZZZZZZZZZZZZZ of the trolley on the wire filled his ears.

"Blow it!" Ray shouted when he was a couple of feet from the ground. "*Now!*"

He dropped, hit the lawn feet-first, and tucked into a roll. He heard the soft *tik* of a button being pushed in front of him as he regained his feet and began running. Less than a second later, the house went up. Heat and pressure propelled Ray forward. He kept his feet, wrapping his arms over his head to protect himself from falling debris.

He didn't look back, nor check the blazing inferno until he was standing safely in the woods beside Warren and behind the folding table filled with computers and cameras. A few of the monitors, from cameras within the house, showed static. Others captured great shots of the burning house and torched deaders. One, however, was a worm's-eye view, looking up at creatures unaware of the fire consuming their dry flesh. They simply kept bowing down and coming back up, chunks of flesh and viscera in their teeth. Ray looked away from the monitor.

"Well, that didn't quite go as planned," Warren said.

"No," Ray agreed. "I was hoping she'd stick around for a while. She would have made great television." He glanced at the trolley that lay against the tree where the now-lax end of the zip line was connected. Gore dripped from its handles.

"If she'd just remembered to remove her gloves," Ray said.

"Think we should have told her about the ones upstairs?"

Ray hesitated.

"No. That would have played to the camera. She wasn't an actress. It wouldn't have looked real."

Warren grunted. "Well I hope I came across as real. I'd hate to be cut in the final edit."

"You did fine, as always," Ray said.

They packed up silently and carried the items to a semi parked at the edge of the house's unkempt lawn, about sixty yards from where their base of operations had been. Paying no attention to the carnage behind, they slipped the items into a crate strapped to one side of the now-empty trailer.

"We have another site picked out?" Ray asked as they climbed into the cab.

"Yeah." Warren started the engine. "A warehouse in New Hope. Gary's team is clearing it now."

"Then I guess it's time to find another assistant and fill the truck with a fresh batch of flesh-eaters."

"And some more cameras."

Ray nodded, his mind already moving on. "I had an idea back there. Think we can track down some fog machines?"

"We can add digital fog in post."

"Yeah, but it won't look the same. I'd rather have the machines."

Warren shrugged. "I suppose. If we can't find them, I'm sure we can build them."

"Fair enough." Ray nodded. "Let's roll."

STORIES OF THE DEAD

KENNETH E. OLSON

Kenneth E. Olson has authored pieces of short fiction for various anthologies including *Steamy Screams* from BloodBound Books, *So Long and Thanks for All the Brains, From Their Cradle to Your Grave, Cesspool, In Shambles* from Harren Press, and *O Horrid Night* from FunDead Publications. His self-published novel, *Ripples*, is available from Amazon.com, as is *Warts & All: A Collection of Previously Published Short Stories, Flash Fiction, Comics, & Drabbles*. Kenneth lives in Minnesota with his wife, two children, and four canine fur-babies.

MEMORIES OF ROMERO

Convention weekends are a great time, but by Sunday the edge of excitement has dulled a bit. Vendors and celebrities alike sit behind their booths with weary eyes and pleasant smiles, hoping for that last-minute sale or autograph. The raucous energy of the previous two days becomes a dull murmur, like bees droning in a hive just out of sight. Persistent, barely heard, but always there.

Unless something happens. Then it gets quiet.

On July 16th, 2017, the Civic Arena in St. Joseph, Missouri went silent. It was the last day of Crypticon Kansas City, and the news had just hit social media. It was as if the last of the fading air had been sucked from the building. Nearly five hundred people, including Eugene Clark and Sherman Howard ("Big Daddy" from Land of the Dead and "Bub" from Day of the Dead, respectively), were momentarily speechless.

And then the memories began. Some, like myself, had never had the fortune of meeting Mr. Romero. Others had, enjoying a handshake and a picture at other conventions they'd attended. And, of course, there were those that worked with him. All spoke highly of him.

To say George A. Romero was influential is an understatement. Any fan of the genre worth his or her salt knows Mr. Romero, intentionally or not, revolutionized horror and gave birth to the zombie sub-genre. Without Night of the Living Dead, The Walking Dead would not exist. Thousands of books would never have been written. There would be no zombie pub-crawls and no zombie proms. His vision created a cultural phenomenon.

We all know this, and we can discuss it until we're blue in the face. But to *feel* it? To be in that moment when the full weight of his importance fell on fans, friends, and co-workers alike? That was something else. Five-hundred people, focused on one man. It created an energy, and not a wholly unpleasant one. Amid the shock and disappointment and sorrow, there was a communion of sorts. A knowledge that we all understood what each other was feeling. A unity.

In the end, the legacy of George Romero is greater than the movies he made and the stories he told. It is the people he inspired, the lives he touched, the moment the horror world held its collective breath. It's hard to express the proper amount of gratitude for that, so I can only say:

Thank you, Mr. Romero.

Thank you for everything.

AFTERWORD

BY
JONATHAN MABERRY

When it comes to George Romero and his ghoulish creations, I have serious history.

When I was ten years old a buddy of mine and I snuck in the back way of the old Midway Theater in Philadelphia to see the world premiere of Night of the Living Dead. We thought it was going to be just another horror film.

Yeah, well…you know what they say about assumptions.

Anyway…let me set the scene. The Midway was one of those massive old Vaudeville theaters, with a huge screen, dark velvet drapes, and lots of disused rooms backstage and downstairs that juvenile delinquents like us used to explore. We never stole anything, mostly because there was nothing left to steal –previous generations of kids had already looted the place and what was left had been gnawed on by rats and roaches. The neighborhood had started sliding downhill in the thirties and by the late 1960s it was dipping below the poverty level. Lots of street violence, domestic violence, racism and sexism. Fun times.

A TRIBUTE TO GEORGE A. ROMERO

My buddy and I were in the process of become hardened by all of this. Bullies in school and abusive parents at home. We watched a lot of horror movies because in those flicks the big bad monster, no matter how powerful, always got his ass handed to him in the third act.

You see, that was the thing we wanted, even if we were too young to realize it. Our fathers were heavy-handed monsters, so we liked seeing monsters lose to ordinary people. And there was always some secret way to do it. Pop a couple of caps worth of silver bullets in the wolfman and he was done. Blow up a castle and drop a hundred tons of flaming debris on the Frankenstein Monster and that was the game. And as for Dracula...that's unlucky S.O.B. seemed to always trip over his cape and fall chest-first onto convenient pieces of sharpened wood. There was always a way to stop the monsters.

Then we snuck in and George Romero proved us wrong.

Understand, this was fall of 1968. No one had ever seen anything like that flick. Nothing. Sure, there were a couple of over-the-top gore films, but they were silly and not at all scary. Something that is simply gross isn't necessarily scary.

And, sure, NOTLD is gross.

But it is scary as hell.

The thing Romero did that so many other filmmakers never even tried to do was present a threat so massive, so pervasive that there was no real way to beat it. Yet at the same time each individual instance of it was something that could be beat. You could kill a zombie. Break its bones so it can't chase you. Shoot it in the head. Break its neck. There was that secret method we'd all come to expect with monster stories. But so what? Kill one, and there's another. Kill five, there are ten more. The math is never going to work out in your favor.

So, as jaded as we were, my buddy and I were not

prepared for that film. No sir, we were not.

At the point where the young couple, Tom and Judy, are killed when the gas pump explodes and the become an all-you-can-eat BBQ for the living dead, my friend bugged out of the theater. He couldn't take it. And, thereafter he never snuck into the movies with me and had bed-wetting issues for years.

I, on the other hand, stayed to see it twice.

And I went back the next day, and the next.

I was a weird ten-year-old.

On the way home from the theater each night I'd try to figure out how I would have reacted. I put myself in the place of the different characters in the movie in that unfortunate little house. Or if I was with the hunters walking the woods. Or in one of the towns around there. I grew up in Philly and Pittsburgh was in the same state. Not close, but still part of Pennsylvania.

I thought about it.

Maybe obsessed over it. How would I survive that kind of thing?

Figuring it out, working out a survival plan, mattered to me. Remember, I had a monster at home and I hadn't yet sussed out the secret way of defeating him. On some level I knew that if I could work out a way to survive Romero's absolutely worst-case-scenario of a horror movie, then maybe all monsters could be defeated.

The inner workings of the preteen mind. The survival strategies of an abused child in the inner cities.

So, what was it about NOTLD that hit me so hard?

Well, the monsters in his stories were not suffering from a curse. They were not patchworks made by a mad surgeon and then galvanized into a cruel existence. They were not Eastern European noblemen feeding on lovely throats in the drawing rooms of London. Nor were they excavated mummies who woke up cranky, lagoon monsters looking for love, or gigantic radioactive fire-breathing cultural metaphors stomping through Tokyo.

A TRIBUTE TO GEORGE A. ROMERO

These monsters were ordinary people. They were Joe Average and Jane Doe who died in pain and misery, killed by their own friends, family and neighbors and then dragged back to life by some reanimating force and driven to be the things that killed everyone they knew.

No, turn that dial to a different setting. They were our friends and neighbors and family members who, in an inexplicably and unfair transformative moment, suddenly turn on us. One minute they are people we know and care about, and who know and should care about us, and the next minute they are not. Suddenly they are alien. And it terrifies us all the more that they wear the cruel disguise of familiar flesh. They have the opportunity to hurt us because they are right here, with us, beside us.

Add to this mix the fact that Romero never adequately explained the cause. In conversations I had with him he lamented the whole 'radiation from a space probe' thing because it had no support at all from science. However, he admitted that this was a theory being floated by politicians and military men who, we are lead to believe, are unreliable narrators of the public message.

So, there was no real answer. No explanation. There was, in that first film, no working mythology. We –the audience—did not have the benefit of decades of movies in what came to be known as the zombie genre. This was the birth of that genre. We weren't prepared for this by the thousands of zombie movies, zombie TV shows, zombie short stories and novels, zombie comics, zombie video games, zombie toys. None of that existed, so for me in that movie theater it was like seeing a truly nasty insect crawling on your arm, with stingers flicking, and you don't know what it is, what it could do, or if you should swat it or remain absolutely still.

We didn't know how to take Night of the Living Dead. We simply did not.

That's something to look back on. George Romero, along with John Russo, created a script and shot a movie that was truly landmark. Who could ever have predicted how influential it is.

And, on a sad and irritating note, that movie came out so long ago that many of the today's millennials don't know that's where it started. For a lot of them it started with The Walking Dead comic and TV show. For others it started with the Resident Evil, or one of the many other games. For some it started with 28 Days Later, which was not actually a zombie film at all, but rather a 'fast infected' flick, part of a different genre, though also started by Romero with his criminally under-appreciated flick The Crazies. I've even met people at conventions, at parties, or at book signings who think that the zombie genre started with Shun of the Dead or The Zombie Survival Guide.

Not hitting them is very, very difficult.

Okay, so back to the kid in the theater. Went in with expectations of seeing just another monster movie and came out marked for life. Changed.

If I'd been a different kind of kid that movie had have hit me with a nihilistic left hook and left me with the belief that the real world, with its own kind of monsters, were like that. Unstoppable, familiar, and poised to turn on you when you are at your weakest.

But that's not how I took it.

The characters in the film died –every single one of them—because they made poor decisions, acted with haste, failed to cooperate, and let panic guide them rather than reason or common sense.

Even at ten I knew I was a different kind of kid. I'd been taking some martial arts classes on the sly because I figured that one of these days my old man and I were going to throw down. This happened, by the way, when I was fifteen. And because I had spent so much time being logical, thinking things through, not being hasty, and learning skills, when the fight happened my old man was the one who went to the hospital.

It was a lesson I learned from Night of the Living

A TRIBUTE TO GEORGE A. ROMERO

Dead, and also from The Crazies. If you can't change the situation, change who you are in that situation. Change how you react to the crisis as it changes. Don't let kneejerk reactions and petty differences drive your survival because that never works.

Why am I telling you all this?

Because I explained all this to George Romero. And he cried. And we laughed together.

I'd met George at a number of horror and science fiction conventions. As happens with professionals who get invited to a lot of events, we got to know each other a bit at first, and after some panels together —and chats in the pre-panel green rooms—we found that we had a lot in common. Then A couple of years ago I called him to say that I was able to generate some interest in a possible anthology of stories set around the events of Night of the Living Dead, and might he be willing to give his blessing.

After hearing me out, he said he would agree on three conditions. First, he wanted to be the actual co-editor of the book. I was stunned, and I agreed. I mean…of course I agreed.

His second demand was that he get to write a short story for the anthology. Um…yeah. As it turns out that could be arranged as well.

Then he hit me with a real humdinger of a sucker punch. George told me that he'd read my novel, Dead of Night, which I'd written a few years before. That book was set in the general area where NOTLD took place, and instead of the space probe thing, I worked with world-class scientists to come up with a really plausible and therefore scary explanation for the zombie apocalypse. George loved the book and said that he wished he'd known something about science when he and Russo wrote the script for NOTLD. Then he said that, as far as he was concerned, Dead of Night was the actually, official prequel. He told me: "Yeah, Jonathan, I think we can both agree that's how it happened. And here's what I want you to do to cement this in place. I want you write a story for our anthology that directly links your novel to my movie."

Yeah, I'm glad this conversation was happening by phone because I now had tears streaming down my face.

So, the agreement was made for us to collaborate on what became Nights of the Living Dead, published by St, Martins Griffin in 2017. As it turned out, this was the last project George completed before he died. The book debuted five days before he passed.

That project was the beginning of what became a strong friendship with George. We talked about his movies and the unexpected phenomenon that was the zombie genre as it is now called. If I expected George to be openly bitter about the millions and even tens of millions being by projects like Resident Evil, World War Z, The Walking Dead, iZombie, and so many others, I was wrong. George had become philosophical about it all even though he wasn't not making big money from the thing he'd started. He told me that it was fine. His wish was that he hoped some people remember where it started. That they remember him and John Russo for writing NOTLD. That they remembered him for that film and others, both in that series –Dawn, Day, Land, Diary, Survival and the upcoming Road of the Dead Films. He hoped he'd be remember for his other works, too. Creepshow, Martin, The Crazies, Knightriders, Monkeyshines, The Dark Half, and the rest.

He wanted to be remembered.

And he is. Not universally. Not nearly as much as he should be.

But he is remembered.

George was a good and decent man, a person of great humor and generosity, and a versatile artist who left behind a legacy whose important and reach cannot be quantified. Hell, there wouldn't even be a Game of Thrones without him. What are the Night Walkers anyway but zombies?

A TRIBUTE TO GEORGE A. ROMERO

The little kid who snuck into the movie theater will always remember George because I picked a damn useful life lesson out of his movie. The young man I became who pushed back against intolerance in all its forms owes a great deal to George's true sense of social justice. The successful writer I've become owes a big chunk of his career to George, because I have written a fair few zombie projects including nonfiction books (Zombie CSU: The Forensics of the Living Dead), comics (Marvel Zombies Return and Marvel Universe vs The Punisher), short stories (Chokepoint and dozens of others), and many novels including the Rot & Ruin series; Patient Zero –first of my successful Joe Ledger thrillers; Dead of Night, Fall of Night, Dark of Night and Still of Night; and others).

And another part of me thanks George. The fan. The reader, the movie watcher, the comic book nerd, the TV addict. George set the bar very high by telling a story that can be enjoyed on many levels –as pure entertainment, as social commentary, as a cautionary tale, and something to provoke thought. And as something that is malleable in order to inspire so many creative writers, from Stephen King to Isaac Marion to Robert Kirkman to craft new tales of zombie horror. We are all the richer for the things we've watched and listened to and read that involve some version Romero's original flesh-eating monster.

So, yeah, thank you George Romero. Thanks for everything. Thanks for stories we'll go back and rewatch endlessly; and thanks for the stories still to come from the countless writers who owe so much of their career and inspiration to you.

You matter to us as an artist and as a man. As a professional creator and as a humanitarian, craftsman, visionary, and decent guy.

Thanks, George. And we all mean that from the bottom of our hearts. I did when I was ten, and I mean it so very much more now. Thanks, also, to the writers and staff who put together this tribute anthology. Then thank you, too.

And, true to the creatures that you created, you'll never die. You'll be with us forever.

Goodnight George.

And thanks….

Jonathan Maberry
Del Mar, California, June 2018

ACKNOWLEDGEMENTS

David would like to thank.

First and foremost, I'd like to thank Duncan P. Bradshaw for wanting to run with this project after I took my initial thoughts to him. Throughout the process, which has been long, hard and frustrating, he showed much enthusiasm, dedication and love towards getting it out there. Thanks, fella. Together we pulled it off! The project, not your coc— Anyway, I'm sidetracking. Also, massive thanks to George A. Romero for the influences—and scares—his outstanding, ground and rule-breaking work has provided me over the years, which, I have no doubt in my mind, will continue to do so.

Thanks to all the people who submitted and congratulations to those who made the table of contents. Without you this book would not have been possible. And last, but by no means least, a special thank you to my entire beta readers, including Jonathan E. Ondrashek, who read my tale before I submitted it. You guys rock!
Cheers,
Dave.

Duncan would like to thank.

A big thanks to David Owain Hughes for approaching me a few weeks after I'd sworn to never do another charity anthology. You proved to be irresistible. I'm sure my laidback attitude grated at times, but we got there, man!

I want to thank everyone who submitted to this project, whether you were accepted or not, we appreciate you taking the time and effort to do so.

STORIES OF THE DEAD

A nod to Jim Krut and David Crawford for answering a message from someone they'd never heard, of to send their thoughts into us. Also appreciate the afterword by Jonathan Maberry, an eloquent finale to this book. A big thank you to Kevin Enhart too for the amazing cover, absolutely smashed it out of the park.

Big thanks to each and every one of you who bought this book. We appreciate it, and hope you got something out of it.

Finally, to George A. Romero. Without your work so many of us would never have started creating. Your dedication, hard-work and sheer determination will always be an example to us. Thank you.

OTHER EYECUE PRODUCTIONS TITLES

All titles by Duncan P. Bradshaw except for EC8

EC1 – CLASS THREE
zombies/comedy

EC2 – CLASS FOUR: THOSE WHO SURVIVE
zombies/survival

EC3 – BOOK OF ISHTAR
both EC1 and EC2 in limited edition hardback

EC4 – CELEBRITY CULTURE
bizarro mind-twister

EC5 – PRIME DIRECTIVE
sci-fi/horror

EC6 – heXagram
genre spanning epic novel

EC7 – CHUMP
zombies/comedy collection

EC8 – TRAPPED WITHIN
charity anthology

http://duncanpbradshaw.co.uk/eyecue-productions/

Lightning Source UK Ltd.
Milton Keynes UK
UKHW01f1821100718
325518UK00001B/160/P